THE LIST THAT CHANGED MY LIFE

Olivia Beirne

REVIEW

First published in eBook in 2018 by
HEADLINE PUBLISHING GROUP

First published in paperback in 2019 by
HEADLINE PUBLISHING GROUP

1

Cataloguing in Publication Data is available from the British Library

ISBN 978 1 4722 5956 1

Typeset in Bembo Std by Palimpsest Book Production Limited,
Falkirk, Stirlingshire

Printed and bound in Great Britain by CPI Group (UK) Ltd, Croydon,
CR0 4YY

MIX
Paper from
responsible sources
FSC® C104740

Headline's policy is to use papers that are natural, renewable and recyclable
products and made from wood grown in well-managed forests and other
controlled sources. The logging and manufacturing processes are expected
to conform to the environmental regulations of the country of origin.

HEADLINE PUBLISHING GROUP
An Hachette UK Company
Carmelite House
50 Victoria Embankment
London EC4Y 0DZ

www.headline.co.uk
www.hachette.co.uk

For my sister, Elle

CHAPTER ONE

16TH MARCH

Amy thrusts her hand towards me and I wince.

No. Please no. Please just leave me here. I can't possibly stand back up. And if I have to throw myself into the air in another attempt at a star jump then I will vomit.

'Come on!' she cries. 'You can do it!'

I blink at her as my chest squeezes out oxygen like I'm an empty tube of toothpaste.

If my cause of death is Zumba then I will be furious.

'No,' I say flatly, 'I can't. This is too much. I'm going home.'

Can't she see I am about to die? I feel as if I'm about to have an asthma attack – and I'm not even asthmatic.

Amy raises her eyebrows at me. 'Get up. You're embarrassing me.'

I screw up my face as thick, purple spots wriggle in front of my eyes. I feel bloody terrible. I thought exercise was supposed to make you feel good! This is like when Amy tried telling me you couldn't taste the difference between white and granary bread. She told me Zumba was 'easy'.

Amy crouches down to my level. 'Come on, Georgia,' she says, 'it's mind over matter. Get up.'

'No,' I say before I can stop myself, 'it's too hard. You're better than me at this, Amy. You're always better.'

Amy lurches forward and yanks me to my feet. I stumble up ungracefully.

Bloody hell, she's strong.

'No, I'm not,' she says firmly. 'I just have a better mindset than you. You've got to go out there and grab life, Georgie. I'm sick of watching you let the world pass you by while you're sat on your arse watching *X Factor*.'

I puff in outrage.

That is so unfair. I do not spend my entire life watching *X Factor*. I mean, for starters it's only on once a year.

I open my mouth to protest but Amy gets there first.

'Now tuck your boobs back in—' she turns to the front, and I begrudgingly copy. 'We're starting crunches.'

Oh great.

TWO MONTHS LATER

'Hi,' I say, 'could you tell me which room my sister is in, please? Her name is Amy Miller.'

My body jars as I hear the words fall out of my mouth. My sister is in hospital. I'm here to see my sister, in hospital.

The receptionist glances up at me, and then back down at her computer screen. She taps away and I stare back at her, desperate to read her face for some kind of clue. I don't have a lot of experience with hospitals. I've never really had to go to one. You only have to go to hospital if something is wrong. Luckily for me, nothing has ever really been that wrong in my life.

Yet.

I glance at my watch.

Where is she? She's here somewhere. I know she is. Mum said it was easy to find.

The receptionist flicks her dull eyes up at me. 'She's in Outpatients, on the fourth floor.'

A tight wisp of air shoots out of me.

'Thank you,' I say quickly, and I race up the stairs.

Amy hasn't been well, and Amy is always well. It started a few weeks ago; she would lose feeling in her fingers and struggle to grip anything. Then, last week, she fell. The day after she was in for blood tests, and then she couldn't stand. She said she was too tired. Amy is never too tired for anything.

Today she is getting the results back. She had to go to hospital to get them. You only go to hospital if something is wrong.

I turn a corner as my eyes prick.

She's fine. She will be fine. She has to be fine. She's always—

'Georgia!'

I jump as I collide with Tamal, Amy's boyfriend. My eyes lock on to him, momentarily blinded by the wave of relief crashing through me.

They're still here. I'm not too late.

'Tamal,' I pant. 'Hi, sorry. Where is Amy? Is she okay?'

Tamal's eyes dart between my face and the room behind me. I try to read his expression, but it remains still.

3

'She's in there,' he says, gesturing to the door behind me.

I nod in thanks and crash through the door. As I enter, all the air inside my body vanishes.

The room is a dull shade of light yellow and has several brown chairs dotted limply in the corners. The wall is littered with paintings and there is a stack of tired children's toys, slumped in a pile. My eyes flit across the room desperately until I spot Amy, curled up on a sofa in the corner closest to the window. I rush over.

'Hey, Amy,' I gasp. 'Are you okay? Sorry, I came as fast as I could.'

I grab a chair and drop into it. Amy raises her eyes to look at me, her mouth twitching into a smile at the sight of me.

'You found it okay then?' she asks lightly.

I roll my eyes. 'Yeah,' I say, 'just about.'

I won't tell her that I almost charged into the maternity ward.

Amy smiles, linking her hands under her bent legs and pulling them close to her chest.

'I have no idea where I parked, though,' I add, my head swivelling around the room as if the car could have followed me in. 'I just left it. I think it was car park J?'

'There is no car park J, Georgia.' Amy grins. 'The car park is labelled in numbers.'

I look back at her, stumped. 'Oh great,' I mutter.

Where the hell did I park my car then?

'I've got the ticket in here somewhere, anyway.' I gesture to my notebook, rammed full with thick pages.

Amy glances down. 'Gosh,' she says, 'you still have that thing?'

I run my fingers over the dented cover fondly. 'Yeah,' I reply.

'I'm not sure what I'll do when I run out of space. It's got everything in it. I think it's more important than my kidney.'

Amy catches my expression and grins into her sleeve. I smile too. There is a silence as she readjusts herself on the sofa and her smile fades.

I shuffle uncomfortably. I look up at Amy and notice her raw eyes, avoiding mine.

I force the words out of my mouth. 'What did they say?'

My eyes search Amy's face as I feel my stomach lurch. My body tenses in the silence.

Amy has always been the prettier version of the two of us. As the older sister, it's as if she got all of the best genes and I was made with the leftovers. She has a heart-shaped face, small pinched lips and deep, oval eyes. Her chestnut hair sweeps over her forehead and swirls down her spine, and she has a smattering of identical freckles all over her nose. I watch as she nibbles her fingernails. Then suddenly she takes a great intake of breath and sits up straight.

I tense.

'I've got MS.'

I hover.

What?

I don't know what that means. I don't know what that is. What does that mean?

Amy catches my eye and smiles, as if she can read my thoughts. 'Multiple Sclerosis,' she adds.

I feel my body sink down into the chair, my bones feeling as limp as strings of spaghetti.

'What is that?' I say.

Amy runs her fingers through her hair, her hands shaking.

'It's a condition which means my nerves aren't working properly. Or the coating, or something. The signals my brain is sending can't get through. That's why I've been feeling so tired, and keep falling over.'

'Is it fatal?'

The panicked words tumble out of my mouth before I can stop them, and the shock of them causes my eyes to sting. My chest aches under the strain and I blink rapidly before meeting Amy's grey, watchful eyes.

There is something wrong. I was so sure there wouldn't be anything wrong.

Amy smiles. 'No,' she says, 'but it is permanent. It's something I have to live with.'

'Can they treat it?'

Amy tilts her head. 'To an extent.' She takes my hand and links her fingers into mine. 'I'm not dying, so stop looking like you're composing my eulogy. It's just a different way of life. These are just the cards I have been dealt. I have to look on the bright side.'

I hold Amy's gaze, and as I do my eyes burn.

'How can you be so positive?' I manage.

Amy squeezes my hand, her eyes shining back at me. 'What else can I do?'

*

'Tea?'

My head jerks up at the sound of Dad's voice. I feel like we have been sat in silence for hours, mindlessly watching *MasterChef*.

'I'll do it.' Mum jumps to her feet, her head snapping around the room as we all nod in her direction. Mum counts us, her arm lingering above Amy, and then exits the living room.

I try and slouch back into the sofa as my skin fizzes with anxiety. Amy is folded into the armchair, next to Tamal. Her hair is tucked behind her ears and her hands are swallowed by her large, bobbly jumper that sags over her stiff frame.

It's her university jumper. She only wears it when she's sick – which is never. She's never sick.

'Oh look,' Dad laughs, pointing at the TV. 'That's like what Mum makes.'

I move my eyes back to the TV as Tamal tilts his head in agreement.

'Amy,' Mum calls from the kitchen, 'what milk do you want? Is it this oat one?'

Amy pushes herself forward and gets to her feet. 'I'll help her,' she says.

All of our eyes follow Amy out of the room and I fight the urge to chase after her. Tamal links his arms across his chest, his face strained.

I take my chance and quickly move into Amy's empty seat. Tamal clocks me and smiles. Tamal has been a nurse for as long as we have known him.

'What do you know about MS?' I say quietly, my eyes flitting nervously to the door. 'I didn't get a chance to speak to anyone in the hospital.'

Dad glances in our direction and then back at the TV, pretending not to listen. I notice Tamal's body tense at my question; his eyes flicker briefly towards me and then back at the pounding TV.

'Erm,' he says, 'well, it's a neurological condition—'

'What does that mean?' I interrupt, every part of me twisting with fear.

'It's to do with the nerves,' he says. 'It's to do with your immune system not working properly. It's different for everyone; for some people, it doesn't affect them that badly. The coating that protects your nerves is damaged, so when your brain sends messages to your nerves it can affect your body's ability to respond. It—'

'What are you doing?'

I jump at the sound of Amy's harsh voice, as she reappears in the doorway. Her eyes are narrowed down at me, and I notice that her hand is curled around the door handle.

I blink wordlessly at her. 'I was just asking about MS,' I mumble, moving back into my chair.

'Why are you asking Tamal?' Amy says coldly. 'Why aren't you asking me?'

My heart jolts.

Amy sat in silence the whole way back from the hospital. We all did.

I can't ask her because I don't want to. I don't want to ask her about her being sick because I don't want her to be sick.

As the silence stretches across the room I hope that Amy has moved on, but her eyes are still fixed on me.

'You can ask me,' she says tightly, 'it's not a big deal. You don't have to go sneaking around behind my back.'

'I wasn't—'

'Don't go talking about me.'

Her voice strikes me and I feel my eyes well up with tears.

'It wasn't like that,' I manage.

'Georgia!' Mum calls from the kitchen. 'Can you come help me carry this in?'

I get to my feet when Amy whips her head around at Mum, who has reappeared in the doorway, carrying two mugs.

'I can help you,' Amy snaps accusingly. 'I'm right here.'

Mum's eyes flit towards me nervously. 'That's okay, love. Georgie can help. Some of the mugs are quite full.'

'So?'

I feel my chest spasm as Amy glares at me. She reaches forward and snatches a mug off Mum with such force that the boiling water splatters down her arm. I watch Amy's face quiver under the pain, but she wills it to remain still and strides towards me, her arm shaking. Her mouth is clenched as she puts the dripping mug on to the table and glowers back at Mum.

'See?' she spits. 'I'm fine. I can carry a cup of bloody tea – ' She shoots another venomous look towards me and walks back out of the room. 'I'm fine.'

CHAPTER TWO

Can I wear pink? An investigation:

<u>PROS</u>

- Pink is secretly my favourite colour
- That great jumper from the charity shop is pink and I want to wear it
- So is that skirt I got for Christmas
- And top
- Having a v. pink face is actually a good thing and isn't something I should feel self-conscious about
- I am a strong independent woman and I should be able to wear any colour I like regardless of Amy telling me I looked 'sweet' (the worst compliment EVER. She might as well have told me I look like an eight-year-old)
- Reese Witherspoon wears pink all the time (not that I look anything like her)
- Pink is the colour of spring – and everybody loves spring

CONS

* I look like Miss Piggy

★

Okay, as an assistant, there are many things that I would argue are not my job.

For example, organising the sugar lumps. Or reloading the paper in the photocopier, or signing for all the packages (I don't mind this one so much, as I see it as an excuse to show off my fancy signature).

But this is too far. Nobody should have to do this.

'I'm sorry,' the bright-eyed salesgirl bats her eyes at me, 'could you repeat that, please?'

Urgh. Please don't make me repeat it. Saying it once is humiliating enough.

I sigh.

'I need to order seven baby doves for the seventeenth of November, please. And they need to be as white as—' I consult my notebook, the tired pages curling under my fingers. 'Rylan's teeth.'

She scrunches up her eyebrows. 'Who?'

I drop my battered notebook on to the counter and meet her baffled eyes. 'He's a celebrity. The doves just need to be white,' I say, cringing as the words fall out of my mouth, 'incredibly, blindingly white.' My eyes flick down again at Bianca's swirly handwriting. 'She doesn't want any ugly little chicks.'

She didn't actually use the word 'chick', but I am a lady and it's not even 11 a.m. yet.

'Baby doves?' the salesgirl repeats. 'We only have fully grown doves.'
I glare at her. Why is this girl being so unhelpful?

'Well,' I flounder, 'are any of them pregnant? Could we get them pregnant? The wedding is in, like, five months. Is that enough time for a baby to be . . . er . . . made? Conceived?'

A frisson of embarrassment shoots up my spine at hearing myself say the word 'conceived' to a complete stranger.

The girl raises her eyebrows at me and pulls open a large catalogue. I inch my swollen foot out of my pointed shoe, trying to ignore the irritation prickling my skin. I am not a PA, I'm not a runner on an elaborate film, and I'm not even a cool spy who needs the doves to catch a homicidal magician.

I sink into a chair and pull out my phone.

I am an assistant designer at Lemons Designs. I'm supposed to be a designer. *A designer.* Yet I have spent the past seven months helping Bianca Lemon plan her big day. I mean, I don't mind. Bianca must trust me if she's allowing me to undertake all of these tasks. It's her wedding, after all. But as a girl who has been single for two years, I know very little about weddings – and even less about organising them.

For example, you have to book the priest. I mean, what? I thought they were just already there.

I turn my dog-eared notebook between my fingers, my attention caught by a loose page that is flapping in the summer breeze. I've had my notebook – or diary, as I like to call it – for years. Although Amy buys me a new one every Christmas, I can't seem to let this one go. I take it with me everywhere.

The girl chews on her lip and finally says, 'Okay, we have three doves which are . . . white. We call them crystal white.'

I bite my tongue.

Ridiculous name for a white dove when crystals are clear. Crystal clear. Everyone knows that.

I take a deep breath and get to my feet.

Calm down, Georgie. It's not this poor girl's fault that you have spent all morning arranging the *circus* that is the opening ceremony of Bianca's wedding, in shoes you can barely stand in. At least I managed to talk her out of arriving on an elephant.

'Okay, great,' I reply. 'I need seven, please.'

The salesgirl sucks her pen. 'Well, we have three.'

'Where are the others?'

'Others?'

'Yes,' I say impatiently, sticking my phone back into my pocket, 'the other doves. Surely you have more than three doves.'

Who only stocks three doves?

'Nope,' the girl closes the catalogue, 'we have three. You can book our three but you will have to hire the other four elsewhere and hope they get on.'

What?

'Get on?' I repeat.

'Yeah,' the girl grins, 'some of the doves can be pretty feisty.'

Feisty?

Oh great. That's all I need at the wedding – a cockfight between all of the crystal white pregnant doves.

I fish out some notes to make a down payment and then leave, hurriedly pulling out my phone.

Where am I going to wrangle four more doves? It was hard enough to find three!

Maybe I'll just ransack some pigeons and get Bianca drunk

13

before they're released. If I dunk them in paint she'll never know the difference.

*

I squint my sagging eyes at my computer screen.

Choose one of these destinations.

My eyes sweep over the four options and I click on a sandy beach layered on a brilliant, blue backdrop. The next question loads.

Choose a cake.

My stomach aches as my eyes fall on four pictures of staggering cakes.

I glance down at my limp sandwich, glumly.

It is so hard being an adult. Every day I find lunch a ginormous disappointment and I have nobody to blame but myself. It's just not fair. Obviously in an ideal world I would buy my lunch from Pret – or that cute little deli round the corner, like Bianca does.

Her laugh swirls through the office door and I shrivel in annoyance.

Bianca always has the poshest lunches. Once she came in with a Quail's Egg Salad with a Side of Promofranochichifitalatah.

Okay, that isn't exactly what she said. Whatever it was, it forced me into hiding my ham and cheese sandwiches from her so she doesn't fire me on the spot for being so dreadfully uncool and common.

I force myself to take a large bite and chew vigorously.

I also accidentally bought wholemeal, low fat bread. Mondays are difficult enough without realising you have to eat an entire loaf of *low fat bread* before returning to your usual delicious, spongy white. With great effort, I swallow the dry ball of congealed sandwich and wince as it parks itself in the back of my throat. I click on the gooiest chocolate cake on my computer screen.

Normally I wouldn't spend my lunch hour sat completing BuzzFeed quizzes, but after Bianca sent me on four hours' worth of errands in relation to her wedding, I feel like I deserve a break. A new question flits on to my screen.

Now choose a colour.

Automatically my finger snaps at the green image.

Normally I would be spending my lunch hour working on my own designs.

I take another bite of my sandwich.

Funnily enough, I didn't apply to work at Lemons Designs to become a wedding planner. I applied because I wanted to be a designer – and I thought that was why I was initially hired.

I jab my mouse at a photo of a black Labrador.

Bianca hasn't asked me to work on a single design project since she hired me, so I've decided to work on the designs by myself.

I move my eyes back to the BuzzFeed quiz as four images of different cocktails pop up and I furrow my brow.

It's all leading up to this big pitch we're having at Lemons, during the same week as Bianca's wedding. I've got it all planned out. Bianca will be really stressed with all of her wedding prep and the big pitch, and will be flapping about the office like a mad parrot. (She loves to flap. Last week our photocopier jammed and she flapped so much I thought she might take flight and emigrate for the summer.) She will turn to me, desperate, and beg me to help, and I will swoop in. I will have planned her perfect wedding, and I will show her my designs for the pitch. She will call me revolutionary and promote me from Assistant Designer to Designer and offer to buy me lunch every day for the rest of my life as a thank you for being the best damn member of staff there ever was – including Sally, the office swot, who drives me crackers.

I click on a photo of a plump cottage and BuzzFeed spins into life.

You will get married in 2075, in a small barn in Swindon.

I drop my sandwich in horror.

What?

2075? I'll be, like . . .

I scrunch up my face and try to work out the maths.

My mouth falls open.

I will be EIGHTY-THREE!

I can't get married when I am *eighty-three*! I'll practically be dead!

And in a small barn in Swindon? Where even is Swindon?

Why would it take me so long to get married? What's wrong with me? Will I not be attractive until I am eighty-three? Will nobody want to marry me until I'm eighty-three?

I puff loudly as heat rises up my back.

Well, there obviously must be some sort of serious fault with this stupid quiz. I will have to write BuzzFeed a strongly worded letter:

Dear BuzzFeed,
Who the hell do you think you are? I am an attractive, strong, VERY MARRIABLE WOMAN who is twenty-six and worthy of a LARGE, GRAND MANOR HOUSE and a—

'Georgie?'

I jolt out of my mad fantasy and spin round in my chair as Bianca strides into the office. I quickly shut my browser down and fix my eyes on her.

Bianca has legs like pipe cleaners and unusual, Titian hair that springs out of her scalp and tumbles down her back. Her long body is wrapped in a purple dress that coils down to her ankles and winds all the way up to her neck. She bats her large, green eyes at me and my spine unrolls.

'Georgie,' she repeats, dropping into Sally's desk chair. 'Sally on lunch?'

I nod, quickly sweeping my tongue over my mouth to check for any loose seeds lodged in my teeth.

Stupid seeds. Stupid low fat, horrible bread. Who puts seeds in bread? Who wants that? Nobody wants a tree sprouting out of their stomach.

Can that happen?

'Right,' she drawls, 'how did you get on this morning? Everything sorted?'

I nod again. 'Yes,' I say, as my heart beats furiously against my ribcage.

Bianca always makes me feel like this. We could be talking about the weather and yet I still feel as if I could pass out with fright at any second. She isn't even a scary woman, she is perfectly friendly, but she also wears spiked heels and snaps her fingers at the receptionists whenever they aren't working fast enough.

I dread the day she snaps her fingers at me. I will probably dissolve into an anxious puddle immediately, only to be yelled at for getting Bianca's designer shoes wet. She once wished me a happy birthday when it wasn't my birthday and I spent an

17

hour convinced she was playing a twisted mind game with me, and let her sing happy birthday to me out of sheer fear. I have since learnt that she is extremely scatty, but she also thinks my birthday is in March, instead of December. I don't think I will ever correct her.

Bianca nods. 'Great,' she says, 'that is great. Thank you, Georgie. There's someone I need you to call this afternoon, okay?'

I flick open my notepad, my pen poised.

Bianca leans into her seat. 'I just feel, like, I want my wedding to be really special, you know? I mean, you only get one, right?'

'Right,' I say.

My eyes fix on my notepad.

'So,' she continues, 'I need you to get someone on the phone, I don't care who, because me and Jonathan have decided that we want this wedding to be really personal. Personal to us, you know?'

I write the word 'personal' in my notepad.

'And we've started calling each other "bear". Like, baby bear; love you, bear; you are my bear . . .'

My face burns with humiliation at Bianca sharing this incredibly personal information with me. That is the worst thing I've ever heard. I will never be able to look at Jonathan the same way again.

'So I think, as a surprise, it would be so cute to have some bears there.'

I freeze.

What?

'Pardon?' I utter weakly.

'You know,' Bianca continues, twiddling a lock of her hair, 'maybe at the ceremony, as we walk down the aisle. I don't know, maybe they could sing or something.'

18

Sing?

What?

Does she know what a bear is? Does she think *The Jungle Book* is a documentary?

'Um,' I say quietly, 'Bianca, I don't know where I will find singing bears. Also, I've just ordered three doves. Won't the bears eat the doves?'

Won't the bears eat *us* is the more important question! Don't bears eat humans? And bears can *climb trees*! I can barely climb a tree!

I open and close my mouth like a dense fish.

Bianca waves her arm in the air. 'Well, they must come with a guard or something, I don't know. Those are the logistics, Georgie.'

Bianca pulls herself to standing and I gape at her.

'Bianca,' I say again, 'I'm not sure how—'

Bianca leans on the door frame of our office and raises her eyebrows. 'Yes, I know it's a challenge, but that is why I am asking you to do it, okay? I know it is hard, but all I'm saying is, if Beyoncé wanted it for her wedding then she would get it, right? So why can't I? If Beyoncé can have it, then I can have it.'

I blink at her. That cannot be the way she rationalises everything.

I open my mouth to respond but Bianca gets there first.

'Look,' she sighs, 'I am feeling super stressed, okay? You know the wedding is now only five months away.' She goes to leave and then turns to face me. 'Honestly,' she says, 'you have no idea how hard planning a wedding really is.'

★

19

Could I get away with killing Bianca?

I watch as boiling water splats into my mug from the kettle.

Probably not. But maybe it would be worth it so I didn't have to spend one more second of my day choosing flower arrangements. As if my day couldn't get bad enough, now I've been roped into turning Bianca's flower ideas into a PowerPoint presentation that she can show Jonathan when he returns from his business trip.

I mean, what? What type of person shows their fiancé a PowerPoint presentation about flower arrangements?

I scoop a large portion of sugar and dump it into my tea.

I could just force her to emigrate. I could book her on a flight to Australia and tell her that she has been summoned to speak at a wedding fair, and then 'forget' to book her a flight home.

Although I quite want to go to Australia myself. It would be a better idea to accidentally book myself a flight and leave her here. But how would I—

'Georgia?'

I duck out from behind the fridge door and spot Sally.

Standing at just under six foot, Sally looks like a highly strung stick insect. She has sleek, dark hair that tucks under her chin and large, bulging eyes that stick out of their sockets whenever she is stressed. Which is, pretty much, every second of every day.

I take a deep breath and force all of my acting skills to stand to attention.

'Hi, Sally,' I say, 'how's your day?'

Sally looks at me as if I've asked her how her menstrual cycle is going.

'Fine,' she barks. 'Did you sort the parrots?'

20

I stifle a laugh. Parrots? Does she think Bianca is getting married on The Black Pearl?

Actually, if that means that Orlando Bloom might be on board then count me *in*.

'Doves?' I say sweetly. 'Yes, I did.'

Sally always feels the need to double-check everything I do. I once thought it would be funny to lie and tell her that I accidentally ordered one hundred chocolate willies instead of one hundred chocolate soufflés, but Sally almost had an asthma attack – and I almost had a written warning – so I have since learnt my lesson.

The lesson being that Sally has a stick up her arse, and my entire office has the sense of humour of a damp tissue.

'Tea?' Sally jerks her head towards my mug.

'Yes,' I reply. 'Would you like one?'

'No.'

'Fine.'

This is how Sally always speaks. Like she's a stuffy old army cadet who hasn't had sex in ten years. She likes to use phrases like 'roger that' and 'not on my watch' and a lot of the time I just want to spike her triple-shot coffee with a bloody sleeping pill.

I steer my way out of the boxy kitchen, edging my way past Sally, who blinks her bulging eyes at me. I begin to make my way up the stairs when I spot Natalie.

'Hey,' I smile, 'you okay?'

Natalie has caramel skin that is constantly contoured and braided hair that is normally twisted down her neck in a thick plait. Her mischievous eyes are framed by cool, square glasses and she's always grinning at me. Always.

21

Natalie is part of the finance team, which makes it very easy for me to listen when she advises ordering a third bottle of wine, as a sensible investment. Although we haven't done that for a while.

'Yeah, fine,' she grins, looking over my shoulder at Sally, who storms past like a premenstrual pheasant. 'What are you doing tonight? Shall we go for drinks? I need something to numb the spreadsheets out of my brain.'

I cup my burning mug close to my chest. 'I can't tonight,' I say, 'I've got to make Amy dinner. Sorry,' I add, 'I don't like leaving her.'

For a split second, I see Natalie's face drop in disappointment. 'No worries,' she says. 'Let me know when you get a night off.'

I smile and make my way up the stairs. 'I will.'

CHAPTER THREE

27TH JUNE

To do list:

- Remind Tina about gas bill (!!!!) (corner her when she is hungover so she cannot run)
- ~~Make Amy lasagna~~ (impossible. How the hell do you make cheese sauce? Leave to Nigella)
- Find seven doves (Bianca. Not important. Wedding is ages away)
- Work on designs?
- Do colour wash (running out of pants, urgent)
- Call Dad

I squirt a generous amount of shampoo on to my open palm and feel my eyes stretch at the purple liquid that snakes out of the bottle.

Oh God, this looks really expensive. Who knew Tina had

such expensive taste? I really should find out what she does for a job. How does she afford any of this? Doesn't our rent bank-rupt her too?

The bottle lets out an almighty groan and my stomach shakes in panic.

Oh no, was that the end of the shampoo? I definitely didn't mean to use it all. I only intended to use a tiny squirt to tide me over until payday.

I glance up at the walls of our dank, grey bathroom. I try to suppress a shudder as I eye the mould, furring up the corners, and the loose tiles that tremble slightly whenever the flat above switches on their tumble dryer.

I never thought I'd live anywhere like this. When I found the job at Lemons, I knew I had to move out. I couldn't stay at home forever. But I'd be lying if I said that I was completely prepared for what my minimum wage salary could afford in London. Amy still lives with our parents, to save for a mortgage. She's always been the sensible sister.

I found Tina online. She said that her last flatmate had packed up and left, so she was happy to snap me up straight away. I didn't even have to sign a contract. Initially, I thought my matchbox room and permanently moist kitchen were charming. I didn't mind the fact that our living-room sofa was lumpy and had questionable stains that I thought were part of the design. Then Tina told me she found the sofa on the street, and I couldn't afford to get it dry cleaned. Then I found mould creeping under my mattress. Then I found the rat.

I massage the shampoo into my scalp and try to ignore the fiery ball of panic forming in the pit of my stomach. Obviously,

I don't usually steal shampoo off my housemate. But after my Elephant and Castle rent shoots out of my bank account, sometimes I'm not left with a great deal of choice.

Amy is the only one who has come to visit me. I won't let Mum and Dad. I don't want them to see it.

I step under the water and allow the shampoo to drizzle down my body.

Oh, this shampoo smells so *nice*.

I would definitely feel better about this if it smelt disgusting, but this smells of a delicious blend of roses and lavender and—

I jolt, as there is a loud knock on the door.

'Georgia?' Tina's voice calls. 'Georgia?'

Oh God. I've been rumbled! Can she smell the shampoo? Can she sense that I'm stealing from her? She's not about to confront me now, is she? I'm naked! And . . . argh! I've got shampoo in my eye!

I ram my head back under the shower in an attempt to wash it out.

The curse of the stolen shampoo!

'Georgia!' Tina shouts, her piercing voice penetrating the bathroom door.

'Yeah?' I manage, madly scrubbing my eye.

Oh God, what's in this? Acid? It feels like acid. Maybe it is. Maybe this isn't actually shampoo at all and Tina filled her bottle with hair-removal cream as a way to catch me out from stealing her stuff.

Argh! How could I have been so stupid?

'Are you nearly finished?' Tina shouts again. 'I'm going out, I need to brush my teeth.'

I feel my body relax slightly as my hands grapple on my head.

Oh, thank God. I think all my hair is still there. The last thing I need is to go bald as punishment for stealing from Tina. How on earth would I explain that to anyone?

I manage to open my burning eye and click the shower off.

'Yeah,' I call back, 'give me a second.'

I clamber out of the shower and wrap my steaming, pink body in my limp towel. I grab my hair and sniff it madly, my eyes darting down to the empty bottle of shampoo lying in the shower.

Oh God, my hair really smells of her shampoo. She's going to know. Can I make a joke out of this? Will she find it funny? Me and Tina have barely exchanged four sentences with each other. She might be totally chilled, or I might wake up in the morning to a horse's head propped in my bed. Both options are equally plausible.

I scoop up the rest of my things and pull open the bathroom door. A waft of steam swirls between us and Tina bats it away from her face.

'Sorry,' I say, slipping past her as quickly as I can.

'Ooooh!' Tina calls, turning to face me. 'You smell nice!'

I freeze.

'Er . . .' I say feebly, turning back to her, 'thank you.'

Tina looks back at me and my eyes dart around the room. Does she know?

'Are you going out?' she asks, gesturing to my towel.

'No,' I say quickly, as the steam around me diminishes and the usual temperature of our ice cube flat puckers my skin. 'Well, I'm going to see my sister. I'm there for the weekend. Are you going somewhere fun?'

Tina's eyes flicker and she looks down at her phone.

'Yeah,' she says, 'I'm out with my girlfriends. I seem to have a birthday every weekend right up until Christmas!'

She laughs loudly and I blink back at her. Apart from drinks with Natalie, I rarely go out any more. Once I graduated from university, I fell into a routine. I like my routine, I'm happy with it.

'Oh,' I say, 'that sounds nice.' I tighten my towel around myself and slowly turn back towards my room. 'Have a nice evening.'

'Thanks!' Tina calls from the bathroom. 'You too!'

'Thanks,' I mumble back, kicking my bedroom door shut, 'I will.'

★

'We should have called a taxi.'

My eyes flit between Amy and Mum as a light wind ruffles my hair and I lean against the bus stop, a blade of sunlight streaming on to my face.

'We can't call a taxi,' Amy says tightly, her eyes scanning the gridlocked road. 'It's a match day.'

I clench my hands as the weighted shopping bags burn into my fingers and I try to ignore the screaming pain in my elbows, which feel like they're going to cut themselves free of my sockets any second.

Bloody hell, these bags are heavy. Why are they so heavy?

'Your dad should have picked us up,' Mum mutters out of the corner of her mouth. 'We should have just waited.'

'He was going to be another hour!' Amy retorts. 'We can't have sat in Sainsbury's for an hour! We can get the bus. It's fine.'

Tomorrow is Sunday, and every Sunday Mum makes a roast

dinner for the whole family. She's done this since me and Amy were kids. But this is the first time she's hauled us both to Sainsbury's and insisted on buying two pavlovas (or pavlov*ARH*s, as Mum pronounced it – apparently, there's a serious difference, and when I said I didn't get it she looked at me as if I'd asked to buy a sex swing).

I tilt forwards as a group of burly men push behind me into the thick of the crowd, all wedged beside the bus stop like passive sardines.

Mum's answer to everything is food. If you're celebrating, heartbroken or shot with nerves, she cooks. I glance down to my splitting carrier bags, overflowing with punnets of fruit and stacks of fancy boxes. Even though she would never admit it, I know what the sudden flurry of all this extravagant dessert food really means.

My eyes stray back over to Amy, who is still glaring at the road. I flinch as the gaggle of men behind me bounce into each other, their beer splattering across the pavement.

We grew up in Twickenham, south-west London. Mum, Dad and Amy still live in our family home, and I moved out earlier this year. It's a lovely place to live.

I was really happy here. Unless the rugby was on.

Then the town is crushed by a swarm of excitable, boozed-up rugby fans, and if you have any sense at all you'll lock your doors, draw your curtains and put *Toy Story* on repeat until the terrible ordeal is over.

You most certainly would not willingly stand alongside a swelling gang of supporters, waiting at a bus stop.

'Be careful!' Mum hisses over her shoulder at a man with a face like a warthog, as he staggers towards us. She holds her arm behind

Amy like a shield and glares at the crowd. I glance nervously towards Amy and see a deep shade of scarlet rising up her face.

I shuffle over as best as I can, but Amy doesn't look at me. I feel my chest twitch.

It's been one month since Amy's diagnosis, and nobody likes to talk about it. Well, actually, that's not strictly true. We all try to talk about it, but Amy won't. She won't even respond.

My eyes meet Amy's briefly before we both look away, staring instead at the congested roads. I see the bus roll into sight and feel the gaggle of drunkards rise as they spot the bus. They all begin to cheer and knock each other across the pavement.

My body stiffens and I fight the urge to hoist Amy in front of me so that I can protect her. I notice Mum's head jerking beside me, her eyes full of worry.

Amy doesn't look ill. This seems to make it harder, because nobody tries to help her. Amy is so stubborn, nobody ever thinks she needs any help at all.

She doesn't want any help. She's never wanted any help.

The bus slowly pulls up and the crowd behind us suddenly sticks together as if we have all been vacuum packed. My shoulders rise up to my ears as a large man with a swollen stomach squashes in next to me, and the crowd funnels towards the doors. I glance towards Mum as I hear her yelp, and then I look at Amy, who hasn't moved. Her eyes are still locked on the traffic, and her mouth is moving slightly, as if she is counting.

The crowd shuffles forward and suddenly I feel Mum barge past me, towards Amy.

My mum is a delicate woman, with dark hair that is cropped behind her ears. As the smallest of the family, she stands at barely five foot tall. I stare at her as she shoves past the giant, roaring

29

men who are blocking her way and wince at the fire in her eyes.

'Excuse me!' she shouts, over the jolly roar of the crowd. 'Excuse me! I need to get through!'

Anxiety spins through my chest as I push my body against the waiting throng, my shopping bags thwacking the backs of my legs. I can barely see Amy now, and as the top of her head is swallowed by the mob, panic grips my skin.

I need to get to her.

'Excuse me!' I hear myself scream. 'Excuse me!'

I angle my shoulders forward and shove myself against the backs of the men in front of me. One of them stumbles sideways, and I take my chance and squeeze through the gap. As I do, I feel one of my carrier bags split open and my aching fingers contract as I hear the crack of boxes of fruit hitting the floor as the bag falls from my hands. With a great push, I reach the front of the crowd, and as I duck forward I hear Mum scream. The remaining shopping falls out of my hands.

My eyes spin around wildly until I spot Amy, lying at the foot of the bus door, her face pressed against the cold pavement and her limbs sprawled out behind her like a broken doll. I watch her in horror as she tries to push herself up and drops back down on to the concrete. Panic seizes my throat, and I charge forward and grab Amy by the elbows. As I try to pull Amy up, I hear Mum scream into the crowd.

'She's disabled!' Mum bellows, her voice roaring above the chatter. 'She's disabled! Look what you did to her!'

I will my limbs not to shake as I haul Amy to her feet. She collapses against the side of the bus, my hands still gripped around her waist.

Mum's voice thunders through the crowd and my grip on Amy tightens.

'What is the matter with you?' she screams. 'That is my daughter! She is not well!'

'Mum!' Amy's voice shoots past my ear, and I feel the heat of her face burn against mine. 'Leave it!'

The line of men stare back at Mum, their drunken eyes wondering. One of them mumbles an apology as the crowd chugs on board, leaving me and Amy slumped against the side of the bus. My eyes fix on Mum's face.

Mum turns her body away from the crowd, and as she looks at Amy all of the anger falls away. She steps forward, her chest rising and falling.

'I'm fine!' Amy manages, glaring furiously in Mum's direction. 'I'm fine.'

I hold Amy below her ribs, my arms burning under her weight as fear snakes up my body and pierces my lungs.

Amy quivers beside me as her final words hang in the air, thick with fear.

'I'm not disabled,' she says quietly. 'I'm not dis . . .'

Her words die and I grip on to her.

Amy is not fine. She is not fine at all.

Chapter Four

18th July

<u>Shopping list:</u>

- 1 loaf of bread (small loaf as spending most of this week with Amy)
- Vegetables (sensible array)
- Healthy yogurt **NOT!!** ROLO OR CHOCOLATE BUTTON!!!!!
- Treats (sensible array)
- Pizza **ONE!**
- Ready meals (sensible array)
- Fancy chicken fillets

'Do you want ketchup?'

'What?'

'Ketchup,' I yell, 'do you want ketchup?'

'Yes, please.'

32

I throw a bottle on to the tray and steer my way into my parents' living room. Amy is propped in an armchair, smiling. Her hair is twizzled into a knot on top of her head and her pinched cheeks are flaring. I hand her a tray and sit next to her.

'Is there anything on the telly?'

Amy shakes her head and picks up her fork. I glance down at my plate bleakly.

God, this looks horrible.

When I offered to cook for Amy, I thought it was a great idea. I was captivated at the idea of whipping up a delicious feast for my sister after a long day at work. I would nip round Tesco, tossing items into my basket, which I would throw together to create a delicious meal. In the depths of my fantasy, I even imagined being snapped up by Joe Wicks for my natural flair for cooking and would end up perched on *This Morning*, lightly discussing my hidden talents.

I spear a limp piece of pasta with my fork and wince.

Cooking has now been added to the growing list of 'things-I-ought-to-be-able-to-do-by-now-but-somehow can't', right before working the tumble dryer and understanding my tax code.

I tear off a piece of garlic bread.

Who knew cooking was so bloody hard? I always thought Mum was just being dramatic.

Amy chews her food and I glance up at her.

After two weeks of managing to create meals that were both undercooked and burnt, I stumbled across the ready meals section of Tesco and have been shamefully lying to Amy ever since. I'm still being a good sister and making her dinner every night. Do you know how hard it is to time an entire meal with only one microwave? Only one little box fits in there at a time. It is actually very advanced and difficult. I think I should get some credit for that.

'What are you doing tonight?' Amy asks.

I look at the wall clock; it's only 6.15 p.m.

I shrug. 'Nothing,' I say. 'Whatever you want to do. Maybe we could watch that new drama on ITV.'

Amy raises her eyebrows at me. 'I thought you were seeing your friend Natalie?'

I force myself to swallow another mouthful.

'No,' I say airily, 'I decided not to.'

Amy picks up the remote and selects an old episode of *The Great British Bake Off*. My eyes widen at the screen.

'Look at that cake!' I gush. 'I don't know how they do it, I am so terrible at cooking.'

Amy twirls her fork around some pasta and cocks her head. 'They've probably had a lot of practice. You could do it if you wanted to.'

'I couldn't,' I scoff.

Amy's eyes dart towards me, slightly narrowed. 'You could.'

I shake my head. 'I couldn't,' I say, 'I could never do that.'

There is a silence as we both watch Mary Berry survey the cakes.

'How was work?' Amy says eventually.

'Fine.'

'Did you show Bianca your designs?'

'No.'

'Why not? They're really good.'

I raise my eyebrows at her. 'She doesn't care, Amy.'

'Well then, make her care.'

I put my knife and fork down. Amy has always been like this. If she worked at Lemons, she would have had Bianca's wedding organised and rebranded the entire company before midday.

She would definitely not eat a squashed ham and cheese sandwich for lunch.

'How was work?' I ask.

Amy turns her body away from me. 'Fine,' she says feebly.

'Did you manage the whole day?'

'Yeah,' she says eventually, 'but I was sat at a desk for the afternoon.'

Amy is a PE teacher, and always has been. She's adamant that this isn't going to change since her diagnosis. Even though everyone has advised her to quit. I've given up telling her to take it easy. It's not worth the fight.

I glance up at Amy, whose eyes are glued to the TV with such ferocity, they could pop out of her head at any second.

I edge my body closer to her. 'Are you okay?' I say.

'Yep.'

'I'm worried about you.'

Amy shifts in her seat and moves her plate from her lap. 'Really?' she says. 'I think I'm more worried about you.'

I blink at her. 'Me?' I reply. 'Why are you worried about me?'

Amy shrugs as the credits roll and the music pipes into the living room. 'I just am.'

★

I rub my eyes and stumble into the living room. I ended up staying at my parents' last night. After me and Amy finished dinner I couldn't be bothered to travel home.

35

'Morning,' I mumble to Amy.

Amy looks up. She is sat at the desk, pen poised. Her hair is scraped back into a tight bun and she is already dressed.

How long has she been sitting there?

'Are you making tea?' Amy says, her eyes snapping back down to her work.

I nod, unable to organise the words jumbling around my brain as I skulk into the kitchen.

'Good,' Amy calls after me, 'make mine a strong one.'

I flick the kettle on and lean against the kitchen worktop. I jump as Mum comes bustling in, laden with Marks and Spencer carrier bags.

'Morning, darling!'

'Hi, Mum,' I manage.

'Goodness,' she turns to face me, 'are you not dressed yet? You know it's almost half past *nine*, Georgia.'

'Yes.'

'What are you planning to do with your day? Are you staying for lunch? Jamil from next door is popping round to discuss the garden plans for his remodel, and then I must start cooking for tonight's dinner with Tim and Linda. You remember them, don't you, love? Well, Linda has just redone her kitchen, so I simply must make a dessert to blow her . . .'

I zone out as Mum witters in my ear, and carry the steaming mugs back into the living room. If Mum had her way, I would be fully dressed by 7.30 a.m. every day, whisking up a savoury crème brûlée for brunch.

I place Amy's tea next to her and zap on the TV. Amy reaches over to grab the remote and zaps the TV back off.

'Hey,' I say, reaching across, 'I was watching that.'

Amy drops the remote on to the chair next to her, her eyes still glued to her notepad, her right hand scribbling.

I lean in to try and catch a glimpse. 'What are you doing?'

Amy dots the paper and continues to scrawl. 'Writing you a list,' she says, not looking up.

I roll my eyes. 'What is it with you and Mum? You're both obsessed with me leaving the house before midday. I'm not going shopping. I can't be bothered, I have literally just woken up. If you have a food craving we can order a takeaway.'

That's actually not a bad idea. I would love a takeaway. What is an acceptable time to order a Chinese on a Saturday? Could I get away with ordering it at, like, 11 a.m.? Surely if I pop a piece of parsley on top I could call it brunch.

'Not a shopping list,' she mumbles, sucking on her pen as she scans her words.

I sink into the sofa and rub my head in my hands. 'Oh,' I say, 'well, can you pass me the remote, please?'

'No.'

'Amy, I—'

'Shut the door, will you?' She finally looks up. 'I need to talk to you.'

I scowl at her as I reluctantly pull myself up from the sofa and click the door shut.

'What?' I say grumpily, slouching back against the sofa cushions.

Amy turns to face me and, for the first time this morning, she meets my eyes. Her eyes are glazed over and sunk into their sockets. Her usually bright skin is dull, as if dusted with a coat of grey, and her lips are cracked and peeling.

I furrow my brow at her. 'Have you been to bed?' I ask.

Amy fingers the piece of paper. 'Yes,' she says, 'but I didn't sleep for long. I've been up since four.'

'A.M..?' I repeat in disgust. 'You've been up since four a.m.?'

The last time I was up at four a.m. was when I accidentally gave myself food poisoning after eating three-day-old pizza (not an experience I ever hope to relive).

Amy takes a sip of her coffee. 'I couldn't sleep. I had something on my mind.'

Mum and Dad converted the study into Amy's bedroom when she could no longer manage the stairs easily. Has she been sat at her desk all night?

I push my fringe out of my eyes, my mind waking up and spinning. She looks serious.

'Okay,' I say slowly, sitting up, 'what is it?'

Amy takes a deep breath. I can tell the words are creeping up her throat, coaxing their way out as I look back at her. Finally, she speaks.

'I didn't tell you this, because I didn't think it was a big deal.'

I blink and try to control the hundreds of possibilities spiralling around my brain.

That is a terrible first sentence. What the hell is she going to say next?

'Right,' I say, trying to keep my voice steady.

'But,' Amy continues, 'before I got diagnosed with MS, I made a list. A bit like a bucket list. It was all of the things I wanted to experience before I turned thirty. It's a mixture of things that I heard about on the radio, or saw online, and I just began ticking them all off slowly. I just wanted to really experience everything I could.'

I take a sip of my tea. My chest burns.

'But now . . .' she pauses, 'obviously there are a lot of things I can't do any more, and I've been thinking about how I can't do them.'

Her voice catches, and suddenly I can't bear it.

'You can!' I blurt. 'You can do anything, you—'

Amy holds up a hand. 'Let me finish,' she says calmly. 'I think you should do them. I want you to do them instead.'

I hover.

'Me?' I say, stumped. 'Amy you're making it sound like you're dying. You can still do them.'

'No, I can't.'

'You can!'

'I can't,' Amy snaps, her fierce eyes flashing up at me. 'Georgie, I can't. I can't do anything any more. This fucking—'

She breaks off and to my horror, her eyes overflow.

I blink back at her, my hand reaching out towards her as she wipes her face with the backs of her hands, roughly.

'Sorry,' she mutters stiffly, 'I'm tired. I didn't mean to do that. Sorry.'

'It's fine,' I say automatically.

Amy takes a deep breath and dabs her eyes. She holds the notepad in her lap and raises her eyes to meet mine.

'I've edited it,' she continues, 'so it's not my original list. That's what I've been doing this morning. I've taken bits out that I know you wouldn't want to do – and I also added some things in there that I think would benefit you . . .' She pauses and I notice a flicker of anxiety pass across her face. 'What do you think? Will you do it for me?'

There's a lump in my throat and tears are straining against my eyes now. I can't see her like this.

'I think we should do it together,' I say evenly.

Amy shakes her head. 'No. I can't.'

'You always say there's no such thing as can't,' I retort.

A laugh escapes from Amy, and the effort of this causes tears to spill down her face.

'Sometimes there is.'

CHAPTER FIVE

I lean back into my desk chair as Natalie buries her head into my new list, which is laid out on the desk.

'So, you have to do everything on here?'

'Yeah.'

I glance at the office door to check that Bianca - or, God forbid, Sally - is nowhere to be seen and then follow Natalie's eyes sweeping across the paper. A dull pang strums in the pit of my stomach as I focus on the list. This feeling is quickly replaced with panic.

Amy has always been the smarter sister, and she demonstrated this once again on Saturday by tricking me into agreeing to the list before letting me see it. I didn't have a single chance to edit it, or negotiate bits out, and by the time she let me read it she'd left for a doctor's appointment and I was left alone, and horrified.

God only knows what she's added or taken out 'for my benefit'. What else could have been on there? Sticking my face in a barrel of piranhas? Tap dancing on the back of a sleeping alligator? Sneaking up behind a gang of drunk girls and running off with their cheesy chips?

Natalie's shoulders shake and I glance over

Georgie's list

1. Have a vindaloo on Brick Lane. (*Is Amy trying to kill me?*)
2. Take a Salsa class. (*Humiliating. Why would she ever want to do that?*)
3. Do a skydive. (*She's definitely trying to kill me.*)
4. Go on a Tinder date. (*Urgh. Why?*)
5. Cycle around Hyde Park. (*May actually enjoy that one, providing I don't pedal under a bus.*)
6. Run 10k. (*Worst one.*)
7. Make the perfect Victoria sponge. (*I may have to come clean about the ready meals.*)
8. Go skinny-dipping in the sea. (*WHAT? Alone? I'll be arrested!*)
9. Try skateboarding at Southbank. (*She does not know me at all.*)
10. Show Bianca your designs! (*Hmmm. Perhaps I'll post them to her and then 'forget' to put the correct stamps on the envelope so she won't receive it until she's ninety and her eyesight has practically gone.*)

Natalie turns the list over and hands it back to me, a wide smile pulling at the corners of her mouth. 'It's not that bad,' she says, 'and some of it may even be fun.'

I raise my eyebrows at her and take the list back. 'I've only got until my birthday to do it.'

Natalie straightens up. 'When's your birthday?'

'Early December,' I reply, 'so I've got a while.'

Natalie frowns. 'But isn't it a list for her thirtieth?' she asks. 'So why isn't the deadline her birthday?'

I place the list inside my notebook and slip it back into my bag.

'Her birthday is a week after mine,' I explain, 'so it's sort of the same. I think she wanted it to end on my birthday so I would see it as some sort of celebration. We usually have a joint party anyway.'

I pull a face at Natalie and she laughs.

Amy said I should do it fast to prove I could do it. She said if I didn't then I might forget about it. I can safely say that there is no way I will forget that I have a skydive looming in my near future.

'Well,' Natalie goes to leave, 'why don't you start with the easiest one? The Tinder date will be done in days.'

'Easiest?' I repeat.

Obviously she has never had any issue with composing a bio that somehow says: 'I'm really fun but not that kind of fun. I'm looking for a relationship, but also I'm not crazy I promise I won't propose to you on the first date' in five hundred characters.

It's an art. Believe me.

'I've always wanted to go speed dating,' Natalie adds.

I shoot her a look. 'Don't you go giving Amy any ideas,' I mutter.

Christ.

I wave Natalie off and pull out my phone, my insides squirming at the thought of going on a Tinder date.

I downloaded Tinder once, and then swiftly deleted it when a man asked for a photo of my big toe and have been successfully avoiding any online apps ever since.

Dubiously, I tap the word 'Tinder' into my App store and watch as the spiral spins on my screen.

This is like something out of a horror film, or a Trevor McDonald documentary. My sister writes me a bucket list, I faithfully agree and am then eaten alive by a crazed maniac after he spikes my gin with heroin. I'll end up on the news and become the face for a safe sex campaign.

Tinder pops open and I feel my insides shrivel. Fighting every instinct in my body, I choose some pictures of myself and tap in a lame bio. One date. I only have to go on one date with somebody. Also, Amy didn't stipulate how long the date had to be. Perhaps I will just say hello and then army-crawl out of the fire exit. Job done.

The first man spins on to my screen and, to my surprise, my heart rate quickens.

Oh wow! He is so good looking! I had no idea such good-looking men would be on Tinder. I thought they'd all have a peg leg and zero teeth. I could happily go on a date with this guy. In fact, I would love to go on a date with this guy! Maybe he is the one! God, this is so easy, the first guy I spot on Tinder and I fall in love instantly. Why haven't I done this sooner? What have I been worrying about? I can't believe I—

I break off my thoughts as I flick down to his bio:
No heffas.

I hover over my screen. No heffas?

Who is this guy?

I look around to check I am still alone, as if the heffa police could storm in at any moment and name me Mayor of Heffaville.

A wave of heat washes up my body as I stare at the screen.

No heffas? Am I a heffa? I mean, I don't think I am. But I did just eat half a packet of Jaffa cakes.

I glance down at my gurgling stomach and feel a surge of defiance.

I am not a heffa. No way. Screw you, *Dave*.

Although, I guess the sensible way to find out would be to swipe right and see if he thinks I'm a heffa. I won't talk to him, obviously, but if it's a match I can be happy knowing that I am living in a heffa-free zone. Surely that is the sensible thing to do.

Before I can stop myself, my finger launches forward and strikes Dave's face right off my screen. I pause as nothing happens.

Oh my God, it isn't a match. I *am* a heffa! All those years of eating pizza for breakfast have finally caught up with me.

I am a heffa. And do you know what comes after heffa? Lump. I am a heffalump.

A bloody lump. A lumpy—

'Georgia?'

I glance up as Sally sticks her head around the door. 'Bianca needs you. Meeting. Now.'

I lurch up from my chair and scuttle after Sally.

'Did you make the coffee?' Sally barks as we speed round a corner.

'Yes,' I lie. 'Of course.'

I feel a pang in my stomach as we power forward.

Shit.

Sally jerks to a halt as we arrive outside the meeting room. She blinks at the empty table.

'Where's the coffee?'

I open my notebook and flick through the pages, pretending to look incredibly busy.

'Coffee?' I repeat, avoiding her eye contact. 'In there.'

Do I have time to make it? Could I tap Sally on the shoulder, duck behind her, and then when she questions me claim she's going senile?

Although she's only thirty-two. That's too young to be senile, isn't it?

Maybe I'm going senile.

'Georgia,' Sally says sternly, 'it's not there. Where is it?'

I could just tell her the truth. That I didn't make any coffee because I was too distracted by Tinder Dave and whether I was, or was not, a heffalump.

If I tell her that I forgot, her head will just explode. It took me three months to get her to stop following me around everywhere. If I tell the truth, she might try and move in with me to track my every movement.

'Did you forget to make the coffee?' Sally's voice slices through me. 'Did you forget to make it? You didn't make it, did you?'

'Yes,' I fire back. 'Of course I did.'

God, she's so annoying.

Who is she to assume that I forgot to make the coffee? Like I'm some sort of imbecile. I am a professional, 26-year-old adult. I can successfully undertake a simple task.

I mean, I know I did forget, but that is beside the point.

'It was here,' I hear myself say before I can stop myself, 'the coffee was here. That's where I left it.'

My neck burns as the lie tumbles out of my mouth.

Right. So I just lied. Why did I just lie? I can't lie. I'm a terrible liar. What am I doing?

Sally's gaze swoops around the room and lands back on me. 'Well, it's not here any more,' she says accusingly.

'Maybe someone stole it,' I retort childishly.

'Sally, get the door!'

My head jerks up as Bianca swans down the corridor. Sally jumps to attention and props the door open obediently as Bianca sweeps through and throws herself into a chair. Her eyes scan the room and my face burns. It is common knowledge that Bianca never starts a meeting without a fresh cup of coffee. It is arguably more important than the meeting itself.

Suddenly, her sharp eyes narrow.

'Where's the coffee?'

Sally springs forward like she's been jabbed with a cattle prod.

'Georgia says it's been stolen,' she says stiffly.

My face burns as I fight the urge to kick Sally in the shins.

Bianca snaps open her laptop and fixes me with a piercing look. 'Stolen?' she repeats, aghast. 'Someone stole our coffee?'

Oh God. Can I go back from this? Say it was all a big joke? Claim April Fools? I mean, it's July, but maybe I could claim it as a monthly gag?

A cold bead of sweat drops down my brow and I keep my face still.

I take a deep breath and try to control my jigging leg. 'Yes,' I say solemnly.

Silence stretches across the meeting room and I avoid Sally's laser glare, burning into the side of my face. She knows I'm lying. She definitely knows I'm lying.

Without warning, Bianca bangs her fist on the table and I leap in fright.

'Bastards!' she cries. 'Who was it, Georgie? Do you know?'

I blink back.

What?

'No,' I stammer.

Bianca swings herself round in her chair, her hair flailing behind her.

'I bet it was that arsehole Dennis from the fourth floor,' she says scathingly. 'He's always trying to sabotage me. You'll have to put in a formal complaint with HR.' She points her pen at me. 'I'll set you up with Sharon.'

I nod feebly.

Please don't set me up with Sharon.

What have I done? What have I started? Am I going to have to make a statement? Will I have to lay my hand on a Bible and swear by the Lord to tell the truth, the whole truth, and nothing but the truth?

Is this how fraud cases start? Am I going to go to prison?

This is bloody awful. My heart rate cannot take this. I think I'd rather have Sally move in with me. Screw it, I'd even opt for bunk beds.

*

Har har! Call the authorities, the old Georgia Miller has vanished. Please make way for the new, improved Georgia Miller who is up at 6.20 (in the *morning*!) ready to go on her first run like a real, in-control adult.

This is not a drill. I have cracked out my trainers (which somehow have *three* holes in them. I really should buy a new pair) and even smuggled my unruly breasts into a sports bra.

I have to say I look fantastic, no wonder everybody loves posting pictures of themselves at the gym. This sports bra has pulled my boobs right up to my chin!

My chin!

I take another smug look at myself in the mirror and fight the urge to pose manically as if I am in the new Nike advert alongside Mo Farah.

I've already texted Amy to let her know about the new me. She replied straight away. I was mildly horrified that she was already awake – it took seven aggressive alarms to wake me up at this ungodly hour. But it has happened! I am ready for a run at the crack of dawn. I'm practically beating nature in my morning routine. Not to mention, like, everybody on my street. Nobody is awake yet! There is not a single soul wandering around my street right now. I am the most productive person in SE1.

I glance out of the window and feel a small tug in the centre of my chest.

But I mean, there is literally nobody out there. Not even the corner shop is open and I could have sworn it was twenty-four hours.

Is it safe to run this early in the morning? Why isn't anybody else doing it?

There isn't any chance I could be abducted, is there?

I scowl at a cat leaping over a fence.

No. Strange men and criminals lurk in the middle of the night, not early mornings. Everybody knows that. That is just basic human knowledge. Anyway, if I do see a serial killer then I am perfectly dressed to run away. Ha.

Unless, that is, they target me at the end of the run when I am thoroughly worn out and already on the verge of death. Actually, that would be the perfect time to abduct me.

Without quite meaning to, I sink back on to my bed as my mind churns like a vat of condensed milk.

49

Is this a terrible idea? Probably not, but what if I'm right? What if I do get abducted?

A bolt of fear shoots through me as another thought drops into my brain.

Mum would be asked to supply a 'have you seen this girl?' photo and she'd definitely use the one of me at my cousin's wedding (where I look like a Christmas pudding but Mum always insists I look 'very nice').

I glance at the clock and jolt. I need to get up and go on this run. I need to get up right now.

Maybe they'd use one of my new Tinder photos. Unless they thought none of them actually looks anything like me. God, that would be mortifying.

My eyes skim back over to the window anxiously, and I spot the cat now sitting on the fence.

Okay, well, there is literally nobody out there. Nobody is going on a run. Obviously none of the locals think it is safe. I mean, where is everyone? This has to be a sign that I, too, should not be going on a run.

Before I can command them not to, my feet pull themselves out of my trainers.

Right. As an adult, I am making the executive decision not to go on this run for the sake of my health and well-being. That is definitely the safe and logical thing to do, and I should not feel guilty about it.

I flop back down on to my unmade bed.

At least I didn't update my Facebook status.

★

'Whisk the eggs, darling! *Whisk!*'

I growl into my bowl of sloppy eggs and shrivel away from Mum. She overheard me asking Siri how to make a Victoria sponge and was suddenly gripped by the idea of passing down her 'baking secrets'. She arranged our baking lesson immediately and, one week later, here I am. Hating life and cursing Amy from afar.

'Darling, you are not whisking properly,' Mum cajoles me, sticking her head into my bowl. 'You need to *whisk*, darling! Whisk! It's all about the wrist action!'

I freeze as my body convulses in disgust.

That is a sentence you should never hear your mother say.

'Mum!' I snap, as she tries to grab my arm so we can whisk in unison. 'Look, I need to whisk at my own speed, all right? I can't whisk under pressure.'

Mum staggers backwards as if I have just asked to be emancipated.

'Well, then!' she puffs in exasperation. 'You can't apply for *The Great British Bake Off*, can you?'

I blink at her, dumbfounded.

What?

'Never have I ever suggested that I wanted to apply for *The Great British Bake Off*,' I say flatly. 'Why would I want to do that? I can barely boil an egg.'

Mum throws her arms in the air. 'Fine,' she says, 'fine! You keep whisking. I want to watch the rest of my programme. Then we can carry on.'

'Fine,' I say, glueing my eyes to my sad eggs as Mum bustles out of the kitchen.

We're not even making a cake! Mum insisted that we needed to 'master the basics' first.

51

This is not how I should be spending my Friday evening. This is not how any 26-year-old should be spending their Friday evening. It's July! I should be sat in a pub garden with a glass of prosecco, not stuffed in a kitchen fighting the urge to thwack my mother with a wooden spoon.

My phone vibrates and I look up.

You have a new match!

Idly, I pick up my phone and click on Tinder. I am desperate to get this bloody date out of the way so I can delete this thing. I never imagined how much admin was required. I woke up this morning to a shirty message from one guy because I hadn't replied to his message in four hours. I was asleep! He messaged me at 3 a.m.!

Honestly, it's not worth the aggravation. I think I'd rather join a nunnery.

My eyes scan my phone as four images spring on to my screen in turn.

Jack, age 28, London.

Oh, I remember him. He's the one with all the group photos. I still swiped right, which is awkward because it must mean I fancy all of his friends.

My phone buzzes again.

Jack has messaged you!

I raise my eyebrows and open the message.

Hi Georgia. How are you? Lovely smile.

I cock my head and type a message back.

'Georgia!'

I jump as Mum swings back into the kitchen, glaring at me.

'Have you been on your phone this entire time?' she cries.

'Have you been wasting time, after I've slaved away trying to teach my daughter the secrets of our family recipes?'

I guffaw at her.

Secrets? Unless Nigella Lawson is my long-lost cousin, there is nothing secret about this.

'Have you whisked the eggs?' Mum demands. 'Have you been whisking? Have you even tried, Georgia?'

Mum always says my name as if I'm a runaway convict.

'Yes,' I say crossly, 'of course I have.'

Mum raises her eyebrows. 'Really?'

'Yes!'

'Well, then . . .' Mum grabs her own bowl and holds it in front of her. 'Let's see if it matches mine. You've had plenty of time!'

I watch in panic as Mum turns the bowl upside down above her head. The eggs stay stuck to the bowl. Mum shoots a look at me as if she's just pulled out the sword of Excalibur.

My insides squirm.

How far will I go to save face?

'Well?' Mum prods. 'Well, Georgia? Did you whisk the eggs?'

I did whisk the eggs. I know I had a small break but I did whisk them. I bloody did.

Defiantly, I grab the bowl and tip it above my head. Before I even have the chance to change my mind, the cold eggs slop on to my freshly washed hair and slide all down my face. I squeal.

I try not to wince as raw egg drips through my eyelashes and runs into my clenched mouth.

Mum shakes her head at me and looks me up and down, then slowly whispers the phrase I hate most: 'Silly girl.'

This is not how I should be spending my Friday evening.

Chapter Six

4th August

To do list:

- TINA. GAS BILL
- Find seven doves (Bianca. Not important. Wedding is ages away)
- Finish design, add to portfolio
- Do colour wash (running out of pants, urgent) !!!!!!
- Call Amy

Oh my God and holy hell. Who needs to join a gym when you have to single-handedly change a double bed?

I don't think I've ever been so exhausted, and I once accidentally walked up the stairs at Covent Garden tube station.

I rub my forehead with the back of my hand and feel irritation growl up my back.

This is such a boring way to be spending a Saturday. I've

been trying to change the damn bed for what feels like *hours*. I wasn't planning on changing my sheets today, but then I caught Tina peering at my fake tan stain and wasn't left with a great deal of choice.

I scowl at the duvet, which is bunched up in the corner of its cover in a sad knot.

I grip the corners of my fitted sheet with my fingers and stretch it across my enormous mattress.

Come on. Come on, you stupid mother—

Argh!

I lurch backwards as the sheet pings back off the mattress and shrinks into a pathetic ball in the middle of the bed. Irritation snarls inside me.

For God's *sake*. Why is this so difficult? Is this my life now? Will I be doing this for ever? Will they find me, aged ninety, gripping the corner of my unmade bed whilst desperately clinging on to a bottle of Lenor?

I'll literally be on my deathbed. My unmade deathbed.

This is so unfair. As an adult, you are expected to know how to master all sorts of impossible tasks without any training or instruction.

I mean, why weren't we ever taught this at school? I have to change my bed once a *week* and I am still waiting for the day when memorising the full digits of pi will come in handy.

(3.14159, thank you very much.)

My phone lights up and my eyes flit down in irritation to the screen, which is flashing amongst my rebellious bed sheets.

After a week of awkward messaging, I am finally going on this Tinder date with this Jack guy. We're meeting at 8 p.m. at a very edgy place called The Hook. Which will be interesting, as there is nothing edgy about me. I have zero edges. If I were a shape, I would be a sphere.

I try to ignore the anxiety snaking up my chest at the prospect of meeting a complete stranger.

But still, at least I am going on the date. One date, as Amy insisted. Then I can delete the stupid app and go back to falling in love with strangers on the tube.

I run my fingers through my hair and drop my phone back on to my bed.

I actually think Amy's list may be having a good effect on me. It is barely 3 p.m. and I am fully showered, moisturised and am willingly changing my bed sheets. Look at me, I am Victoria Beckham.

And I went on a run this morning, *and* I didn't die in the process!

I pull myself back to standing and glare at my naked bed.

Urgh. Why is this so hard? Is it supposed to be this hard? I wish there was someone who could do this for me. Not like a maid. But a self-changing bed?

Actually, that's a great idea. Maybe I'll take it to the Dragons and make my fortune, and then I can just buy a boyfriend instead of going on this stupid Tinder date.

Although, I don't want to date a gigolo.

I stride down the street and try to ignore the pain searing through my feet as they pulsate in my pointed heels. I glance at my watch.

8.07. Shit.

A gust of wind whips up my back and I push my fingers through my hair as the August sun beams between the tall

London buildings. This is not how I wanted to be seen arriving on my date. Late, windswept and phoneless.

Shortly after my bed fiasco my phone decided to throw itself into the bath. Thankfully I had already organised with Jack where I was meeting him, but now my phone has been laid to rest in a giant bowl of rice.

I turn a corner and finally spot The Hook. I suppress the urge to roll my eyes.

Obviously it is covered in fairy lights and bunting. I wouldn't be overly surprised if I were served a drink by a man dressed as an avocado.

I blink as I scan around the entrance, waves of heat crashing through me. I can't see him. Oh no. Why can't I see him? Why isn't he here? Where is he? He said we'd meet outside. He said he'd be wearing green. He's not here.

Nervously, I push my way inside.

Oh my God, he's not here. Where is he? He's stood me up. This is awful. Will I just have to go home? I can't believe I—

Oh. He's there.

My frantic eyes land on a young guy walking out of the toilet. He has dark hair, stubble that runs across his jaw, and is wearing a green jumper.

I relax slightly.

I take a deep breath and walk over. He looks up and smiles at me.

'Hi,' I say. 'Jack? I'm Georgia.'

Jack's eyes flick down my body and then meet my eyes. For a second, he almost looks surprised to see me.

'Hey,' he says eventually.

'Sorry I'm late,' I say. 'Shall we get a drink?'

Jack's mouth twitches, he glances over his shoulder and then back at me.

'Sure.'

★

Amy lies on her stomach and pulls the Monopoly board closer towards her.

'I think,' she says slowly, 'I'll buy Mayfair.'

I scowl at her.

'You only want Mayfair because you know I want Mayfair,' I say.

Amy grins. 'No I don't. It's a good investment.'

I make a loud, jokey sigh and glance at my stack of fake money piled up next to me. I wish I was actually this rich. Could I persuade anyone it was real money?

Mum pops her head around the living-room door. 'Roast will be ready in half an hour, okay?'

'Thanks,' we all say in union.

Tamal fishes my phone out of the bowl of rice and looks at it. 'Has it been in here all night?'

'Yes,' I say. 'Thank you so much for trying to fix it.'

'No worries.'

'So, you weren't tempted to make it work when you got back in from your date?' Amy asks in a lofty voice, her eyes still glued to her cards.

'No,' I reply, 'I just went straight to bed.'

'Ah,' says Amy, playing with the plastic houses, 'then you must have been quite tired when you got in.'

I laugh. 'If you want to ask me how the date went, just ask me.'

Amy looks up at me and grins. 'Do I have to?'

To be honest, I have been desperate to speak about it since I arrived. I glance over my shoulder to check Mum isn't feathering about in the corner. The last thing I want is for her to hear I've been on a good date. She'd update her Facebook status in seconds.

'It was really fun,' I grin, 'we got on really well. We just stayed in the bar and chatted all night. I got quite drunk actually,' I add.

A smile spreads across Amy's face and she pulls herself up to sitting.

'Good!' she says triumphantly. 'I knew you'd have fun! Are you going to see him again?'

I feel my cheeks flush. I want to see him again, and he did kiss me. That's a good sign, right?

'Hopefully,' I say.

'Well!' Amy grins at Tamal. 'Hurry up and fix Georgie's phone so we can see if he's messaged you!'

Tamal looks up from the phone and raises his eyebrows. 'Good news,' he says, 'I think it's working.'

Despite myself, I feel my stomach lurch. I have been wondering all morning if Jack has messaged me. I quickly move over to Tamal as my phone springs to life.

Ah ha! It worked! It's alive!

I grin at my lit-up phone. I feel like Dr Frankenstein.

I eye Amy and Tamal, who are grinning at my phone like toddlers.

Oh God, I don't know how I feel about my sister and her boyfriend seeing this. What if Jack's messaged me something totally inappropriate? Or something really soppy and embarrassing? I should put a stop to this.

I carefully lean over to try and grab the phone, when it vibrates.

Jack has messaged you.

My stomach jerks. Amy squeals and I snatch the phone out of Tamal's hand before he can open it. I need to read this first. I click on the message excitedly, and as my eyes scan the message the bubbling excitement turns into prickling fear.

Amy and Tamal lean in towards me, waiting.

'What?' Amy presses. 'What did he say?'

My eyes are glued to the phone. I take a deep breath and read the message aloud.

'It says,' I gnaw my lip, '"Hey, Georgia, sorry this is late notice but it looks like I can't make tonight after all. Let me know if another night works for you."'

I raise my eyes to meet Amy's. She's blinking at me in confusion.

Amy looks at my phone, her eyes wide. 'What time did he send that?'

'Half eight,' I say weakly. 'Half an hour after I met Jack.'

'But,' Tamal screws up his face, 'you went on a date with him?'

I shrug limply. 'Apparently not.'

'Well, then . . .' Amy turns to face me. 'Who did you go on a date with?'

I drop my phone in my lap, anxiety squeezing at my heart.

'I don't know,' I mumble.

Who did I go on a date with?

CHAPTER SEVEN

Running schedule:

04/08   1k   ✓   (August is not the time to start running.
                  Sweat patches are uncontrollable.)

I stare blankly at my computer screen, mindlessly typing figures into one of Bianca's budgeting spreadsheets. For once, I was relieved when Bianca asked me to balance her wedding budget. Since Sunday, my brain hasn't stopped spinning.

I attempt to swallow the dry lump lodged in the back of my throat.

Who did I go on a date with? I'm sure I asked his name. I spent an entire evening with him, laughing, sharing stories. Who was he? I didn't mention this to Amy, but I told this guy a lot about me. All about my job, my family, my life. I don't even know who this guy is, and now he knows so much about me.

I glance up as Natalie slips into the office and shuts the door behind her. She pulls Sally's chair over and slots down next to me. Sally has been in meetings with Bianca since 9 a.m., thank God.

'How'd it go?' Natalie grins, picking up my hand cream and squirting a generous amount into her open palm.

I avoid looking at her. 'How did what go?' I ask, knowing full well what she's talking about.

'The date?' Natalie asks.

Panic spikes inside me at the mention. I sigh.

'Yeah, great,' I say bitterly. 'But it wasn't him.'

Natalie frowns at me. 'What do you mean?' Her mouth falls open as the thought hits her. 'Oh my God. Were you catfished?'

'No!' I retort. 'The opposite. Dogfished. I was dogfished.'

Natalie screws up her face. I pull my tired, square eyes away from the spreadsheet and explain the whole story, my stomach squirming at every detail.

'Wow,' Natalie breathes when I finish. 'Well, I didn't think you were going to say that.'

I shrug and pull out my phone. 'I know.'

'Well,' Natalie says, 'look on the bright side. At least you can cross one off your list, right? You said to Amy you'd go on one date.'

I cock my head. I hadn't thought of that.

'Good point,' I say, as I reach into my bag to get my diary. My hand claws at the inside of my bag hopelessly. Panic pricks at my skin. I bury my head inside the bag.

Where is it?

'You all right?' Natalie asks, as my head is engulfed by the lining.

'No,' I say, my heartbeat starting to race. 'No. I can't find my . . . my diary's gone.'

'Your diary?' She repeats, 'Your notebook, do you mean?'

'Yeah . . .' Panic spins up my throat. 'You know, the notebook I take with me everywhere, I just call it a diary. It's got all of my . . . stuff in it. I need it.'

I ram my fingers through my hair, fear clawing at my body. Where is it? Where *is it*?

Natalie leans forward. 'Did you leave it at home?'

I begin taking all of the items out of my bag frantically. 'No,' I say quickly, 'I always keep it in this bag. This is the only bag I use. I take this bag with me everywhere. I never take it out. It's not here.'

I pull the final objects out of my bag and then look up at Natalie. Her almond eyes are wide behind her thick glasses. My list was in that diary. Amy's list. Why isn't it in my bag? Where has it gone?

I can't have lost it. I can't.

Natalie looks at me helplessly and I gape back at her. She opens her mouth to speak when my phone vibrates next to me. My eyes flick down and land on a text.

Hi. It's Jack from Saturday, you left your notebook with me. I'm free tomorrow night if you want to meet back at The Hook. Let me know x

My stomach drops.

'What?' Natalie catches my expression. 'What is it?'

'It's him!' I manage, my throat burning. 'Jack! Fake Jack! He's got my diary! He *stole it*! He wants to—'

'Georgia?' Sally's sharp voice interrupts me. 'Where are you? Ah. We need you in this meeting.'

Olivia Beirne

I blink at Sally, a cold sweat forming on my brow.

I can't go into a meeting now. I can barely speak. I need a serious lie-down and a shot of whisky.

'Sure,' I say weakly, as Sally raises her eyebrows at me expectantly. 'I'll be right there.'

Sally sweeps out of the room and I turn back to Natalie.

'You have to go see him,' Natalie says at once, 'and get your stuff back. Who does he think he is? What has he been doing with your diary? What a freak!'

I nod, my mouth dry. 'Yeah,' I say. 'You're right. What if he kills me?' I suddenly blurt. 'What if this is his trap to lure me back to his, so he can chop me into tiny pieces and bury me under his floorboards?'

Natalie hovers. 'You've been watching too much *CSI*.'

'Natalie!' I whine.

Natalie stands up. 'I'll come with you,' she says defiantly. 'Tell that weirdo you'll meet him tomorrow after work. I'll come with you and sit two tables away. He won't know who I am, and if anything happens you can give me a code or something and I'll step in.'

I pull my wobbling legs to standing, feeling as if I may crumple back to the floor at any second.

'Right,' I say, fighting the urge to vomit, 'okay. I'll do it.'

*

I flick open my compact mirror and take in my reflection. Needless to say, I did very little at work today and spent the majority of the afternoon frantically reading horoscopes in case any of them hinted that I was about to be murdered by this Jack freak.

64

They didn't. Although one said that I should expect a 'financial development', which I am certainly looking forward to.

Somehow, me and Natalie managed to barricade ourselves in the office toilet for the last forty minutes of the day and Natalie sculpted my face from scratch. I look like an entirely new person. Ironically, Jack may not recognise me. I snap the mirror shut as the train rocks around another corner and panic tickles my heart.

'Are you okay?' Natalie asks.

I nod rigidly. 'I think so,' I say, fixing my eyes on a tube advert of a swollen cat, sucking on a thermometer. My stomach lurches and I try to ignore my dry throat, twitching with panic. I scrunch my eyes shut and then open them again and glance down at my freckled hands, which are shaking slightly.

Ever since I received Jack's message, I keep getting overwhelmed by waves of hot emotion.

The first emotion is horror. I don't even know who this guy is, and he has my diary. My personal diary and my list. What has he read? Why does he want to meet me again? What does he want?

The second emotion is anger, which wraps itself around my ribcage like fire. He lied to me. I thought he liked me, but I don't even know who this guy is.

The third is anxiety. The worst one, the hardest to control.

This thought cues the familiar violent beat of panic to smack at my chest, and I blink quickly to try and steady my vision. I try to moisten my mouth and take a deep breath, which rattles through my twitching body. I never confront anybody. I never argue. I have very clear boundaries that make me feel safe, and I never stray outside them. I know what I can and can't do, and I can't do this. I can't storm up to a stranger and demand my diary back. I don't know how. That isn't me. I haven't got the power. That's Amy. Amy always argues for me.

My eyes sting as the anxiety pulls at my throat and I shake my head. The thought of Amy summons a sudden wave of indignation and I straighten my spine defiantly and squash the anxiety back down. I can't let Amy know I lost that list. It was so personal. I just need to get it back.

'Such a freak,' Natalie mutters, scrolling through her phone. 'I can't wait to see what he looks like.'

'Shh,' I hiss, glancing around the tube.

Natalie looks up. 'Is he here?' she whispers, barely moving her mouth.

I shake my head as the tube pulls into Tottenham Court Road and we stand. He's not on this carriage, unless he's disguised himself. Who knows? Maybe along with being an identity thief he's also a shape shifter.

Natalie links her arm into mine as we stride through the tube station. We spent the majority of the afternoon planning via email how this evening is going to run. Natalie will enter first, get a drink (Diet Coke – she needs a level head in case anything happens, plus we haven't been paid yet) and sit down. I've described to her what fake Jack looks like. So if she spots him, she will sit two tables away and get out her magazine. Then I will enter, go to the bar and order a gin (I also can't afford it, but I need the liquid courage). If he's already there, I will storm over, like Beyoncé, and demand my diary back (this was Natalie's input). If he's not, I will find a seat and idly look at my phone (my input).

I grab Natalie's arm as we reach the corner leading up to The Hook. My stomach spasms.

'Okay,' I say, 'it's just round that corner, so we'd better separate.'

'Right,' Natalie nods, 'see you inside.'

I nod weakly in response.

Oh God, I am so nervous. How do private detectives do this on a daily basis? I mean, I know they don't do this exactly. At least private detectives have guns and Swiss Army knives. The worst I could do is brandish my blunt nail file and pray Jack doesn't challenge me to any form of duel.

I glance down at my watch. Okay, it's been two minutes. Thirty more seconds and then I'll go in.

My stomach squirms.

I just need to get the list and leave. That is all I need to do. It is simple. I don't even need to talk to him. I could just take it and walk off. No need to engage in conversation. Strictly speaking, I don't even need to look him in the eye. I could even just—

'Georgie?'

I jump as my eyes snap up and land on Jack, standing in front of me. His mouth is curved into a kind smile, and as soon as my eyes meet his a current of anger fires through me.

He leans in to kiss my cheek. I flinch in shock, but he doesn't notice.

'Why are you waiting out here?' he asks, gesturing around. 'Aren't you cold?'

His green eyes glint at me, and I finally find my voice.

My list. He's stolen Amy's list. My sister's list.

'Hello, Jack,' I say coldly, 'if that even is your name.'

That is the line me and Natalie have been rehearsing all day.

A flicker of amusement passes over Jack's face. 'It is my name,' he smiles. 'Shall we go in?'

'No!' I cry, furious at his casual response. 'I don't want to see you! I want my diary back.'

I keep my eyes on his face as anger bites my skin. To my horror, I even feel a knot pull its way up my throat.

Jack's eyebrows twitch slightly. 'That's a shame,' he says. 'I wanted to see you. I thought we had fun.'

'We . . .' I splutter. 'I don't even know who you are!' I burst out, trying to control the heat storming up my face. 'You pretended to be my date! I can't believe you—'

I suck in a great breath of air. I cannot lose myself over this.

'I just want my diary back,' I say firmly, 'please.'

Jack looks back at me, his eyes etched with concern. He opens his bag and begins to rummage around.

'Sorry if I upset you,' he says. 'I was just, you know, at a bar and a good-looking girl asked if I wanted a drink.' He cocks his head slightly, his green eyes locked on mine. 'I thought it would be fun.'

To my annoyance, I feel a ripple of excitement when he calls me 'good-looking'. I lift my chin.

'I had fun anyway,' Jack adds, finally fishing out my diary.

My body jars as I notice the list poking out between the pages. I am never letting that out of my sight again. Jack is still staring right at me. I flinch.

'Well,' I say tightly, 'I did too. Or I thought I did. Until you stole from me.'

Jack goes to hand me the diary and freezes. 'Stole?' he repeats. 'Stole what?'

'My diary!' I snap, the hot emotion returning behind my eyes. 'And my list!'

Jack frowns at me, his eyes flitting quickly to my diary, suspended from his fingers.

'Diary?' he repeats. 'What diary?'

I reach forward and snatch it out of his hands.

'This!' I cry, flapping my battered notebook in his face. 'This! My diary. My *personal* notebook with everything *personal* in it that you *stole*. You thief.'

'I didn't steal it,' he says evenly. 'You left it on the table.'

My stony face quivers.

Oh.

'Whatever.'

'Why would I steal your diary?' Jack asks, his voice suddenly sharp. 'What use would that be?'

I stuff my notebook back in my bag, wincing as the pages crumple under my shaking hand.

'I don't know,' I say bitterly, ramming the diary down. 'I don't know the motives of a criminal.'

A small laugh escapes him. 'A criminal?' he repeats.

I feel a swell of fury.

'Yes!' I cry. 'You stole from me and you tricked me! How could you expect me to want to ever see you again? I don't even know who you are! You took advantage of me!'

A full laugh, coated with sarcasm, pumps out of Jack now. 'Took advantage of you?' he says. 'How? You came on to me. I just said yes.'

'I did not come on to you!' I puff, my face flaming. 'You—'

'You came up to me and asked if I wanted a drink,' Jack says mildly. 'I'm just putting two and two together.'

I swing my bag over my shoulder, hearing my heartbeat thumping in my ears.

'Only because I thought you were someone else. I would never come on to you,' I say indignantly. 'You're a freak.'

Jack steps back, a shadow passing over his face.

'Okay,' he says, tucking his hands into his pockets. 'Fine. Well, I'm going to go and get a drink. Do you want one?'

I gape at him. 'No!'

Jack shrugs. 'Suit yourself,' he says, as if I have just turned down a cup of tea. 'See you around, Georgie. Also,' he adds, 'I think pink looks nice on you.'

My eyes fly over my blue jumper.

What? Pink looks . . . what?

My heart jars as he walks past me.

I'm not wearing pink. Why would he say . . .?

'Did you read it?' I hurl after him.

He turns to face me. 'Read what?'

'My diary!'

He keeps walking backwards and I see a tiny smile play at the corners of his eyes.

'Nah,' he says, 'of course not.'

He turns away and my fingers coil around my diary instinctively, defiance spiking behind my eyes.

He read it. He read my diary.

I glare after him as Natalie scurries round the corner, her face flushed.

She reaches me and looks back over her shoulder. 'Was that him?' she says. Her eyes scan my face and her brow knits. 'Are you okay?'

I nod and turn, my eyes fixed on the spot where Jack left. 'Fine,' I say quietly, 'lucky escape. He was a freak.'

CHAPTER EIGHT

Georgie's list

1. Have a vindaloo on Brick Lane.
2. Take a Salsa class.
3. Do a skydive.
4. Go on a Tinder date. ✓
5. Cycle around Hyde Park.
6. Run 10k.
7. Make the perfect Victoria sponge.
8. Go skinny-dipping in the sea.
9. Try skateboarding at Southbank.
10. Show Bianca your designs!

I look up at the garish red sign, looming over me and flashing uninvitingly.

SPORTSWEAR!!!!!!! SHOP TODAY!!! HUGE SALE!!!!!!!

I massage my forehead with the back of my hand and try to

fight the birth of the migraine I will inevitably get from laying eyes on that hideous sign.

Why are there so many exclamation marks? Who needs that many? Who is that excited? And to buy *sportswear* of all things?

I glance around dubiously, as if a nice stranger will appear and tell me that I don't really need to go inside. I can buy the trainers online and Sally was just trying to scare me as punishment for accidentally (on purpose) giving her decaf coffee.

I scrunch up my face and tuck my bag under my arm defiantly.

Come on, Georgie. You have to buy running shoes. If you are going to take on this darn list then you must run, and to run you must own proper running shoes. You cannot run in Primark platform heels.

Well, I can actually, as I've had to run for the bus many times after a few too many Chardonnays with Natalie. But that isn't an experience I would willingly relive.

Sally told me that I needed to buy 'actual running shoes' that 'fit me properly'. She told me I needed to have my 'running style assessed'. Which, to me, sounds absolutely dreadful. It also sounds made up. I mean, do people actually assess other people's running styles for a living?

She also said that I would get some 'handy running tips'. The only running tip I would happily receive is 'don't'. I did say this to Sally, but she didn't find it very funny – which I should have seen coming, as Sally doesn't have a sense of humour.

Right. The sooner I get in the sooner I can get out, get back to my flat and watch *RuPaul's Drag Race*.

I suck in a deep breath and power through the entrance to

the store. I am greeted almost immediately by a burst of music and enormous cardboard cut-outs of perfectly sculpted bodies. My eyes flit over to a cardboard man, towering over me.

Wow. I wonder if you buy a pair of shoes you get to take him home for free?

'Can I help you?'

I stop and snap my head round, my cheeks flaring as my eyes land on the shop assistant.

'Err,' I stumble hopelessly, 'yes, please.'

Wow, he's good looking. I can't have him serve me, he's too good looking. How am I supposed to concentrate?

He steps forward and smiles. I hover on the spot awkwardly.

'What are you looking for?' he asks, his face breaking into a smile.

Oh God, he's getting really close to me. Why is he getting so close? Is this a normal distance? It doesn't feel like a normal distance. I feel like he's about to kiss me.

Maybe he is. Maybe that's how everybody hooks up these days. Maybe this is where I'm going wrong and this is why I'm single.

'Sports stuff,' I blurt, and then immediately want to kick myself.

Urgh. No, that is why you're single. Because you cannot answer a simple question from an attractive man without sounding like a moron.

'Trainers,' I add quickly, leaning on my back leg. 'I need some new trainers. For running. Running trainers.'

His face doesn't move. 'Okay,' he says pleasantly, 'well, we have lots of trainers here. I'll show you.'

I nod and follow him as we delve further inside the fluorescent shop floor.

'So,' the assistant says conversationally, 'what sort of running are you into?'

I blink at him.

What sort of running am I into? What kind of question is that?

'Oh, you know,' I fumble, 'a bit of everything.'

My eyes flit over to an old woman, peering at the trainer socks.

I must look pretty fit for him to keep asking me all of these sports-related questions. I mean, I know we're in a sports shop, but he didn't ask these questions of Old Mother Hubbard in the corner.

'So . . .' he stops as we reach a section filled with stacks of boxes, 'we have these new ones in. Perfect for long-distance running.'

I hover as his words sink in.

Long-distance running.

'Do you do long distance?'

I pause, stumped.

Does 10k count as long distance? I mean, I think it sounds pretty long.

What does Mo Farah run?

'Yes,' I hear myself say.

Well, how is he to know that I'm lying? I could easily be a long-distance runner. I mean, my hair is in a ponytail.

Maybe I could be, maybe this run will be the making of me and I will be so good at running that I'll enter the London marathon.

Excitement grips me as this new idea seeps into my mind.

The marathon! Yes! Why didn't I think of it before? Mum and Dad would be so proud and I'd finally shift my extra chin.

'These are the trainers for you, then.' He smiles as if he is reading my thoughts. 'What size are you?'

'Six!' I gabble.

He nods and moves towards the boxes and pulls one down.

Excitedly, I drop down on to the stool and pull off my heeled boots. I glance down at my feet.

Thank God I'm wearing matching socks.

I take the shoes from the shop assistant and slip them on my feet. They slide on as if they were crafted personally to the shape of my foot, and I feel a warm glow rise up inside me.

I spring to my feet and look down in awe at my new footgear.

Wow. They look amazing! I look amazing! Why don't I ever wear trainers? They look so fantastic. They—

'Okay, so if you'd like to step on the treadmill.'

His voice breaks my thoughts and a bolt of alarm shoots through me.

What? The what?

'I'm sorry?' I say.

Why did he say treadmill?

'That treadmill,' he repeats pleasantly, gesturing to an ugly machine looming impressively in the corner.

I gawp at it in horror.

Okay, what on earth is a treadmill doing in a shop?

'No, thank you,' I say lightly, 'I'm happy with these shoes.'

He looks back at me, the fixed smile on his face twitching at my words.

'We need to test that they support you properly when you run.'

I blink back at him.

When I run?

He gestures back at the treadmill and I feel panic ring in my ears.

When I run?

Do I have to run? Here? In the middle of the shop? Shops aren't made for running! They're made for shopping!

I look away from the treadmill and jump slightly as I catch the shop assistant's knowing eye.

He's going to make me run, isn't he? I mean, what else can I do? I am going to have to run, in the middle of a shop, in front of this very attractive man.

Well, I guess this is it. Goodbye, pride. So long, integrity. It was nice knowing you, self-respect.

Numbly, I step on to the treadmill.

'Okay,' he says, moving over to the front of the machine, 'so we will only do a short run.'

My body convulses in relief. A short run. I can manage that. Surely, I can manage a short run.

He presses a button and, to my alarm, the floor below my feet skids backwards and I feel myself jolt into a horrible jog. I am not prepared for this. I'm wearing hooped earrings! I can't be expected to run wearing hooped earrings!

What if I have a heart attack? Will he be able to resuscitate me? I don't want him grappling around my breasts! Not when I'm unconscious anyway.

I try to smile weakly at the shop assistant, then I notice his eyes are glued to the figures dancing about on the screen. My stomach lurches.

What do they all mean? Is that my heart rate?

My body stiffens in fear.

Is that my weight?

No, of course it's not. Regardless of the amount of chicken nuggets I ate on Saturday, there is no way that I weigh forty stone.

I continue to bounce on the treadmill uncomfortably as my chest jiggles vigorously.

This is hideous. I feel as if I'm about to be sick. My chest burns as I glare up at the assistant, willing him to let me stop running.

Please let me stop. Please, oh please, let me bloody stop. This has been going on for ages! Why can't it stop? He said a short run! This isn't a short run! This is an actual run.

He leans forward, and thankfully clicks a button, and the treadmill slows to a halt. I clasp the sides of the treadmill in desperation as my chest burns in relief. I swallow in a poor attempt to control my erratic breathing. If this is what proper running feels like, then I'm out. Why on earth does Amy enjoy it so much? I feel dreadful.

I need a glass of water and a sit-down pronto. My legs feel like unset jelly and my top lip is damp and quivering.

This is terrible. Twenty minutes ago I felt great and now I feel repulsive.

'Okay,' he says, his eyes still glued to the treadmill, 'well, the shoes seem to support your weight well.'

I jolt in alarm.

My weight? Why is he bringing up my weight?

I stagger off the treadmill and pull the trainers off my pounding feet.

'They seem to be the right fit for your running technique too,' he adds.

I smile weakly.

Running technique? Do I have running technique? I must do.

Heck, maybe I'm better than I thought.

'But you should work on your cardio,' he says. 'For long distance your cardio needs to be in better shape.'

I blink back at him.

'Right,' I say tightly.

Well, that isn't the can-do attitude I expected from a supportive shop assistant! Who is he to say I can't do it? I'll show him when I win the London marathon and appear on the news for completing it in record time. I'll even mention him in my victory speech:

And to the man who thought I wasn't fit enough to run the race . . . well, I bet you feel pretty ridiculous now.

I sashay over to the till, restored to my usual height in my heeled boots, and tap in my pin number to pay for the trainers. He hands me my bag and smiles.

'Good luck with everything,' he says. 'I hope the running goes well.'

I pull the bag off the counter and flash him a smile.

'Thank you,' I say, 'me too.'

★

I concentrate fiercely on my computer screen and attempt to drown out Sally, who has been pacing round my desk for the past four hours as if she's The Flash.

Jonathan arrived home from his business trip yesterday, and Bianca is giving him and the rest of her family a tour of the office. Then, myself, Sally and Bianca will have a meeting with the family to discuss 'wedding progression'.

Cue the biggest eye roll ever known to any living creature.

I mean, what? Have you ever heard of anything so ridiculous? When I lightly mentioned how perhaps we should be preparing for the big pitch, Bianca tried to assassinate me with her eyes and Sally almost gave birth in the kitchen – and she isn't even pregnant. I'm just hoping Bianca doesn't ask me for a bear update.

'Purple and gold,' Sally is muttering as she flaps past my desk, 'with a light scent of lavender to match the colour scheme.'

'Sally,' I burst out, desperate to stop her obsessive pacing and muttering, 'why don't you sit down for a minute?'

Sally staggers to a halt and snaps her head round to face me. 'What?' she says stoutly. 'Sit?'

Her eyelids flick over her protruding eyeballs and I try to ignore the purple vein throbbing at her neck.

'Yes,' I lean back in my chair and gesture to her own, 'sit down for a minute and tell me about your weekend.'

Sally gawks back at me, flabbergasted. Her feet are still marching on the spot as if her legs haven't caught up with her brain.

'Just for a minute,' I add, forcing my face into a smile.

I relax slightly as Sally sinks into a chair surreptitiously. I swivel round in my chair to face her.

'So,' I say, feeling like her therapist, 'how was your weekend?'

'Good,' Sally fires back like a well-programmed robot, 'fine.'

I try not to flinch at her abrupt answers.

'Good,' I say soothingly. 'What did you do?'

Sally pauses. 'Not much,' she says, 'went running.'

'Oh!' I say, pleased that we finally have something to talk

about. 'I've started running,' I say. 'I'm actually training for a 10k.' I add idly.

Har har. Just lightly slip that in there.

As much as I am hating the idea of running 10k, it is no secret that I love showing off about it at any given opportunity. Finally, I am one of those adults who willingly takes part in an activity that counts as productive. Although, I did catch myself shoehorning it into my conversation with the postman today, which almost feels like a step too far. Especially since I have only been on one run and I had to stop when I stubbed my toe on the dog poo bin.

Urgh, that was a real low point for me. The dog poo bin strikes again.

Sally jerks her head. 'You're running a 10k?' she says.

I take a sip of my tea and nod, trying to control the smug grin peeling onto my face.

Look at me. Chatting to a colleague about fitness and training for a 10k. God, I am adulting well. Maybe I'll start throwing impromptu dinner parties and serve amuses bouche. Whatever the hell that is.

'When?' Sally asks.

I cock my head. 'In a few months?' I guess. 'I'm running it for my sister.'

'We should train together!' Sally almost shouts, launching back to her feet.

My sweet sense of smugness is suddenly washed away..

Oh no. *No*.

'I have a strong training ritual,' Sally instructs, marching back around the room. 'It comes with a training diet. You can start both.'

No. Absolutely not. I need to put a stop to this.

'Sure,' I manage, 'the thing is, I—'

'Georgia!'

I jump as Natalie charges into the office. She grabs on to the door frame, her hair whipping round her shoulders. I almost fall off my seat in fright.

She never calls me Georgia.

'God!' I say before I can stop myself, clutching my chest. 'Bloody hell, Natalie, what is it?'

Natalie's eyes dart towards Sally and then back at me. 'I need to talk to you,' she shoots.

I eye Sally, who has finally stopped marching. Her head is bouncing between me and Natalie as if she's watching the Wimbledon semi-final.

'Now?' I say blankly.

Has she forgotten Sally is my line manager? I can't just start up a casual conversation now.

'I'll have my lunch break soon,' I add as Sally starts scooping up files, indicating that I should do the same.

'In half an hour!' Sally says briskly, charging past me. 'We are needed in the meeting room now,' she adds sharply.

I spring to my feet.

'I'll come see you at lunch,' I mutter to Natalie quickly.

She gapes back at me like an anxious fish. What's wrong with her?

'Have you done the coffee?' Sally barks as we storm down the corridor.

Bloody hell, my feet hurt in these shoes. Christ. Why do I ever wear heels? Maybe I should start wearing those trainers with wheels in the bottom. That would make my life a hell of a lot easier. Not to mention how cool I would look.

Olivia Beirne

'Yes,' I say, thankfully being honest. 'I've had it delivered. It will already be there.'

'Unless it's been stolen,' Sally snips, and I scowl at the back of her bob.

We spin round the final corner and into the immaculate meeting room. Sure enough, the coffee has already been laid out. I quickly rearrange the chairs as Sally slams the presentation packs down on the desk. I try to control the bubbles of irritation that pop every time Sally rearranges another pencil, and I line up the final chair.

Bianca wanted to host a business lunch for all of her family today. Which basically means she wants to show off how successful the company is. I just hope I get one of the free fancy biscuits later.

'She's coming!' Sally practically screams.

I lurch forward and dart towards the front of the room, taking my cue from Sally. I stand next to her awkwardly.

Great. We look like a set of passive prison guards.

I hear the clack of Bianca's shoes and I smooth down my fringe as my heart rate returns to normal.

What shall I have for lunch today? I decided that I would treat myself today and buy lunch, a very rare occurrence. Do I go full out and order something wild, like a Five Guys? Or should I be sensible and order a salad?

Actually, no. Ridiculous idea. Salad is not a treat, it's mild punishment.

'Right, through here,' Bianca sings as she reaches the meeting room. Her smile stretches as she spots Sally and myself. 'Hello, darlings!' she says. 'Everyone, this is Sally and Georgie who work on the design team. They have been simply wonderful, helping with the wedding – and Georgie makes fantastic coffee.'

I fix my smile as the back-handed compliment strikes me in the face.

Slowly, Bianca's family troop in, all 'ooing' and 'aahing' in the process.

'Do sit down,' Bianca says. 'Sally, Georgie . . . this is my mother, Pauline . . . and my father, William.'

I smile and nod politely as each family member enters.

'Obviously you know Jonathan,' she continues, 'and this is my brother, Jack.'

My face twitches as the last introduction sinks in and my eyes land on the final member of Bianca's family entering the room.

What?

No.

Oh no. Oh my God. Oh no.

I watch in horror as Bianca's brother walks into the room. Bianca's brother, Jack. Bianca's brother, Jack, who I yelled at yesterday. Jack.

He meets my eyes and I see a flicker of surprised recognition sweep over his face.

Oh my God. I've kissed my boss's brother. I shouted at him. I called him a freak. I said I never wanted to see him again.

And he's *right here.*

My entire body burns as he walks past me and slips into one of the chairs. I wobble next to Sally, barely able to stand.

What do I do? What can I do? What the hell is he doing here? He can't be Bianca's brother. He can't! Surely this is all some sort of practical joke. Surely to God I haven't yelled at my boss's brother.

Nooooooooo.

Can I jump out of the window? My eyes dart around the room as my heart beats furiously in my chest.

Argh! There are no windows! We are in a windowless room!

What did I say about Bianca? I can't remember! Did I say anything? He told me he was in London to help with preparations for his sister's wedding but I had no idea it was . . .

I didn't even know Bianca had a brother!

I need to leave. I need to leave right now.

'Thank you both so much,' Bianca coos. 'Is the wedding presentation ready?'

'Yes,' Sally says swiftly, 'all ready.'

Bianca smiles. 'Great,' she says. 'Well, then, take it away.'

Sally strides forward and picks up the remote.

Oh my God, I'm going to have to do my presentation in front of him. This is awful. This should be illegal. This is the worst day of my life.

I catch Sally's eye and jump as she glares at me. 'Lights, Georgia,' she hisses.

I quickly jab the lights off and try to ignore Jack's penetrating stare, burning into me.

I will have to quit. I will have to hand in my notice immediately and become unemployed. I will have to run away and create a new life for myself in the hills. I can't handle this.

I glance up at Sally and try my best to look incredibly interested as she talks through Bianca's first dance options.

Okay, I just have to get through this next bit. Then I can go for lunch and lock myself in the toilet at Pret. Nobody will look for me there. Everyone knows I can't afford it.

'And now,' Sally says, 'Georgia is going to talk you through the buttonhole options.'

I stare back at her imploringly, silently begging her not to make me speak. Sally blinks back at me, a strained look in her eyes. Weakly, I take the remote off Sally and turn to face the room.

Buttonholes?

If I get through this presentation without accidentally calling them 'bottom holes' then I deserve a knighthood.

Chapter Nine

<u>Ways to handle Jack situation:</u>

1. Quit job and become a nun
2. Quit job and become an artistic/painting nun (do they exist? Must research. VITAL)
3. Quit job and become very successful painting nun (research local nun houses. Will they accept me after university?)
4. Stay at job and change identity
5. Stay at job and pretend I have no idea who Jack is
6. Stay at job and pretend I have sudden amnesia (best idea yet. Pursue)
7. Call Jack out in middle of work canteen in *EastEnders*-style fight (would give me the chance to wear Pat Butcher earrings)
8. Pretend to Jack that I knew all along who he was and that I tricked *him* (would give me the chance to be smug and superior)

9. Hide from Jack for ever in work basement
10. Pretend I've forgotten how to speak (take up sign language?)
11. Emigrate

Have you spoken to him?!!??!?

My eyes flick to the right-hand corner of my monitor as Natalie's email pops up. I glance at Sally, who is barking orders down the phone to Bianca's vegan caterer. (She's having four caterers. I don't even know what the other three are doing. Bianca is on the Atkins diet.)

No.

I quickly hit send before my face peels off from my skull under the pressure. I pull up the wedding spreadsheet and try to silence my anxiety by staring at columns of numbers.

Twenty minutes of dreadful presentation later (and a surprise Q and A that Bianca decided to chuck in) and Jack, thankfully, did not acknowledge me. He is probably still furious that I called him a freak. And a criminal. And a thief.

I take a slug of water as I try to tame the sparking panic that is popping under my skin.

As soon as the meeting finished, I bolted down the corridor. I've been successfully avoiding Jack since. Or, he's been avoiding me. Either way, I haven't seen him. Perhaps he has spent the rest of the day reciting extracts from my diary to Bianca.

My eyes flick down to check the time on the digital clock. Four fifteen. I only have to hide for forty-five more minutes and then I can run home and pretend this never happened. I stare mindlessly at my open spreadsheet and obediently type in the receipts, my brain aching. Is this karma for going on a Tinder date? Is this the universe trying to tell me that Tinder is a terrible idea, like I always knew it was? Perhaps it is the universe's way of telling me I shouldn't be dating.

I have been single for two years now. Happily single, I might add. But still, very much single. And then the first date I venture out on turns out to be my boss's closet brother. If that isn't some awfully big sign, then I don't know what is.

Maybe I will just become a nun. Maybe that's what I'll do after I've been fired for calling Jack a freak. Perhaps that is the next chapter in my life. The nuns will accept me and love me for who I am. That is, until they hear me sing and my monotonous tones shatter their precious church windows and I'm sent into exile.

I jump as Bianca's knuckles rap at the door. Her eyes scan the room, passing over Sally, and then land on me. A spasm of fear clutches at my body.

'Georgie,' she says, 'you can go home, you've done enough today.'

I freeze, anxiety closing up my throat.

Is she . . . is she firing me?

'Really?' I say weakly.

Bianca nods, pulling her wrist up to check the time. 'Yeah,' she says lightly, 'if you think you've completed everything.'

I blink at her. Is this a test? Is she speaking in riddles? Is she trying to trick me into a confession?

Bianca waits in the doorway and I slowly put my belongings in my bag and get to my feet.

'Thank you,' I say quietly.

Bianca looks up from her phone and smiles. 'No worries,' she says pleasantly. 'See you tomorrow.'

My body sags in relief.

Okay, see you tomorrow. Tomorrow. That means I'm not fired. Maybe she is just being nice. I nod weakly and turn, then suddenly find myself face-to-face with Jack. My stomach leaps into my mouth and I almost collapse in shock.

I pull my eyes away quickly and scuttle down the corridor, my face burning.

At least this terrible day is over and I will never have to see Jack again and I can pretend this never happened. Thank God for that.

★

I stuff my foot into my sparkly new trainer and try not to laugh at Amy's aghast expression.

'I hope you're happy,' I say. 'Is this what you wanted? Was this your plan all along, to get me nearly fired?'

Amy starts to laugh. 'That is mad.'

'I know.'

She runs her fingers through her hair. 'It could only happen to you, though.'

I puff at her. 'Is that supposed to make me feel better?'

Amy pulls the list out of my bag and I flop down next to her.

Amy grins. 'Well done,' she says, smiling down at the list, 'one down.'

I nestle into her shoulder. 'I know.'

Amy fingers the list, where a circular coffee stain is smeared into the top corner.

'What did you do?' she asks. 'Did you spill coffee on it? You don't drink coffee, do you?'

I scowl at the corner. My body tingles as if tiny spiders are crawling up my spine, and anxiety pulls at my throat.

'No,' I say, touching the stain myself. 'Not very often.'

I frown.

Jack must have read it.

'Right,' Amy says suddenly, 'you need to hurry up and go on this run. *Doctor Foster* starts in half an hour.'

I jump to my feet and point a foot at her like a ballerina. 'How do I look?'

Amy folds her legs under her and smiles. 'Like a pro,' she says, 'like you were born to run.'

I snort and pick up my water bottle.

'I wish you could come with me,' I say. 'I hate running, I'm so rubbish at it.'

Amy pulls open her book and raises her eyebrows. 'Mind over matter,' she says knowingly. 'You're better than you think.'

I roll my eyes and walk out of the living room.

'Mind over matter' is Amy's favourite expression. I, on the other hand, think it's a load of codswallop. Amy always says it works in every situation, which I have several issues with. What about if you have your leg chopped off by accident under surgery? Or you're teleported back to the Stone Age and are being chased by a T-Rex? Or you accidentally develop thrush? How will mind over matter help with any of that?

It won't. Repeatedly thinking 'I don't have thrush' will not free you from thrush. Take it from me.

I push my way out of the back door and gasp as the cool air whips around my ears. I crick my neck and kick the door shut behind me. Right, a run. A simple run. If I do the run around the park then I can warrant cracking open that cheesecake I bought for Amy. I bounce on the balls of my feet and begin to lightly jog up the street.

I have to admit, I do look pretty cool in all my running gear. This would be a great time to bump into someone I went to school with – or my old PE teacher, who laughed when I got stuck on the gymnastics horse. Or, like, Jack.

God, it would be great to glide past Jack now. Head to toe in sports gear, in new trainers, casually running. Although it would mean that I would have to speak to him again. And I do not want that.

I shake my head as I dodge a street light.

Stop thinking about Jack. He's gone now. Thankfully.

I turn another corner and will myself to keep running as the familiar ripple of anxiety creeps through me.

He must have read my list. He must have done. I feel as if he's read a private conversation between me and Amy. I would never allow just anyone to read that list. It's private.

I suck in a great gulp of air.

Don't think about Jack.

I glance at a stray cat, eyeballing me whilst perched on a parked car, and try to ignore the aggressive pounding in my chest. My eyes flick down to my flouncing breasts in alarm.

What? What are they doing? How are they doing that?

I glance away and then back down at my chest in alarm.

Okay, I don't mean to sound dramatic, but my sports bra is certainly not working. Is it supposed to feel like this? I feel like my breasts have transformed into violent pots of uncoordinated jelly.

Without quite meaning to, my hands grip my boobs to clasp them in place.

Okay, ouch. This really hurts. Surely it's not supposed to hurt.

I can't have this! What if I stop running and the force of the run has permanently dislodged my breasts, and one is suddenly much higher than the other? I can't have one boob up by my chin and the other perched on my hip bone.

I turn a corner, my angled elbows jabbing forward as I run. It really is quite difficult to run when you don't have any arms.

This is ridiculous! How long can I run whilst holding on to my boobs? I don't think I can run any more like this! What if some youths see me, take a picture and turn me into a meme, and I go viral? All for the sake of a bloody run.

Argh! I knew I hated running for a reason! This is a disaster!

How is mind over matter supposed to help me here? What am I expected to do now – simply will my boobs to stay in place? If I had the mental power to command every aspect of my body to change then I would make some serious edits. Starting with my nipples.

I turn another corner of our street and, to my horror, spot a crowd of teenagers lurking around a parked car. Before I can stop myself, I spin round on the spot and jog in the opposite direction.

That's it. I am going back home. I will not run past a group of youths whilst clasping my breasts in fear of one of them falling off. That is not going to be how I go viral. I just won't allow it.

★

I cross my legs and attempt to defuse the panic bubbling in my chest. I fix my eyes on the back of Jack's brown, curly hair as he takes a sip of his coffee.

He's back.

He was here when I came in this morning and he hasn't left. He is still here, drinking coffee and chatting to Bianca like everything is completely normal and fine. Whereas I am hovering at the back of the meeting room trying not to develop an instant hernia every time he opens his mouth.

What is he doing here? Why is he here? He left! He came for the tour, and then he left. What good reason could he possibly have for coming back?

Sally marches through the door, her bulging Filofax stuffed under her arm, and I turn to face her.

Thankfully, Jack has barely looked at me all day. Maybe he doesn't recognise me. He sure is acting as if he doesn't recognise me.

'Right . . .' Bianca flips open her notebook and snaps her eyes around the room, her back poker-straight, 'so the wedding is now in about three months, okay? Sally,' she locks her eyes on to Sally, who blinks back at her as if she is about to receive missionary orders. 'I need to see a new draft of the schedule.'

'Roger that,' Sally barks.

I fight the urge to roll my eyes. For goodness' sake.

'Jack,' Bianca says, 'how are you getting on with your speech?'

I look at Jack. He's doing a speech?

'Fine,' Jack says idly.

I hide a smile as Sally jolts forward in alarm. There isn't a brother's speech in the schedule.

'How long is the speech?' she almost shouts. 'How many minutes?'

Jack angles his shoulder backwards as a smile plays with the corners of his mouth, and his eyes flit towards me.

'Are you Sally?' he says.

My stomach drops. Why did he look at me before asking that?

'Yes,' Sally says, her head dropping into a neat nod.

Jack grins and he looks back down at his notepad. Everyone stares at him.

'Jack!' Bianca bursts out, thwacking his arm with her pen. 'Sally asked you an important question. How many minutes will your speech be?'

'Oh,' Jack says, his eyes flicking towards me again, 'I'm not sure. An hour?'

'An hour!' Sally squawks, leaping from her seat as if she has just sat on a hedgehog. 'I mean,' she quickly composes herself, her face glowing, 'we just . . . it's just . . . the schedule,' she trails off weakly.

Jack's grinning. He's winding her up.

'An hour?' Bianca repeats, twisting her body towards Jack. 'You want to make a speech for an hour? Oh!' she coos, clutching her chest. 'Are you going to re-enact moments from our childhood?'

Sally flicks her hair out of her eyes as she scribbles viciously in her notepad.

'Maybe,' Jack says, shrugging.

'Oh, Jack!' Bianca cries. 'That is so touching! Sally, can we add this to the schedule?'

Sally whips her head up from her notepad and blinks at Bianca, aghast.

'I think we can.' Jack's eyes flit back towards me, the sides of his mouth curling. 'Right, Georgie?'

I jolt involuntarily at the sound of my name being spoken by Jack's voice.

Why is he calling me Georgie? He can't call me Georgie here! Nobody at work calls me Georgie apart from Natalie.

(And Bianca, because I am too scared to correct her.)

Bianca peers round at me expectantly.

'Sure,' I say weakly.

At my words, Sally almost collapses into her chair.

I stand up. 'Shall I make some coffee?' I say, desperate to end this conversation before anyone works out that we know each other.

Bianca flicks one leg over the other and nods. 'Yes please, darling.'

'I'll bring some in,' I say, and carefully duck out of the door and into the kitchen, my pulse thumping in my ears.

'Want a hand?'

I spin round and spot Jack, leaning on the door frame. My face flames and I hover uncertainly. He's asking me a question. He's talking to me. Why is he talking to me? What does he want? What is his motive? Why can't he just *leave me alone*?

I blink back at him.

Damn. I'm going to have to speak to him. Unless I just shake my head. I could pretend I've lost my voice. Or that, since we met, I've taken up a new life as a full-time mime artist. I'm pretty good at that 'trapped in a box' shtick.

I turn my back to him, trying to ignore the heat licking my ears.

'No, thank you,' I say calmly, reaching and pulling down mugs.

If I engage in minimal social contact then perhaps he will leave.

'I'll help you carry it,' Jack says.

'I'm fine,' I say tightly.

How patronising. I can perfectly well manage carrying a tray of coffee down a corridor. I am a strong, independent woman. Thank you very much.

'Okay,' Jack says mildly.

I'm hoping at this he may leave. But, to my annoyance, he is still leaning on the door frame.

'So,' Jack says, 'you were right about Sally. She's a real character.'

I spoon instant coffee into the identical mugs and feel a wave of indignation rise inside my chest. I'm the only one who is allowed to moan about Sally. He doesn't even know her. Who is he to judge her?

'That was really mean,' I say quietly, 'what you did to her back there. That will have really stressed her out.'

I glance back at him and see his eyebrows rise in amusement. I turn back to the coffee.

'Coming from the girl,' he says lightly, 'who swapped her Pro Plus for Tic Tacs?'

I freeze.

How does he know that? Nobody knows that!

(Apart from Natalie.)

'That's different,' I say coldly, refusing to turn my body to meet him.

Jack laughs. 'Well,' he says, 'I know how much she winds you up. I just wanted to get her back for you.'

'I don't need,' I snap, spinning round to face him, 'anything from you. We don't have anything.' I wave my arms in front of me. 'We are not anything. There is nothing here. This is my place of work—'

I break off, my face burning. Jack looks back at me, his face blank.

I turn back as the kettle clicks off behind me and try to avoid the great puffs of steam wafting around my face.

I can't believe he is here. Why is he here? Why is he talking to me?

I stack the steaming mugs on the tray and turn. To my irritation, Jack is still standing by the door.

'Do you want me to carry it?' he asks.

'No,' I say stubbornly, even as my arms burn under the weight of the tray. 'I'm fine. Thank you.'

★

'He's read my diary,' I hiss to Natalie, as she twirls pasta on her fork. I glance around the work canteen to check Jack or Bianca aren't lurking at a nearby table. They should rename the canteen *Fifty Shades of Grey*, and not because of its overwhelming sex appeal.

Natalie looks up, her manicured hand touching her high, purple neckline and her glasses slipping slightly down her nose.

'He's read your diary?' she repeats. 'Your notebook, you mean? That's weird. How do you know that?'

I lean in and wrap my hand around my mug of soup. 'Because he keeps dropping in things about me that he shouldn't know.'

Natalie looks at me. 'Like what?'

'Like, how I don't think I can pull off pink and that Sally annoys me.'

'Sally annoys everybody,' Natalie notes.

'Yes, but . . .' I eye her, 'he knows about the time I swapped her Pro Plus for Tic Tacs.'

Natalie chews another mouthful and blinks at me.

'Are you sure you didn't just tell him that on your date?' she says mildly. 'You were pretty drunk, weren't you?'

I shake my head, irritated at her bringing up the date.

'No,' I say firmly, 'I didn't. I wouldn't have.'

Natalie shrugs and goes back to her pasta. 'Why is he here?' she asks. 'Does he, like, work here now?'

I shrug. The thought of Jack permanently working here causes my stomach to grind.

'No idea,' I say. 'Hopefully, he will go soon.'

Natalie looks up. 'Do you still fancy him?'

'No!' I retort instantly. 'I've never fancied him. I never would.'

Natalie grins. 'You fancied him enough to kiss him on the first date.'

'That was different,' I say haughtily, leaning back in my seat. 'That was only because I thought he was somebody else.'

Natalie cocks her head. 'Well,' she says, 'I guess you will just have to avoid him.'

I shrug and glance around the canteen. 'Yeah,' I say, knowing full well that is near impossible.

'Anyway,' Natalie says, pushing her food around with her plastic fork, 'how's Amy doing?'

My heart twinges at the mention of Amy, and I smile.

'Fine,' I say, 'she's okay. She's still working. I think she's finding it quite hard. She's tired a lot.'

Natalie puts her fork down. 'I bet she's happy you're completing her list.'

I nod, a familiar weight forming in my chest.

'Yeah,' I say. 'I just wish she would do it with me. I feel like she's given me her dying orders. It's her list.'

Natalie smiles and pulls out her phone. 'I need to get back,' she says. 'Do you fancy going for a drink after work?'

I stand up. 'I can't,' I say. 'Sorry. I've got to be back to see Amy.'

Natalie shrugs as we walk towards the doors. 'No worries,' she says. 'Let me know when you can.'

Chapter Ten

Amy's smoothie recipe:

100ml almond milk (only have semi-skimmed milk, sure it's fine)
50g blueberries (guessed, don't own scales)
1 banana (don't have)
1 handful kale (I have small hands)
1 tsp goji berries (what)
2 tbsp natural yogurt (only had strawberry mousse?!)
50g strawberries (guessed)
1 handful spinach (no)
1 cup protein powder (refuse to buy)
Dash of vanilla essence (don't have, so used 3 scoops of vanilla ice cream instead)

I push my way through the front door, my arms sagging under the weight of bulging carrier bags and my damp fringe smeared on to my forehead.

'Amy?' I shout. 'It's me.'

I hear a muffled noise as I kick the front door shut. Mum has Zumba every Tuesday. Amy used to go too. I stagger into the kitchen and drop the bags, and then I spot Amy, curled up on the sofa. Her hair is scrunched up on top of her head and her eyes are sunken, the lids swollen and pink. My eyes flit down to her clothing and I realise, with a dull ache in my stomach, that she has spent a full day at work.

She peels an eye open to look at me, but within moments it droops shut again.

I kneel next to her and place my hand on her arm. 'You okay?' I say quietly.

'Tired,' Amy grunts, her lips barely parting.

I nod and pull myself back to standing. 'I'll start dinner, okay?' I say, walking back towards the kitchen. 'That will make you feel better.'

I walk back through the kitchen and flip over the ready-meal box I grabbed from Tesco on my way over here. We have tried telling Amy to cut her hours down, or at least try to get a different job where she could sit down more. She won't listen. She never does. I don't think the kids in her class even know how sick she is.

I stab the plastic film with a fork and slot it into the microwave, when my phone vibrates. I pull it out of my pocket and my body lurches.

It's a message from Jack.

I freeze. My eyes are glaring down at my phone.

Why is he texting me? What does he want now? What could he possibly have to say to me? We had an accidental date, we realised he is actually related to my boss, and we've addressed the awkwardness of the awful coincidence. There is nothing more to be said!

I had planned to ignore him, and volunteer to complete the pile of shredding in the basement until the wedding is over and he can scoot back to wherever he is actually from. Why is he texting me?

I glance around, as if Bianca could be lurking behind the fridge, ready to jump out and unravel the whole mess. Hardly daring to breathe, I open the text.

Hey Georgie, sorry about today. Hope you're okay. Great coffee. Jack x

I blink at the message as anger foams beneath my skin and my mind compiles the aggressive list of everything annoying about the text:

1. Stop calling me Georgie. My name is Georgia. He does not have permission to call me Georgie.
2. Of course I am okay. Why wouldn't I be? Who is he to think that I would be affected by some man I barely know?
3. Everyone knows I am terrible at making coffee, so that is another sly dig.
4. Don't put a kiss at the end of the message.

The microwave zings, and before I can command myself otherwise, my finger swipes my screen flamboyantly and the message is deleted. As of tomorrow, I shall completely ignore him. I've got enough on my mind without him occupying even the tiniest corner of brain space.

I cut the steaming pie in half and walk into the living room.

Amy struggles to open her eyes and look at me. She rubs her face with the back of her hand and scrunches up her nose.

'What time is it?' she says. 'It feels too early for dinner.'

I hand her a bowl on a tray and slot down beside her. 'It's almost eight,' I say. 'You must have been asleep for a while.'

I notice a shadow of worry pass through Amy's eyes. 'Oh,' she says, 'yeah. I guess I was.'

Amy picks up her fork and stabs the pie. I watch, my chest aching. Amy never used to sleep in the day.

'You know,' I say, 'I've been thinking, and I think we should do the list together. I could book us in for the Salsa class this weekend. What do you think?'

Amy blinks down at her dinner, her shoulders sagging into her chest. 'I can't,' she says quietly.

'Sure you can!' I say instantly, desperately trying to imitate the burning enthusiasm Amy used to spring on me. 'It will be fun. We can be rubbish together.'

Amy shakes her head and laughs softly. 'I can't even manage a whole day at work. I feel terrible. I can't go dancing, you know I can't. I'm sorry.'

'But I really think—'

'Georgie,' Amy snaps forcefully. 'I can't. You go. I need to rest.'

★

I eye my grey, misshapen sandwich in dismay. My stomach shrivels as my lunch taunts me from the edge of my desk.

When will I be the type of person to buy lunch? When can I throw away my hideous roll of cling film and stop buying Lidl cheese?

More importantly, when can I stop shopping in Lidl? Amy shops in Sainsbury's. Maybe I should shop in Sainsbury's. Bianca shops in Waitrose, which is obviously too extreme.

I click on an email and force my eyes to focus as Bianca's trail of correspondence spills on to my screen. I cannot wait until this wedding is over. Maybe then I will finally be paid to design.

I notice Sally, buried in a stack of paper, and I click on my latest design and swell with excitement as it springs to life on my screen. This is what I'm meant to be doing with my life. I am meant to be a designer.

I glance up at the sound of Bianca's pointed knuckles rapping on the door. She prowls into the office, designer shoes first, and scans the room with her beady eyes. Sally's head quickly pops up from her pile of paperwork, and instantly snaps back down, as if the contracts have invisible lassos coiled around her eyeballs. Bianca's gaze lands on me and I see a flash of satisfaction sweep over her face. I have started to let go of the idea that she is limbering up to fire me. After I made her fourth coffee of the morning, she called me a 'darling lamb', which Lord Sugar certainly doesn't say to his boardroom casualties. So I think I'm safe.

'Georgie,' she says, angling her body to face mine.

Involuntarily, I feel my body tense.

Oh God, what? What is she going to ask me now? Can't she just leave me to answer emails and ignore the phone, like a normal assistant?

'I need your help, darling,' she continues, leaning nonchalantly against the door frame and pulling out her iPhone. 'The brides-maid dresses are ready. They are at the tailor's. They need picking up.'

Right, then. I guess that means I have to pick them up.

I pull out my notebook and scribble down 'bridesmaid dresses'.

'Okay,' I say.

'They're at 613 Tottenham Court Road,' Bianca adds, easing herself away from the door frame, 'under my name. Obviously.'

I get to my feet and hook my bag over my arm. 'Okay,' I say again.

'There are six bridesmaids . . .' Bianca says, as she moves down the corridor.

I scurry after her, as best as I can with my average-sized legs.

'. . . so Jack will help you carry them.'

I jolt to a stop.

'Oh?' I manage.

'Yeah . . .' Bianca reaches her office and finally peels her eyes away from her iPhone, 'he's in the lobby. You'll need a cab.'

She turns and clacks through the open door, her long hair swishing behind her.

I hover, uncertain what to do next.

Great.

I take a deep breath and turn on my heels, making my way towards the lobby on my unstable legs.

Okay. Well, that's okay. I will just act as if Jack is a normal colleague. There is nothing odd about this situation, and certainly nothing to feel uncomfortable about. I shall just behave like the ultimate professional that I am.

I push my way through the door and spot Jack, leaning on a pillar and scrolling through his phone. He is wearing a suit today, and his dark stubble enhances the taut line of his jaw. He looks really good in a suit. To my annoyance, my heart flips at the sight of him.

Stop that, heart. Stop that right now.

I march towards him and feel my brow crease into a knitted frown. Jack looks up as I approach him, and smiles.

'Hey, Georgie,' he says, and moves forward.

I lurch backwards in horror. Oh my God, is he going to try and kiss me? In the lobby? At my work? Shirley the receptionist is sat right there! Oh good Lord, this is dreadful. What is he going to try and do next? Wink at me? Start a mating call?

'Hello, Jack,' I say stiffly. 'If that even is your name.'

I freeze in horror as I hear the last sentence shoot out of my mouth.

Argh! What am I doing? I said that last time! I can't say that every time I see him!

'Shall we?' I almost shout, before he has the chance to respond to my ridiculous greeting. 'The taxi is outside.'

I turn abruptly on the spot and march towards the door, feeling unnervingly like Sally.

Well, that was a disaster.

Right. From now on I must behave professionally, as if nothing has happened. Maybe I'll pretend I don't remember him at all. If he brings it up I can be, like, 'Sorry, who? Oh goodness, I go on so many dates I don't remember, har har I'm so sociable and popular.'

Although I literally saw him yesterday, so he may then speak to Bianca about getting me sectioned.

I loiter on the pavement and stick out an arm, trying to look like this comes completely naturally to me, and I casually hail black cabs all the time.

If I'd known I would have to spend time with him then I would have at least worn something nicer, and clean. Not that

105

this isn't clean, but you know. I would have ironed it. Or worn something with a hint of breast.

Not that I care about Jack, because I don't. And I most certainly do not want him looking at my boobs. Absolutely not. The very idea.

'How are you?' Jack asks.

'Fine, thanks,' I fire back, my eyes glued to the road. 'You?'

Jack tucks his hands in his pockets. 'Yeah, fine, thanks. I bet you weren't expecting this.'

Oh God. My arm has been hanging out for such a long time. This is getting embarrassing. Why aren't any cabs stopping? I really need a taxi to pull in ASAP or I'm going to have to turn it into some sort of weird yoga pose. The only yoga pose I know is the downward dog, which is totally inappropriate before you even take into account how grossly unflattering it is.

'Yeah,' I say. I narrow my eyes and succeed in making eye contact with a driver, who finally signals and pulls in to stop. My mouth curls into a smug grin. Oh, thank God. I am a Londoner after all.

I pull open the taxi door and slide in.

'You weren't surprised?'

'What?'

For the first time, my eyes focus on Jack's appearance. To my irritation, I feel a fizz of excitement. He's wearing tailored blue trousers and a crisp, white shirt. His neat, dark hair frames his chiselled face and his green eyes spark as I meet them. He looks gorgeous.

I feel a spasm of annoyance at my heart's girlish reaction to Jack.

No, he doesn't. He looks ordinary. Unmistakably, undeniably ordinary.

Jack clips his seat belt on.

'Where are you going?'

I look up as the taxi driver speaks, angling the rear-view mirror towards us.

'Oh,' I gabble, '613 Tottenham Court Road, please.'

The taxi driver nods and pulls out into the thick London traffic.

I glance up at Jack, and realise I still haven't given him an answer.

'No,' I lie, forcing my voice to sound as casual as possible. 'No, I wasn't surprised. I mean, I was, obviously,' I add quickly, 'but, you know, nothing really surprises me.'

Jack blinks at me.

What am I talking about? Why am I talking like James Bond?

Jack smiles. 'Well,' he says, 'this whole thing has been a shock for me. I had no idea the wedding you were helping to plan was my sister's. I thought I'd never see you again.'

A dart of panic shoots through me.

Reluctantly, I flick my eyes towards him again. 'Did you . . .' I start, in my best nonchalant voice, 'did you mention to Bianca—?'

Jack shakes his head. 'Nah,' he says, 'she's got a lot on.'

'Oh.'

What does that mean?

'Did you get my text, by the way?' Jack asks as I pull out my phone.

'No,' I blurt, using all of my energy to try and control my cheeks from flaming.

I glare out of the window as I notice Jack peering at me. He must know I'm lying. I am a terrible liar.

107

Jack takes out his phone and starts texting. Did I ever ask him what he did for a job? If I spoke about my work, surely I would have asked him back. Hopefully I'm not a huge narcissist. I can hardly remember anything about him.

Bloody gin.

'Your top's nice,' Jack says lightly, his eyes briefly flitting up from his phone.

I feel a zap of joy at the compliment.

'Thank you,' I say, running my hands over my top. 'It's actually . . .' I trail off as I notice Jack's mouth twitching. I glance down at my top and my stomach lurches.

I'm wearing a pink top. I'm wearing a bloody pink top. Damn. He's going to think I'm wearing it because he said I look good in it. Because he read my diary where I said I didn't think I could pull it off.

He's mocking me. Again.

My face burning, I twist my body round to face the window and glare out at the traffic furiously, refusing to make eye contact.

'Why are you here?' I say, sounding more annoyed than I intended.

Jack crosses one leg over the other, still tapping at his phone. 'Bianca wanted to make use of me whilst I'm in London. I'm happy to help, my work can wait. Obviously I know the bridesmaids.'

'Of course you do,' I mutter under my breath. 'Did you trick them into dating you too?' I add before I can stop myself.

Jack grins as I turn back to face him. 'Why do you want to know?' he says. 'Are you jealous?'

'No!' I retort, my face flaming. 'Of course not. And I'd appreciate it if you'd act like a professional. This is my work.'

I look daggers at him and Jack shrugs, raising his phone. I turn away and glare out of the window again, my face hot. The driver pulls up outside the tailor's and gestures at the staggering amount displayed on the meter, flashing above his head. Jack idly reaches into his pocket, but I get there first and quickly shove some notes through the driver's window. I'm not having him pay for my taxi as if we are some sort of item. We are two professionals on a business task. Why shouldn't I pay for the taxi?

Jack glances at me and I pull open the door coldly.

Also, Bianca gave me the taxi fare earlier, so it's not like I'm paying for it out of my own pocket.

'Here we are,' I say, marching up to the tailor's door as efficiently as I can in my heels. 'You really don't need to help me,' I add pointedly, raising my chin as Jack stands beside me. 'I can manage this on my own.'

Jack looks at me. 'Have you seen the bridesmaid dresses?'

'No,' I falter.

Jack slips his phone back into his pocket and nods. 'I have,' he says. 'Trust me. You're going to need my help.'

*

I frown at the stack of bridesmaid dresses, forming a tower on the cash desk. Jack wasn't joking. To my horror, each dress is laced with painfully expensive stones and weighs about seven pounds each.

Bianca has six bridesmaids.

The sales assistant smiles at us. 'Here you are,' she says sweetly, 'reserved for Bianca Lemon. Now,' she bats her eyes at me, and then at Jack, 'will you be okay carrying all of these?'

I turn my attention back to the dresses, transfixed.

If I summon all of my internal strength, I will be able to carry one of those dresses at the very most. I mean, for one thing, they are all floor length, and Bianca must be having a bridal party of glamorous giraffes because the trains of these dresses are enormous. There is no way I can hoist six of them off the floor. Even in heels I stand at a very firm five foot four.

Also, they look like they cost more than my entire year's rent, and that's saying something. I live in Zone Two.

Jack notices my expression and looks back at the sales assistant. 'What time do you close?' he asks.

'Four,' she answers politely.

Jack nods. 'Great,' he says. 'Can you please hold these for us? We'll be back later.'

The sales assistant nods and Jack turns and walks out of the shop. My head turns to see him disappear into the street, and then I look back at the sales assistant hopelessly. Where is he going?

I scurry after him madly.

As annoying as he is, I need him here! There is no way I will be able to carry six of those dresses single-handed. I can barely pick up one!

I push my way out through the revolving doors and finally catch up with him.

'What are you doing?' I say roughly.

Jack turns and faces me, his phone in his hand. 'You hungry?' he asks.

I blink at him, bemused.

'What?' I spout. 'What are you talking about?'

Jack looks back down at his phone. 'I'm hungry,' he says,

ignoring my response, 'let's get lunch. We'll come back for the dresses. Do you like French food?'

'We need to get the dresses,' I say stiffly. 'We don't have time for lunch. We need to get back to the office.'

Jack looks up from his phone, his eyes spark. 'We'll get them later,' he says idly. 'There's a great place over there I used to go . . .' He looks behind him and I root my feet to the ground.

'I'm not hungry,' I lie, my stomach burning at the idea of a delicious, surprise hot meal. 'Besides,' I add, as I notice Jack about to speak, 'I have lunch back at the office.'

Oh yeah. My festering cheese sandwich which I almost certainly sat on during my morning commute. Don't want to miss out on that beauty.

Jack puts his phone away and steps forward. 'Fine,' he says, 'have a coffee.' He turns and starts walking. 'Or a wine. I won't tell Bianca.'

I glare at the back of his head as he swans down Tottenham Court Road. I hover, feeling like a lost duckling. I don't want to follow him, but I can't carry the dresses back to the office on my own.

I huff loudly and storm after him, begrudgingly. This is ridiculous. He has tricked me into going on another date with him.

I catch up with him and he glances at me, a small smile creeping across his face. We stride alongside each other and I fix my eyes ahead, desperate not to give him the satisfaction of acknowledging him.

'You know,' he says lightly, his hands tucked into his pockets, 'I know you don't like me, but everything I told you on the date is true.'

I flash him a look.

'Your name is Jack?' I say.

Jack nods. 'Correct.'

'You're twenty-eight?'

Jack nods again.

'You're obsessed with me and that's why you've shown up at my work?'

The last bit fires out of my mouth before I can stop it, and Jack laughs.

'I'm in London to help my sister plan her wedding. I used to work in digital marketing.'

I nod and keep my eyes locked forward, and we fall back into silence.

I won't lie, his name and age are pretty much all I can remember about him.

Did I solely talk about myself on our four-hour date? What is wrong with me?

'It's just here,' he says, as we reach a small cafe tucked in the heart of Soho. I follow him inside as we are guided to a table and handed menus. As my eyes scan the list of food my stomach aches.

'I think,' he says lightly, 'I'm going to get the steak. I've been craving this steak for years. I used to get it all the time. What do you want?' He looks up from the menu at me and I flush.

'Nothing,' I lie.

Jack raises his eyebrows. 'You have to have something. I know you like steak. Come on,' he smiles as the waiter appears, 'the food here is really good.'

The waiter looks at me expectantly and I gnaw my lip as my stomach groans. Now that I am here, I am really hungry. I can't just sit and watch him eat a steak, of all things. I'll faint. Just because I am having lunch with a man doesn't make it a date, this could easily be a business lunch.

'Okay,' I say eventually, my eyes flitting back to the menu, 'please can I have the steak too?'

Jack grins as the waiter takes our menus away.

'How do you know I like steak?' I ask.

Jack shrugs. 'An educated guess.'

'You mean you read it,' I say pointedly, 'in my diary?'

Jack takes a sip of water. 'I didn't read your diary.'

'Liar,' I say, as I feel myself relax.

'Says you?'

I frown. 'What?'

Jack shoots me a knowing look. 'You lied to me earlier.'

I hesitate as the waiter starts laying our table.

'No I didn't,' I say. 'When?'

'When you said you didn't receive my text,' Jack says, leaning back into his seat.

My face burns and I try to ignore the hot sweat that prickles at my upper lip.

'It's fine,' Jack shrugs, 'I get it, you're mad. I annoyed you yesterday and I'm sorry.' He looks at me, finally the smug smile gone. 'I shouldn't have acted that way around you. I was just pleased to see you. But you're right,' he sighs, 'business setting and all that. I'll be professional from now on. This is strictly business. Tell me about the last sales quarter at Lemons.'

I smile slightly. He was pleased to see me? I was certainly not pleased to see him.

I look up as the waiter reappears with two identical steaks. My stomach swells in excitement. I haven't had a steak in weeks, let alone in the middle of the day. I pick up my knife and begin to carve, my nostrils quivering as the rich smell of the food wafts up from the plate.

'Anyway,' Jack says, 'what are you doing this weekend?'

I look up as I swallow my first mouthful.

'I think I'm going to a Salsa class on Saturday,' I say as casually as I can.

That sounds so ridiculous coming out of my mouth. There is nothing casual about me announcing a weekend Salsa class.

Jack nods. 'Oh, cool,' he says, 'whereabouts?'

I put my knife down. 'I found a great class over in Covent Garden,' I say. 'They have one in the daytime, which I guess means it will be quite casual. Nobody who's that into Salsa would go at midday.'

Jack swallows another mouthful. 'That sounds fun,' he says. 'I might join you.'

'You can't,' I blurt, before I can stop myself.

He can't come with me to a Salsa class!

Jack looks up, a slight look of surprise etched on his face. 'Why?'

I blink back at him.

Why? Is this guy a moron? Oh, I don't know, maybe because Salsa is the sexiest dance form ever, and spending my Saturday grinding my pelvis up against my boss's brother seems like one step away from being fired for sexual harassment.

I put my knife and fork down, my appetite slowly vanishing. 'I think,' I say, as if I am talking to a small child, 'under the circumstances it would be best to keep our relationship professional. I know we had that weird date thing,' I laugh awkwardly as Jack stares at me, poker-faced, 'but that was a mistake.

Colleagues don't go Salsa dancing together. Sorry,' I add, 'I hope that makes sense.'

Jack puts his knife down and rubs his hands together, then smiles lightly. 'Sure,' he says, 'I understand completely.'

CHAPTER ELEVEN

Potential outfits for Salsa class:

1. Red floaty dress from first year uni (no idea where this is)
2. Jeans and a red top (cool and aloof. Although what if need to do high kicks? Minimal leg leverage in jeans)
3. Year 11 prom dress ? (Would certainly be overdressed but perhaps would make important statement)
4. Cool dance clothes (Would have to buy cool dance clothes)
5. Outfit like girl from *Step Up*? (Own nothing like this. Also look nothing like her)
6. Cool charity shop dress?! (Would need to lose two stone before tomorrow to fit into it)
7. Zumba outfit (gross and unflattering)
8. Eva Longoria's outfit in *Grazia*?! (Would need to find outfit in shops + £1 million to pay for it)

The List That Changed My Life

I lean back into my seat as the car chugs along the winding country road. I glance at Amy and feel a snake of anxiety worm its way through my body. We are on our way to Amy's hospital appointment. I can tell she is annoyed that we are all squashed into Dad's Ford Focus; she wanted to go on her own and went on a huge rant this morning about how she is an adult and doesn't need her entire family coming along to a hospital appointment. Obviously nobody was going to stay at home. Also, Dad is quite pleased because it means he can visit the garden centre on the way back.

Amy glares out of the window, her eyes fixed on the smudges of green and brown that whizz past the car as we curve round another bend. Tamal is slotted in between us on the back seat, his hand wrapped around Amy's, and his eyes locked on the road ahead.

'For goodness' sake!' Mum parps up from the front, gripping on to the corners of her seat. 'Will you slow down, Ian!'

Mum clasps her hands dramatically and flings herself against the door. Dad's eyes flit towards her and then back at the road.

'I am doing the speed limit,' he says tightly. 'I am driving at—'

'You are not!' Mum interrupts. 'You are driving at fifty miles per hour. You are a speed demon. You are not a boy racer, Ian Miller, you are almost sixty years old. Stop showing off to Tamal.'

At this, Tamal jerks slightly and Dad scowls.

'Don't be ridiculous,' Dad says, as he changes gear.

Mum pulls out her notepad and begins fanning herself, rolling her eyes at Dad. I shift my gaze back to the view out of the window as the sun pours in and spills on to my lap. It is just a routine appointment; Tamal has said that there is nothing to worry about. Even though Tamal's a nurse, I'm not sure if Amy believes him. I don't know if I believe him either. We thought there was nothing to worry about when she kept falling over. I glance at Tamal and notice his eyes are etched with concern, and I feel a pang of guilt.

'How's work, Tamal?' I ask, moving my body to face him in the tightly packed car.

Tamal smiles. 'Fine,' he says, 'thank you. Busy as always. How's your job going?'

I cock my head as I consider my answer. 'Yeah, fine.'

'Have you shown your boss your designs yet?'

I look up and can't help but smile. This is another example of why Amy and Tamal are a power couple. They agree on everything, and are obsessed with me showing Bianca my designs.

With her eyes still fixed on the window, Amy speaks for the first time. 'No,' she says, 'she hasn't.'

I shrug apologetically at Tamal. 'It's difficult,' I say.

'No it isn't,' Amy says, 'you're just being lazy.'

I pull my eyes away from Tamal, stung by Amy's comments. I know this is a hard day for her, but she isn't usually mean.

I tuck my hands under the backs of my legs and look out of the window again as we finally exit the country lane.

'I'm going to a Salsa class today,' I say quietly.

Tamal grins. 'Great!' he says. 'See, Amy,' he adds, nudging her in the ribs, 'she isn't being lazy. It takes guts to go to a Salsa class on your own.'

I smile weakly as the memory of Jack's proposal to join me wafts through my mind. It is much better to go on my own, obviously. Maybe I'll get paired up with a sexy Spaniard. Maybe he will be the love of my life and we'll have a Salsa-themed wedding and enter *Britain's Got Talent* as an epic duo.

Mum puffs in outrage in the front seat as her window slides up. She jerks her body round to face my dad's.

'What are you doing?' she snaps.

Dad enters a roundabout. 'We have the air con on,' he says calmly, 'we cannot have the windows open at the same time. Think of the ozone layer.'

Mum glares at Dad and rams her finger back on the window switch, which politely shimmies back down, revealing a gust of air that whips me in the face.

Here we go.

'The air con isn't working,' Mum says crossly. 'I am too hot.'

Dad clicks the switch and the window glides back up again. 'If you give it a minute then it will work.'

'Ian!' Mum barks. 'I am a fully grown woman. If I want the window open then I shall have the window open!'

Mum's window clicks back down again and Dad mutters something under his breath as he turns into the hospital and slots the car into a neat parking space. We all fold ourselves out of the car. I catch a glimpse of myself, reflected in the chrome of the car, and wince.

What is it about car reflections that make you look so obscene? I thought I looked quite nice this morning, but according to the car door I look like the splatted version of Humpty Dumpty. I turn and walk over to Amy, who is nestled into Tamal's chest.

'It's just an injection,' Tamal says to Amy. 'We'll be in and out in no time. Then we can go get some lunch or something.'

'You could come to the Salsa class with me!' I say.

Amy glares at me.

'That's okay, Georgia,' Tamal says kindly. 'I think we're going to spend the afternoon together. It's rare I get a whole day off with Ames, and I want her all to myself.' He squeezes Amy's shoulders and I notice her eyes are wet.

My stomach twinges. Amy never cries.

I nod as my heart pricks with anxiety and we make our way towards the hospital. Dad appears next to me and hooks his arm over my shoulders.

'Don't look so glum, George,' he says, steering me towards the entrance. 'It's just a routine appointment.'

'I know.'

'You haven't sent me any drawings recently.' He turns to face me, his eyes smiling. 'Is work keeping you busy?'

I look up at Dad. I used to send him cartoons every day whilst at work. It is only as he mentions it that I realise I did it right up until Amy got ill. I hadn't even noticed I'd stopped.

I shrug. 'Something like that.'

★

I wrap my arms across my chest and peek around the corner apprehensively.

Oh my God, what am I doing? What am I doing?

I wince as a leggy woman sashays past in a ruffled fluorescent dress and loud, bright bangles. I glance down at my faded black leggings and my grey baggy top. I thought this is what you were supposed to wear. This is what I used to wear to Zumba whenever Amy would force me to go. Why didn't anyone tell me I had to dress like an extravagant toilet-roll holder?

Not that I would have done, if they had. Obviously. Imagine being perched on the Jubilee Line with a glittery flower pinned to my head! I mean, it's the middle of the day!

I booked on to the class last night and paid ten pounds for a one-hour class. Which, now I'm here, seems a bit ambitious. Can I Salsa dance for an entire hour? Can anyone? I can barely manage running for more than eight minutes! (My most recent personal best.) Amy said it takes her an hour to run 10k. Which means it will take me about four days, providing I've eaten a good breakfast.

I glance up in horror as the largest man I have ever seen strides towards me. He has dark hair, slicked down his neck and is wearing a crimson shirt that splits open in the middle to reveal a forest of curled hair. Slowly, my fearful eyes creep up his towering body.

I cannot get paired up with him. I refuse. He looks like an actual bull. If we stood facing each other my nose would slot right into his navel.

As carefully as I can, I scoot away from him and back into another corner. I notice a frilly woman who is stretching in the corner, skimming her eyes over him in delight, and I feel myself relax slightly. Oh good, she can go with him.

God, this is so awkward. Who am I going to be partnered with? I am going to have to do the sexiest dance in the world with a complete stranger, sober, in the middle of the day. At least when me and Natalie lock our crotches with strangers in O'Neill's we're always one glass of wine short of being an actual grape. Maybe I should have said Jack could come, at least then I would have a guaranteed partner.

Suddenly the pool of lacquered men and ruffled women spill

through the open door. I manoeuvre my way to the back, and scuttle through into a tiny dance studio.

Oh my God.

To my horror, each wall is layered with giant mirrors. I gape at my awkward reflection as the women of the class greet their reflections as if they are being photographed for the cover of *Vogue*.

Oh my God! Mirrors? Who thought that was a good idea? It is bad enough that I am going to have to conjure up every ounce of sex appeal I have (which is obviously a limited supply) to get through this class, but I also have to watch myself doing this? I quickly slot myself in the back row, blocking my reflection behind a large skirt.

'Okay!' A piercing voice shoots through my ears, as a woman in heeled shoes clacks her way to the centre of the room. '*Hola*, señors and señoritas! I am Gabriella, let's dance!' She claps her hands together, and to my alarm, loud Latino music pumps through the room and everyone begins to thrust their hips in time with the music.

I'm sorry, what? What are they doing? Should I be doing that? How do they all know what to do?

The teacher faces the front and starts sashaying her hips either side in time with the music. Dubiously, I copy.

Why on earth did Amy ever want to do this? What is fun about this? What am I supposed to be getting out of this? This is absolutely humilia—

Oh shit, she's changing direction.

I manoeuvre my legs to copy the teacher, feeling as sexy as an uncoordinated octopus. After what feels like one hundred years, she stops. She claps her arms in the air and turns to face us.

Is that the end? Please let it be the end.

'To Salsa,' she cries, launching her arms into the air, 'you must feel the music in your bones!'

I glance at the couple next to me, who are nodding intently as if she is preaching from the Bible.

'It is all about passion!' she continues, pointing at an unsuspecting couple. 'It is about emotion, and above all,' she turns back to the front, 'it is about sex!'

My body jars forward.

Arghhhhhhhhhhh! She can't just say 'sex' in the middle of a dance class! In the middle of the day! Who is this crazed woman? Oh my God, what have I signed up to? Am I about to be tricked into having an orgy?

'Partner up!' she cries, clapping her hands again. 'Let's start with a simple step.'

My eyes flit around in alarm as the men and women shimmy across the room to greet each other like sexually charged flamingos. I hover. Nobody is coming towards me, thank God.

That's okay. I can just dance by myself, I don't want a partner anyway. This actually works out quite—

'You!'

I jump in fright as the teacher jabs her arm towards me. Everyone twirls round to look at me, and my face burns.

'Where is your partner?' she yells.

I blink in horror. 'I . . .' I stutter, 'I don't have—'

'To the front!' she cries, spinning on the spot to face the mirrors. 'You shall demonstrate with me!'

I freeze.

What? Demonstrate? I can't go with the teacher! I'm a beginner!

Can I leave? If I ran out of the door would anyone notice? I could pretend I suddenly really need a wee and then just not come back. Or I could—

'Now!' she demands.

I jump forward and scuttle towards the front.

Oh my God. As if this isn't mortifying enough, now I am going to have to try and be sexy, dancing with a woman who terrifies me. What will happen if I accidentally tread on her foot? I glance down at my clumpy trainers and wince. Everything about this is awful.

'Now!' She clicks the music on and steps towards me, her narrowed eyes locked on to mine.

My God, she's intense. I feel like she's trying to possess me. I blink back at her, desperate to look away but worried that if I do I'll get told off.

This is ridiculous, I am a 26-year-old woman! Why am I so scared of the teacher?

'Hands!' she shouts, raising her hands up.

Everybody faces their partners and links their fingers together. Anxiously, I fold my hands into hers.

Urgh, God. I don't even know her and now we are holding hands. I don't even like holding hands with Mum.

'Feet!' she commands. 'With the music. I shall lead.'

Wait, what? What did she say? What am I supposed to do with my feet? Can't she see I'm a beginner? I'm wearing trainers!

She pushes me backwards and starts clicking her feet in a rocking motion. As carefully as I can, I copy, and to my annoyance accidentally catch sight of myself in the mirror. I shudder.

Oh great. I look like a penguin in desperate need of a wee.

'And that,' Gabriella shouts, finally releasing my clammy hands, 'is how we Salsa!'

She claps her hands in the air and everyone applauds each other, batting their eyes provocatively at their dance partners and peeling their hips away.

Thank god that hour is over.

I stagger backwards and quickly march to the back of the class, desperate to sink back into the crowd and stop being the centre of attention.

God, that was horrible. Nothing about that was enjoyable. What was Amy thinking?

I grab my water bottle and slot in behind the class, my top lip damp and quivering. At least now I can go back to the flat, put a wash on and watch *Gilmore Girls*.

I wipe my forehead with the back of my hand and feel my damp fringe stick out at odd angles. I glance at the woman next to me, whose hair is still sculpted to her face like she painted it on this morning.

How do they still all look so perfect? None of them look out of breath at all. Although I suppose none of them have spent the best part of an hour fighting off a panic attack as a result of being the class demonstrator. Slowly, we feed out of the classroom and back down the stairs.

'Please!' Gabriella calls as we file in a line out of the classroom. 'Sign up here for my next class.'

I reach the front of the queue and smile at Gabriella awkwardly as she wafts the clipboard under my nose. My eyes flit down.

She wants me to sign up again? Is she kidding? There is no way I am ever going to anything like this again ever. Not even if—

I stop in my tracks as my eyes land on a name on the clipboard. Without quite meaning to, I take it out of Gabriella's hands.

Jack Lemon.

'Would you like a pen?' Gabriella asks, peering over my shoulder.

I jump. 'Err . . . no,' I say, giving the clipboard back to her, 'thank you.'

That's Jack. That's Jack's name.

Why is Jack's name on her list? Has he signed up to a Salsa class? Why? Because of me? It must be!

I funnel out of the class and feel a fresh wave of heat ripple through my body.

What is he doing?

CHAPTER TWELVE

<u>Georgie's list</u>

1. Have a vindaloo on Brick Lane.
2. Take a Salsa class. ✓
3. Do a skydive.
4. Go on a Tinder date. ✓
5. Cycle around Hyde Park.
6. Run 10k.
7. Make the perfect Victoria sponge.
8. Go skinny-dipping in the sea.
9. Try skateboarding at Southbank.
10. Show Bianca your designs!

'Why are you going to a Salsa class? My Salsa class. Why are you going to my Salsa class?'

The words jumble out of my mouth and I glare at Jack, my face burning. I knew he'd be in the kitchen. He always makes a tea as soon as he comes in.

Jack continues to pour the steaming water into his mug and looks up at me, frowning.

'Your Salsa class?' Jack repeats, glancing back down at his tea. 'I didn't know you taught Salsa. You want a tea?'

A bolt of annoyance zaps through me.

Oh, har har. Like I could ever *teach* Salsa. After Saturday I can barely walk up the stairs.

'The one I go to,' I snap. 'You're going too. Why? To see me?'

I stare back at him, heat licking up my neck. To my annoyance, his face doesn't change.

God, he is so *infuriating*. Why isn't he responding? He's acting as if I'm asking him about the weather. He doesn't even look like he's listening!

I tried to let it go. I really did. I tried to sit at my desk and get on with my work and forget all about the fact that he magically happens to be going to the same Salsa class as me. My Salsa class.

But I'm sorry, it's now 9.07 and my willpower cannot hold out any longer. I need answers.

'To see you?' he echoes.

'Stop repeating everything I'm saying!' I burst out. 'Why are you going?'

Jack drops his tea bag in the bin and smiles. 'How do you know I'm going?'

'Because I saw your name on the list,' I say tartly. 'So, whatever your plan is to keep seeing me, you can just stop it. I told you we aren't dating and we're not.'

I turn to stalk back out of the kitchen when Jack laughs.

'Hang on,' he says, 'you're the one who worked out when I

was going, and it's you who has come to find me at work to ask me about it. Are you sure you don't want to see me?'

What?

I gape back at him, my mouth opening and closing furiously. 'I . . .' I splutter mindlessly, 'I don't . . . I don't want to see . . . *no!*' I manage finally, my face flaming.

A small grin pulls at the sides of Jack's mouth as he finally finishes making his tea and angles his whole body towards me. To my annoyance, my eyes flick down his chest.

'Okay,' he says eventually, 'well, good. I'm glad we got that sorted.'

I stare back at him, my brain whirring.

'I need to get back to work,' I say tightly. 'I'm very busy.'

Before Jack can say another word, I turn on my heels and stagger back towards my desk.

Urgh. Well, that did not go very well at all.

★

I narrow my eyes at my computer as I select a shade of buttercup yellow and swish it across the screen. With my eyes still fixed on my design, I coil my fingers around my tepid mug and take a slug of tea. Bianca has been in meetings all morning, which means for once I have been allowed to get on with designing uninterrupted. Our big pitch is for a clothes retailer, to design their summer rebranding. I have been working on a collection of designs for months. I will show them to Bianca; I just have to wait for her to be in a good mood and not be so manically stressed about the wedding. Although, it's starting to feel like that time may never come.

I glance up, distracted momentarily by Sally, who is scrunching her hair on top of her head like a damp sponge and rapping her pen on the desk.

Sally is a great designer. She may actually be better than Bianca. Everything she designs is perfect, and she will not finish a piece of work until it is exactly that, which makes her an exceptional employee in a design firm, but doesn't do her many favours amidst Bianca's wedding planning.

I put down my mug and peer at her as she mutters into her notebook.

'Sally,' I say quietly. 'Sally?'

Sally's head jerks up and she blinks at me as if she has just been woken out of a deep trance.

I flinch. 'Are you okay?' I ask.

For a second, Sally's shoulders sag at my question, as if she was expecting me to ask her to recite Bianca's wedding vows in Latin.

She nods slightly and I lean forward.

'Do you need any help?' I say. 'I'm just working on some ideas for designs, if you want an extra pair of hands with the wedding planning.'

Sally's eyes swell and for an awful moment I fear she may burst into tears.

'Could you?' she says. 'I am trying to work out who has confirmed attendance. If I read them out, could you write them down?'

'Sure!' I say brightly, picking up my notepad and pen.

A smile dashes across Sally's taut face. 'Okay,' she says, 'these are the people who are coming.'

'Great.'

'Flementine Darlington.'

I pause, my pen poised.

What? Surely that isn't someone's actual name.

'And her husband, Felix.'

I look up, waiting for Sally to crack into a smile, when I remember she doesn't have a sense of humour.

Flementine and Felix?

I madly scribble the names down, guessing how to spell 'Flementine'. What do they call her for short? Flemy?

'Mr and Mrs Boikskin-Chester.'

I force my face to stay composed as a laugh creeps up my throat. Who are these people?

'Granny Porpington.'

At this, a laugh bursts out of me. I clasp my hand over my mouth and look up at Sally, who is blinking back at me, baffled.

'Sorry,' I say, trying to compose myself as another chain of giggles shoots out of me, 'sorry. But, Granny Porpington? That sounds like a character from Paddington Bear.'

Sally's face twitches as her eyes dart above my head. I frown at her.

'Our Grandma actually loves Paddington,' Jack says cheerfully, 'so I think she'd be quite pleased with that.'

I jerk round to see Jack standing at the door carrying a stack of paper. Sally snaps back into attention mode and consults her list manically.

'We were just amending the guest list,' she yelps.

I glance back at Jack and then pull open the design file on my computer, trying to control my flushing face.

'Sally,' Jack says, looking over my shoulder, 'can I borrow Georgie for a minute?'

Sally opens her mouth to reply but I get there first.

'No!' I cry, before I can stop myself.

Sally blinks at me.

'I mean,' I say quickly, trying to compose myself, 'we are very busy here, Jack. Sorry. Maybe later.'

Sally's fixes me with a stern look. 'Georgia,' she says firmly, 'you can help Mr Lemon. I will be fine.'

Urgh. Mr Lemon.

'Oh, and . . .' Sally stands up, 'I bought this for Amy, it's about yoga.' She hands me a book and smiles unnaturally. 'I thought it might help her.'

I flounder as I gape at Sally. She bought Amy a present? To help her?

'Thank you,' I manage, as I put the book down on my desk. 'Thank you so much, Sally. She will really appreciate it.'

Sally smiles stiffly and drops back into her seat. 'Not at all.'

I glance back down at the book as I feel hot emotion pull at my throat. I think that's the nicest thing Sally has ever done for me. She cares about Amy and she's never even met her.

I pick up my bag and follow Jack out of the office. As soon as we're alone, the familiar spark of irritation flares in the pit of my stomach.

'What do you want?' I say coldly.

Jack turns to me, bemused. 'I need help finding the order form for the bridesmaid shoes,' he says. 'Bianca said you would know where it is.'

I look back at him, embarrassed at the realisation that he has a genuine need to speak to me.

'Oh,' I say, lifting my chin, 'okay. It's this way.'

I begin to walk down the corridor and Jack follows, his papers tucked under his arm. We march in silence until we reach the filing room. I push the door open and pull out a cabinet drawer, which pings open in front of us.

'It will be in here,' I say crisply, 'probably near the back.'

Jack looks at me for a second, and then moves towards the open cabinet. He drops his papers to the floor and starts searching. I roll my eyes and grimace at the back of his head, when my phone vibrates. I pull it out of my pocket. I don't care if Jack sees me texting at work. My eyes land on a text from Amy and my body turns cold.

Hey, been sent home from work. Going to bed. Tamal at work. Bring your keys later x

I hover over my phone, my eyes stinging dangerously. This is the first time Amy has been sent home from work. She has always refused to take any days off sick. She must be feeling really terrible.

I run my hand over my forehead as anxiety claws at my throat. I need to help her, but I don't know how. I don't feel like I'm helping her at all.

'Is this it?'

I look up at Jack, and to my horror the sudden movement of my eyes causes tears to spill down my face.

Jack jumps back, alarmed. 'Are you okay?' he says.

I quickly slip my phone back into my pocket and dab my face with the back of my hand, furious at myself for crying in front of him.

'Yes,' I say quickly, 'fine. Yes, that is the file, now shall we go?'

I turn to leave the room, but Jack doesn't move.

'What's the matter?' he says.

'Nothing,' I say firmly, taking a deep breath, 'nothing at all. I'm just tired.'

Jack shuts the filing cabinet and raises his eyebrows questioningly. 'Is it something to do with Amy? Is she okay?'

My eyes burn at the sound of Amy's name. How does he know about her?

'That,' I say tersely, 'is none of your business.' I pick up my bag, desperate to leave before I burst into tears. 'I have a lot of work to do. See you later.'

I push my way out of the door as my face crumples.

I need to help her. I need to do more. I just don't know how.

★

I watch dubiously as the nifty skateboarders, all crouched low over their boards, swoop and flip over the Southbank ramps. I glance down at my own skateboard, and feel an involuntary stab of fear.

Nothing feels more unnatural than the idea of standing on a flimsy board with wheels and rolling towards any of these ramps. Especially that big one over there, which looks like the Grand Canyon's less reliable sister. My eyes scan the ramps and I screw up my face determinedly.

Come on, Georgie. If you do this one thing, you can tick another item off this list and be done with it. Amy didn't stipulate how long you had to skateboard for, you could just roll across the ramp once and call it a day. You could even . . .

I pause as my eyes lock on a character, jumping over the ramps with ease. I feel my eyelids twitch.

Is that Jack?

I take a step forward and narrow my eyes as if I have an internal zoom option.

Oh my God, it is! What is he doing here? I watch in surprise as he flips over another ramp.

Wow, he's actually pretty good. How does he know how to skateboard?

I squeeze my eBay-bought skateboard, tucked under my arm, and turn my attention to a small, inoffensive ramp sat in the corner. It looks like the child's ramp. It must be for beginners. Okay, I shall just roll over a gentle slope and leave before Jack sees me. I can do this.

I inhale a great mouthful of air and puff out my chest. I stride towards the ramp, trying to ignore the sound of my boots snapping on the tarmac and reverberating around the skate park. Some of the skateboarders eye me, as if I'm the grown-up who is about to lecture them all on why a good education is more important than flipping off a ramp, and I flash them an unnerving smile.

I reach the ramp and drop the skateboard to the ground. My stomach twinges.

Wow. Now I'm here it does actually look a lot higher than I first thought. It's actually pretty steep. I peer down the ramp slowly. Is it too steep?

I'm sure you're not supposed to skateboard with a handbag tucked under your arm, but I am not leaving it lying around in a skate park.

I can't believe I'm about to do this. Why did Amy put this on the list? What's the point?

I hold my handbag under my arm and step on to the skateboard slowly.

Nobody else here has bags, how do they do it? I guess they all use their pockets, which is actually pretty—

WHOOSH!

Without warning, the skateboard lurches forward and shoots off. I hurtle down the ramp madly and crash to the floor, my legs twisting underneath my body.

Arghhhhhhhhhhhhhh!

My heart jitters in panic as I lie crumpled on the floor. Hot pain seeps through my body and I wince.

What happened? How did that happen?

I try to lift myself up, but my head rattles with pain.

I don't know if I can stand.

'Georgie?' I hear a voice. 'Georgie, are you okay?'

*

I lean back into my seat and eye my ankle as an agonising throb ripples up my leg. I shut my eyes and try to fight the tears stinging behind my eyelids. I pull one eye open as Jack reappears, holding two polystyrene cups. He hands one to me.

'Thank you,' I say quietly.

'No worries,' he replies.

Jack took me to hospital and we have been sat in A&E for what feels like hours.

I couldn't even stand – he had to carry me to the taxi. I bury my face in my cup as embarrassment courses through me. I didn't want him to carry me, obviously, but I was in no position to argue. If he hadn't have been there, I don't know what I would have done.

'You don't have to stay,' I mumble. 'I'm sure they will have my results soon.'

Jack puts his coffee on the floor and shakes his head. 'It's fine,' he says.

He's mad. Of course he is. I have been nothing but rude to him since I realised who he was. He has only been nice to me: he didn't tell Bianca who I was, and he helped me today. But then, he did read my diary.

I look back up at him. 'Why were you at the skate park?' I ask.

Jack settles back in his seat. 'I was skateboarding,' he says plainly.

Hmm.

He must have known I was going to be there.

I nod, taking a sip of my tea, and recoil as the liquid lava singes my tongue.

'Shit!' I cry, pulling the cup away from my mouth.

Jack's eyes flit over to me, then he pulls out his phone.

'It's hot,' I say quietly, holding my mouth with my hand. 'Be careful.'

His lips curl slightly. 'Thanks,' he says.

'Georgia Miller?'

I jolt upwards as a nurse appears, holding a clipboard.

'Hi,' I manage, 'that's me.'

Her eyes scan the room and smile as they land on me. She walks over.

She sits next to me and my stomach spasms.

Please don't say my foot's broken. Please. It can't be broken. It can't.

'So,' she says, consulting the chart, 'it's just a sprain. You will need to wear a support. You can pick one up from most super-markets, and just take it easy. Okay?'

Her kind smile stretches over her face, and to my alarm my eyes start to prick.

'Thank you,' I gush, failing to control the tears seeping from the corners of my eyes. 'Sorry,' I gabble, dabbing the side of my face with the back of my sleeve, 'I've just . . . I've got this 10k, and I need to be able to run. It's important. I just—' I break off, finally pulling myself together. 'Thank you.'

The nurse smiles and stands back up.

'Glad you're okay, but I'd recommend staying away from running for a week or two,' she says kindly. 'And you need someone to drive you back home,' she adds, 'okay?'

I nod, lifting my leg off the chair as she leaves my side. I glance up at Jack and notice he is staring at me.

'Thank you,' I manage, 'thank you for taking me, and helping.'

Jack doesn't say anything, his green eyes round with concern.

'Are you doing the run for Amy?' he asks.

I look back at him. My former rage at him for knowing about Amy is replaced with a wave of relief.

I nod. 'Yeah,' I say, 'she isn't well.'

He sinks deeper into the chair. 'I know,' he says.

'Yeah,' I laugh lightly, 'you read it in my diary, right?'

Jack sighs. 'I told you,' he says, 'I didn't read your diary.'

'Well then, how do you—?'

'You told me on our date,' he says. 'You told me about the MS.'

I pause, my stomach lurching queasily. I look away, my face prickling with embarrassment.

Oh. I hadn't thought of that.

'How is she?' Jack asks.

I hold his gaze, the truth itching at the back of my throat.

I lock my moist fingers together. 'Not great,' I manage, 'it makes her really tired. I don't know what to do. She's losing herself. It's eating her up.'

'Excuse me?'

We both turn as a lady with auburn ringlets and a broad chest appears, jingling a bucket. 'We're raising money for the Red Cross. Do you have any spare change?'

I stick my hand in my pocket and fish out some coins, and watch as Jack slots in a note. The woman nods her head appreciatively and edges around the room.

'She used to be so motivated,' I say, watching the woman approach another set of people. 'I don't know how to instil that in her again. That's what she has always done for me.'

'Well,' Jack says, looking down at the Red Cross leaflet, 'maybe we need to find something to motivate her.'

Chapter Thirteen

<u>Georgie's list</u>

1. Have a vindaloo on Brick Lane.
2. Take a Salsa class. ✓
3. Do a skydive.
4. Go on a Tinder date. ✓
5. Cycle around Hyde Park.
6. Run 10k.
7. Make the perfect Victoria sponge.
8. Go skinny-dipping in the sea.
9. Try skateboarding at Southbank. ✓
10. Show Bianca your designs!

I wiggle my feet in my trainers and grab my water bottle determinedly. Two weeks after my ankle injury, and I am ready to enter the battleground again.

Right, third run. I can do this. I can run for twenty minutes. I am even wearing two sports bras - which took me ten minutes alone to put on. Honestly, getting in and out of a sports bra should be counted as a sport within itself. Christ.

I glance outside and push my way out of the flat, making a mental note of everything I need.

Right, then. Phone, water, keys—

I manically pat my body.

Oh my God, where are my keys? Have I left them in the flat? Oh my God, I'm so stupid! How will I get back in? I'm locked—

Oh wait, they're in my pocket. Cool.

I bounce gently on the balls of my feet and then set off in a light jog down the street, catching sight of myself in a shop window. I really am nailing this whole 'casual runner' look and, as this is my third run, I am officially classing myself as a runner. I have even bought a handy armband to lock my phone in. I am one sweatband away from being Jessica Ennis-Hill.

I glance at my phone with pride and notice it's flashing. I scowl.

Why is it flashing? Who is texting me at 7.30 a.m.?

I focus on the road and try to ignore the curiosity tugging at my mind.

It can't be important. I'm only running for twenty minutes, I will look when I get back. It can wait twenty minutes.

What if it's Amy? Maybe something has happened to her. Although nobody would text me to let me know. They'd call. I know for a fact Mum can barely turn her mobile on.

I turn a corner. The crisp air fills my lungs as if I have inhaled a tube of toothpaste.

It could be Jack. But then, why would he be texting me at 7.30 in the morning? He rarely texts me, and that is how it

141

should stay. Friends don't casually text each other first thing in the morning, that would be weird. But who else could it be? It must be Jack. Since I deleted Tinder, he is the only person to text me at all.

Why is he texting me so early in the morning?

Oh God, what if he has sent me a soppy, totally inappropriate message? Actually, it is totally inappropriate for my boss's brother to text me. Full stop. Urgh. I wish he didn't have my number. What if he is texting me with Bianca? What if they are having breakfast together – totally plausible – and he's lightly tapping away at his phone? She could see! And then she'll say, 'Who are you texting?' and he will say, 'Georgie,' and then she will say, 'Georgie? My assistant? Why is she texting my brother? That is so weird, they must be having sex. I shall fire her.'

I feel my insides twist as my stomach performs somersaults.

Argh! I need to check. I have to. I need to tell Jack to stop texting me right away. The idiot. Why on earth is he texting me? Is he trying to get me fired?

Without checking my surroundings, I ram my feet into the ground and skid to a halt. My chest burns at the sudden chance to catch my breath and I buckle over, my hands grasping at my phone.

I frown. It's an email. What? Who is emailing me at this time?

I click on mail and fight the urge to throw my phone in the bin as an email from Bianca appears.

Bianca had the dreadful idea yesterday of installing our work emails on our phones, after Sally asked to leave early for a doctor's appointment. Why is she emailing me at this time? This should be illegal. Furiously, I jab the email open and scowl at the message that lights up on my screen.

Georgie. I need you to visit London Zoo before the meeting at 10.30. I have a bear tip. Ask to speak to Charlie. B x

I glare at the screen in horror.

A bear tip? London Zoo? She wants me to gallivant off to London Zoo? I'm supposed to be a designer!

I shove my phone back into my armband and continue to run, fuelled by a fresh injection of irritation shooting up my body.

And before 10.30? It's almost 8 a.m. now!

I pummel my legs into the ground furiously as I storm on to a stretch of grass.

Maybe I'll just pretend I didn't get the email. Or that my phone is broken. Although, what is this bear tip? Maybe going to the zoo will solve this ridiculous problem and I can stop pretending to need a wee every time Bianca brings it up.

I feel another zap of irritation as my phone vibrates again. My eyes flit down to my armband and my flashing phone.

What now? Is she emailing me again? Is this a follow-up email? I could be asleep! For all she knows, I could be doing something really important.

I rip the phone out of the armband.

My legs slow to a gradual halt as my eyes focus on my phone, and Mum's name flashes on to the screen.

Mum? Why is Mum calling me?

'Hello?' I press the phone to my ear, anxiety washing over me.

'Hello?' Mum's voice spills out of the phone excitedly. 'Hello? Oh Ian, look! It's working!'

I scowl at the screen.

What is she talking about?

'Keep running, darling!' Mum says. 'Keep going!'

I start running obediently and then stagger back to a halt.

'Hang on,' I say, 'what? How do you know I'm on a run?'

My eyes dart around the park expectantly. Is she here?

'Amy set up this great application!' Mum trills. 'It means we can run with you!'

I look around, baffled.

'Run with me?' I repeat. 'What? Are you here?'

A horsey laugh fills my ear as Mum and Dad chuckle in unison.

'No, darling!' Mum cries. 'Of course not. It's Tuesday!'

I continue to stare at my phone. What's that got to do with anything?

Am I dreaming?

'We thought—' I hear as Dad takes the phone. 'We would log on to the application.'

I try to squash the burst of irritation that squirms inside me.

App. It's called an app. Urgh.

'And join you on your run,' Dad continues. 'We can see you! You're right by the park, aren't you?'

At this, I fully spin on the spot.

Where the hell are they? How are they doing this?

'Something to do with your location settings,' Dad finishes.

I glance down at the phone and feel my eyes roll into the back of my head.

'Oh, and Georgia!' Dad quips. 'I got your cartoon email this morning. Very funny! Look, I put it on the fridge.'

I hear a scuffle of noise and then an expanding silence.

Dear Lord. He thinks we're FaceTiming.

Why is technology always so difficult for parents to understand?

'Oh well done, darling,' Mum coos in the background, 'you've already run 1k. You are doing well.'

'Thank you,' I say, picking my pace back up and breaking into a run.

'This is fantastic!' Dad cries. 'We can see exactly where you are!'

Oh God. I hope they don't log on to this app randomly to see what I'm doing as a fun joke. I don't want Mum working out how much time I spend in McDonald's.

I jog around another corner and try to zone Dad out. This is a bloody nightmare. How am I supposed to run with those two in my ear, acting like they've discovered the first life on Mars?

'It really is amazing!' he continues. 'Modern technology. I don't know how I—'

'Oh!' Mum shouts in the background.

I screw up my face as her pinched cry shoots into my ear. I hear another muffled sound as Mum snatches the phone off Dad.

'Georgia!' Mum calls. 'I've just noticed that there is a Cook store right near you! You are a five-minute jog away from it!'

I narrow my eyes. I hope I don't know where this is going.

'Right,' I say slowly.

'Will you pop in for me on your way back?' she says. 'I'm sure it opens at eight. I'm having a dinner party this weekend and could really do with some Chicken Alexander.'

I furrow my brow. 'Who's Alexander?'

'It's a meal!' Mum snips. 'Will you pop in and get me some? Oh! And some Tagine Cups.'

'Mum,' I whine, 'I'm on a run! I haven't got time!'

Mum puffs down the phone. 'Well!' she cries. 'Do you think

I have time to make twelve mini quiches? Of course I don't.
And if there was one little thing that could make my life easier
then I would have thought that you, as my daughter, would—'

'Urgh!' I cry. 'Fine! Fine! I'll go and bloody get them.'

'Oh good. Thank you, darling. Oh, could you also pick up
twelve mini spotted dicks? Your dad loves those.'

I gape at the phone.

If that is any form of innuendo then I am putting myself up
for adoption.

∗

I eye the large, grand sign dubiously and sigh. I cannot believe
I am about to enter London Zoo in a pencil skirt. I feel like
I'm on *The Apprentice*.

I tug my skirt down and shimmy in, like an anxious penguin,
as nerves dance around my chest. I glance at my phone: 09.55.
Okay. I have half an hour to speak to Charlie. Whoever the hell
that is. I hope it's a real person and this isn't some sort of code.
Maybe Bianca actually doesn't want bears at all, and she's speaking
in cockney slang. What could 'bear' mean in rhyming slang?

Chairs?

Actually, that is totally feasible. She could easily be asking me
to source chairs for the wedding. Shit. Am I being a total idiot?
But then, why would she send me to London Zoo? They don't
sell chairs here, do they?

I waddle up to the reception desk and glance at a woman
who is dressed head to toe in large, stained overalls. Her hair is
scraped off her face and she has a heavy nose ring hanging from
her left nostril. Her thick arms are slumped forward, forcing her

back to arch, and there is a smear of mud on the side of her neck.

Or, at least, I think that's mud.

'Hello,' I say awkwardly, 'I'm here to see Charlie.'

The girl looks up and her brow knits. 'I'm Charlie,' she says in an unfriendly voice. Her eyes flit up and down my body and her frown deepens.

Oh, right. Well, that was easy. I think.

'Ah,' I say, 'hello. I'm here on behalf of Bianca.'

The girl stares at me, her lazy expression hanging.

I hover uncertainly.

'Bianca Lemon?' I offer.

The girl's eyes show no flicker of recognition at my question. Eventually, she speaks.

'Who?' she grunts.

I flinch, a cold sense of dread washing over me.

'I . . .' I stumble, my face hot, 'I'm here on behalf of Bianca Lemon.' I start again. 'She said to ask for Charlie—' I look around. 'Maybe a different Charlie.'

'I'm the only Charlie here,' she growls, as if I have questioned her very being.

I blink back at her. Have I got this totally wrong? Was this some form of office joke at my expense?

I pull out my phone and quickly jab Bianca's phone number.

'Sorry,' I say to Charlie, holding my phone to my ear, 'one second.'

I turn away as the phone trills in my ear and my face burns. Am I going mad? There is only one London Zoo, right? Have I completely—?

'Hello?'

I jump slightly as Bianca's flowery voice swirls down my phone.

'Hi,' I say, trying to stay calm, 'Bianca, it's Georgia.'

'Hello, Georgie darling,' Bianca says. 'How are you? Did you get my email?'

I scowl at the phone. 'Yes,' I reply, 'I'm here now. I'm with Charlie, she says she . . . err . . . doesn't know you.'

The last bit tumbles out of my mouth awkwardly and I falter, hoping she doesn't take offence.

'Oh yes,' Bianca says casually, 'I don't know Charlie— Oh no, this is no good, I need it with much more froth than that, please,' she instructs. 'Thank you.'

What?

'You,' I say slowly, 'you don't know Charlie?'

'Oh no, darling,' Bianca says, a tinkle of laughter dancing down the phone.

I feel my face burn.

Well then, why the hell did she send me here?

'My friend does,' Bianca continues. 'Charlie is my friend's second cousin. She said that she worked at London Zoo and I just thought, now there is an idea. I thought you could ask her about the bears. As a way in, you know.'

I fight the urge to hurl my phone at the wall.

'Are you with her now?' Bianca says.

I glance back at Charlie, who is still eyeing me expectantly.

'Err,' I mumble, 'yes.'

'Oh good,' Bianca coos, 'ask her now, will you? While I'm on the phone.'

I blink back at the phone.

What? No! I can't ask that incredibly stern woman if she has a troop of singing bears!

Can I get out of this? Hang up on Bianca? Pretend my phone has broken?

'Georgie?' Bianca persists, her sharp voice piercing my ear. I stand on the spot mutinously.

Slowly, I step towards Charlie, who slumps her head in her hands. I force my eyes to meet hers.

'Hi,' I say again, 'I've got my boss on the phone. Bianca Lemon.'

'Hello!' Bianca calls from down the phone, and I jump as her pinched voice thunders into my eardrum.

A smirk pulls at Charlie's mouth, and my face burns.

'Ask her about the bears,' Bianca orders.

Urgh. This is going to be the worst moment of my life. I really hope they don't have CCTV. I don't want to end up on the news as a hysterical joke.

I look at Charlie, praying she can read the apologetic under-tones of my question. I don't even know how to word this, it's so ridiculous.

'She,' I begin, 'she, err . . . she is getting married, and she would like some bears at the wedding . . .'

I pause, my forehead peppered with beads of sweat that cling to my fringe. Charlie's eyebrows creep up her face. She pulls herself up to her full height and towers over me, like a large, ominous gorilla.

'Bears?' she repeats.

I nod gravely.

Charlie's eyes flit to the phone, and then back to me.

'Real bears?' Charlie says slowly.

I nod again.

God, this is so humiliating.

'Tell her I'll pay for them!' Bianca barks down the phone. 'No expense spared!'

Charlie glances back at the phone as Bianca's crisp voice spills into the room. She runs her hands through her coarse hair and shakes her head.

'Nah,' she says, her mouth splitting into a wry smile, 'nah, we can't do that. You can't hire the bears. Sorry.'

'That's okay,' I gabble quickly, desperate to leave before Bianca can speak again. 'Thank you for your time. Goodbye.'

I spin on the spot and march out of the zoo as quickly as I can.

Bianca sighs down the phone. 'You know,' she says wearily, 'we really need to work on your negotiating skills.'

CHAPTER FOURTEEN

Running schedule:

04/08	1k	✓	(August is not the time to start running. Sweat patches are uncontrollable.)
10/09	2k	✓	(Actually isn't that far at all! Who knew?)

'You're in a good mood.'

I angle my head round to face Amy as we lurch into downward dog.

Oh God, I hate this position. Who on earth ever invented this? How was it discovered? Surely this position was stumbled upon whilst having sex. But then, how could anyone ever have sex like this? I've only been in it for about thirty seconds and I feel like my head is about to explode, and not in a good way.

'Am I?' I reply.

'Yeah,' Amy says, as we curl into the cobra position, 'you're all twinkly. And you're wearing make-up.'

151

I glance down at Sally's book, propped open on the settee. I smile at Amy.

'I am just pleased,' I manage, all the air from my body squashed inside my stomach, 'to be spending time with you. It is nice to see you doing things.'

Amy looks quizzically at me but doesn't say anything.

Good Lord, this is uncomfortable. I thought yoga was supposed to be relaxing.

'How are you feeling?' I ask, trying to look at Amy without moving my head. If I move any of my body too much I will certainly topple over.

Amy keeps her eyes on me. I tense. This is the question Amy seems to hate the most. This would be the moment when Amy snaps. To my relief, her face curls into a smile.

'Fine,' she says calmly. 'I'm actually feeling good this week,' she says. 'I'm feeling better at work and it is so nice to be doing yoga again. I'd forgotten how much I enjoy it.'

I smile as a wave of affection for Sally spreads through my chest.

'Okay,' Amy says, 'now we need to lean on one side and put an arm in the air. It's quite hard, it's called "wild thing".'

I snort and Amy shoots me a look. 'Why is that funny?'

'Oh, come on,' I say, firmly stuck in my cobra position. 'Wild thing? What is wild about yoga?' My eyes flit down to the picture and I see the pose. 'Oh my God,' I say, 'how on earth do you do that? It looks impossible!'

Amy grins. 'You can do it. Come on, follow my lead.'

Experimentally, I get to my feet and bend my back to copy Amy. I frown at the picture. I am definitely doing this wrong.

'So,' Amy says, 'has that guy been back at your office?'

I curl my arm backwards. Okay, wow, this is really hard.

'Guy?' I repeat, knowing full well that she means Jack. 'What guy?'

'Jack,' Amy says, not missing a beat.

I feel my cheeks flush. 'Yeah, he has, actually. He's sort of working with us. He's all right, you know. He was the one who helped me with my ankle.'

Amy twists her head round to face me. 'Did he now?' she says suggestively.

I scowl at her. 'We're just friends,' I say, moving my head, 'honestly, I—'

I go to twist my head round to face her, but suddenly lose my balance and topple into a huge heap.

'You idiot,' Amy giggles.

'It's not funny,' I grumble, laughing myself. 'That really hurt. Hey,' I say, suddenly able to look at Amy properly, 'you're doing it!'

Amy curves her back, perfectly sculpted into the pose as if she was drawn from a book. She shakes her head so her chestnut hair tumbles towards the floor, her pink cheeks flaring.

She flashes me a grin. 'So I am.'

★

I eye my fat ankle, stuffed into my boot and frown. I really hope this is just a swelling and I don't have a permanently fat ankle. That would be unfortunate to say the least.

I look up slowly as Sally appears next to my desk.

'What are you doing?' she says sternly.

I jump slightly in alarm. 'Balancing the spreadsheet,' I say carefully.

Why is she asking me that? I'm doing exactly what she asked

me to do. Is this a test? Am I supposed to be doing something else? Sally's face doesn't move.

'Next Wednesday,' she says tightly, 'what are you doing next Wednesday? In the evening.'

I blink up at her, bemused.

'Err . . .' I say, 'nothing really. I mean I—'

'Good,' Sally nods and marches back to her desk. 'We shall go running together. You need to be careful with that ankle, and I'll help you.'

I gape at her as she drops into her chair and begins tapping at her keyboard.

Oh great. I walked straight into that one.

'That's okay,' I say quickly. 'I think, actually, I—'

My words are lost as the office door thuds under the rap of Jack's knuckles. I glance up and he flashes a grin at me.

'Hey,' he says, 'you got a minute?'

I glare at Jack and then cock my head meaningfully in Sally's direction. He can't just saunter in here in the middle of a working day, when Sally is sat right there!

Thankfully, Sally doesn't look up from her computer.

'It's to discuss spreadsheets,' Jack adds, smirking over at Sally.

'You're going to get me into trouble,' I hiss, shutting the office door behind me.

'What for?' Jack says, affronted. 'People do talk to each other at work. We're only colleagues. I want to ask you about the company's net profit.'

I raise my eyebrows at him and lean against the office door.

Oh please, like I have any idea what that is. I don't even know what net profit means. Is it the amount of money Bianca spends on nets?

Why would Bianca want any nets?

'What do you want?' I ask, a smile tugging at my face.

Jack's eyes spark. 'I've got an idea . . .'

'Oh?'

'About Amy,' he finishes. 'About how to make her feel better.'

The smirk is abruptly washed off my face. About Amy? He's been thinking about Amy?

'What do you mean?' I manage, confused.

Jack grabs my arm and pulls me into a seat, propped in the corridor. He drops into the chair next to me and leans forward.

'You know your list,' he says, 'Amy's list. The one she made for you?'

I nod.

'Why don't we make one of the tasks on there for charity?' He looks up at me. 'We could raise loads of money for MS. She could get involved. It might make her feel better, give her something to focus on, and it'll also be for a good cause.'

I stare back at him, my body inflating like a hot-air balloon.

'I thought maybe,' he says, 'we could do a sponsored 10k or something.'

We. He thought *we*.

'Amy loves running,' I say.

'Exactly!' Jack says excitedly. 'What do you think?'

I glance down at my hands, a warm glow filling my chest. I smile.

'I think that's a really good idea,' I say. 'I think she'll love it.'

Jack grins and runs his hands through his hair.

'Great,' he says, 'we could do it around December time, so we have plenty of time to plan it. As the last thing for you to complete on the list. You know, to celebrate.'

I look back at him. He's really thought about this. He really wants to help.

'I'll help you plan it,' he says, getting to his feet. 'We need to raise a load of money.'

I stand too and, before I can stop myself, my arms wrap themselves around his neck and I squeeze him into a hug.

Jack flushes slightly as I let him go.

'Let's go out for dinner tonight,' he says, pulling his phone out of his pocket, 'to discuss it all.'

I pull a face and he raises his eyebrows.

'Not a date,' he says, rolling his eyes, 'don't panic. I'll meet you downstairs at five. I'll make it worth your while.'

With that, he walks back down the corridor and I'm left standing, floundering.

Well, if that doesn't sound like a sexual offer then I don't know what does.

*

'Just here,' Jack says, sliding into a chair, 'that's perfect,' he looks up at the waiter, 'thank you.'

I sink into my seat and glance around anxiously at the deep-red walls. I try not to brush against the couples sat on either side of us, our shoulders almost touching.

'If you're going to have a vindaloo,' Jack says, hooking his jacket on the back of his chair, 'you really need to have it here. Amy was right to send you to Brick Lane, they really are the best curries.'

I smile weakly as my eyes fall on the menu.

Okay, this is not how it was supposed to happen. If I'd

realised Jack meant this when he suggested dinner, I never would have agreed. I can't eat my first ever vindaloo in front of Jack. I never eat curry. I have no idea what will happen when I do. How will my body react?

If I accidentally fart in front of a man I barely know I will leave the country.

I tune in as I realise Jack is still talking.

'This place in particular is really great,' he says. 'I used to come here all the time.'

I cock my head. 'Do you not live in London any more?' I ask.

Jack shakes his head. 'Nah,' he says, 'haven't for years. Love it, though.'

'Why did you move?'

Jack looks behind my head. 'I had to,' he says absent-mindedly. 'Hi,' he says as the waiter appears, 'can we have two vindaloos, please?'

I lurch forward in horror as I hear him order.

Already? We've only just arrived!

Oh no. I am not ready for this.

'And a beer.' He leans in towards me. 'I'm going to have a beer, do you want one?'

No! I want water. A bucket of ice water and a fire extinguisher.

'No,' I turn to the waiter, 'thank you, just water. Thank you.'

The waiter nods and walks back towards the kitchen.

Why does everything on Amy's list make me feel like I'm on the verge of a panic attack? Was this the whole idea? To increase my heart rate and endanger my blood pressure?

Nothing about Amy's illness would stop her eating a curry either. She must have added this on especially for me. *Why?*

'I've been thinking about what you said,' I say to Jack. 'Amy works at a school, as a PE teacher. She leads a running club with some of the kids. Maybe they could be involved.'

Jack grins, the spark in his eyes flashing. 'Great idea!' he says. 'We could have a sponsored run, and maybe, like, a bake sale. Hey,' he looks up at me, 'maybe your Victoria sponge could be the centrepiece.'

He grins mockingly, and I scowl.

'Did you read all of my list,' I say, 'or just my diary? You know that is a huge invasion of my privacy. You're lucky I'm even speaking to you.'

The waiter places our drinks down and Jack scoops up his beer.

'I told you,' he says, 'I didn't read your diary. And to be fair,' he adds, 'I didn't mean to read your list. It fell out of your notebook when I picked it up.' He shrugs apologetically. 'Curiosity got the better of me.' He sips his beer. 'I didn't realise what it was at first,' he continues. 'I just assumed it was a bucket list. I thought it was a nice idea.'

I curl my fingers around my glass as realisation seeps into me.

'Is that why you were at the skate park?' I say. 'And why you came to the Salsa class?'

Jack shrugs. 'I thought it looked like a good to do list.'

I open my mouth to reply when a bright bowl of something orange slides in front of me, steaming viciously.

Oh my God.

Jack grins at his bowl. 'Looks great!' He looks up at the waiter. 'Thank you.'

I mindlessly mouth something at the waiter as he ducks behind us. My eyes focus on the curry ominously.

What is going to happen when I eat this? What will happen to me? Will I be okay? Or will I die?

I stab a piece of chicken with my fork and carefully slot it into my mouth.

Stay calm, Georgie. Everything is going to be okay. People eat curries all the time. Lots of people eat curry, and they don't die. Everybody in India eats curry, and they're all fine. You can do this. It's just a curry.

'So,' Jack says, already finishing his first mouthful of curry, 'when shall we start planning? It's almost October, so we've got, like, a couple of months.'

I force down the curry nervously. Okay, so far so good. That actually tasted quite nice.

'Let me talk to Amy,' I say, 'and see what dates work for her. See what she thinks.'

Jack nods and spoons another portion into his mouth.

'It's really nice,' I say, my eyes flicking up at Jack, 'for you to help me with this.'

Jack shrugs, his eyes fixed on his plate. 'Well,' he says, 'I know what it's like to have a sister who needs you.'

I smile, forking another piece of chicken. 'Yeah. It's nice for you to help Bianca with her crazy wedding.'

Jack's face twitches at the word 'crazy'.

'She deserves it,' he says. 'She really deserves the perfect day.'

I scoop up another forkful and feel myself relax.

Wow, I am actually enjoying this. I am having a curry, on Brick Lane, with a guy (three things I have never done before), and I am enjoying myself! I never thought I—

I pause as a tickle of heat pinches my throat. My eyes widen in alarm.

Oh no. Oh *no*. What's happening? What was that?

I swallow my mouthful slowly as I feel a rumble of heat, stirring in the pit of my stomach.

Okay. What is that? What is *that*?

Oh my God. I think this is really spicy.

I open and close my mouth frantically, as all the moisture that once sat in my mouth evaporates.

It is! It is really spicy! Oh my God. Oh my God.

I pull my eyes away from Jack and try to distract myself as I feel the heat race up my body like a forest fire. As it reaches my throat, hot daggers of spice stab at my insides and I feel scorching heat rip through me like fire. All the blood inside me rushes to my head and I glare at my bowl of curry helplessly, feeling as if I've been incinerated internally.

Oh my. That's really . . . I need to . . .

My hand springs forward and I grab my glass of water and chug it down in one gulp. The fire inside my throat calms for a second, and then spreads through my chest, more furious than before.

I need more water! Why did he give me such a tiny glass? What is the point in that? Who wants such ridiculously small glasses?

Arghhhhhhh!

Jack peers at me. 'Are you okay?'

'Fine,' I blurt, swivelling my body round and searching desperately for the waiter.

Another wave of unbearable heat swarms over my body. Oh my God, how is this so spicy? I need liquid. I feel like someone has set me on fire!

'Are you sure?' Jack says.

I whip my head back round to meet Jack, and then, before I can think of anything else, I grab hold of his beer and gulp it down, desperate for it to douse the fire storming up my throat. I slam the empty beer bottle down and lock eyes with Jack, panting.

'That's really,' I pant, 'it's really . . . spicy.'

Jack gapes at me, his mouth hanging open, and I stare back at him.

Suddenly he throws his head back and laughs, a real laugh pumping from the depths of his stomach. A laugh I have never heard before.

'It's not funny,' I manage, although I feel a chain reaction of giggles bubbling up too. 'Stop laughing.'

Jack holds his stomach as the corners of his eyes crease and his smile widens.

'I'm sorry,' I add, 'I'll buy you another beer.'

'Stop,' Jack gasps, waving his arm across his chest. 'Stop.'

A full laugh shoots out from my chest now, as I lean forward and hold my head in my hands. My chest aches as laughter tickles every part of me and forces its way out of my mouth in loud, vibrant bursts. My laugh seems to make Jack laugh even harder and the couple next to us shoot us a disapproving stare.

'Sorry,' I grab the waiter as he walks past, 'can we have another beer, please?'

Jack holds up two of his fingers. 'Two,' he manages, between laughs, 'make it two. I don't trust you any more. You're getting your own.'

★

'Amy?' I crash through the house, my shopping bags banging behind me. 'Amy?' I shout again, 'are you awake?'

I kick the door shut behind me. There is no answer. It's almost eight, she shouldn't be in bed already.

'Amy?' I call again.

'Hey, Georgia . . .' I look up and spot Dad, making his way down the stairs. 'Amy is in the living room. She doesn't feel great today.'

My eyes stray to the living room door. She will definitely be able to hear me. Why is she ignoring me?

'She will,' I say fiercely. 'I've got good news.'

I power through into the living room and Dad follows. Amy is curled under a blanket on the sofa, her skinny legs poking out at odd angles and her head resting limply on her hands as she stares at the TV. Her usually bright hair is hanging from her scalp and her pale skin is speckled with flecks of green.

'Hi, Amy,' I say, dropping the bags to the floor.

Amy pulls her eyes away from the TV, but she doesn't speak.

'How was work?' I persist.

Amy doesn't answer, her eyes glueing themselves back to the screen. I try to silence the annoyance rippling through my body.

'Fine,' I say calmly. I step forward and reach the remote, zapping off the TV. Amy finally raises her dull eyes to meet mine. I smile, the excitement zinging around the pit of my stomach.

'I need to talk to you,' I say, grinning. I drop to the floor, cross-legged, and Dad slots down next to Amy on the sofa, hooking his arm around her shoulders. He pulls Amy up from her slouching position and into his chest, and Amy slumps forward like a puppet with no strings.

'What's up, Georgia?' Dad says brightly.

I look into his face gratefully. At least one of them is happy to see me.

'Where have you been?' Amy scowls at me from under her cuffs, masking her face. 'It's almost eight.'

'I went out with Jack,' I say. 'We had a vindaloo on Brick Lane.'

Dad smiles. 'Ah!' He nudges Amy. 'Another thing ticked off the list! Well done, Georgie.'

I smile. 'So,' I say, 'we've had an idea about your list, Ames. We thought that we could make the 10k a charity event, for you.' I look up at Amy, who is staring back at me, her face unchanging. 'And, like, raise money for MS.'

I stare at Amy hopefully and she looks back at me blankly. She doesn't say anything. Dad looks down at her and then back at me.

'I think that's a great idea,' he says.

I grin, excitement shooting through me.

'We thought,' I continue, 'we could host it with your school. Maybe get the kids involved. We could raise loads of—'

'What?' Amy cuts across me, her voice cold.

I falter. 'Host it at your . . .' I trail off at Amy's scowling expression. 'What?' I say defensively. 'What is it?'

Why is she so angry?

Amy pulls herself away from Dad sharply. 'Why would I want to hold an event at my school celebrating how sick I am? What . . . like, have everyone there watching me? Poor, sick Amy. Isn't her life so sad?'

I blink at her, winded by her reaction.

'It's not,' I stumble, 'that isn't—'

'I'm fine,' she snaps. 'I'm not a charity case. I'm fine.'

'Amy, I didn't—'

'You should go,' she cuts across me, getting to her feet. 'I need to go and lie down. I'm sick, remember.'

I stare after her and blink as my eyes prick. I hang my head in my hands and scrunch my hair. This isn't how it was supposed to go at all.

'Hey . . .'

I look up at Dad, who has reappeared after following Amy.

'. . . are you okay?'

I shrug. 'I just,' I say thickly, 'I just want to help her. She won't let me help her.'

Dad shuts the door behind him and perches back on the sofa.

'Just give her some time,' he says gently. 'Today was a bad day. Don't give up on it.' He smiles at me. 'She'll come round.'

CHAPTER FIFTEEN

<u>Reasons Not To Go Skydiving:</u>

1. Terrified of heights. Genuine fear. Should not be mocked or taken lightly.
2. Unnatural. Humans were not built to drop from the sky and survive. 'It's raining men' is a song, not an observation.
3. Weight. Is there a weight limit? Me + someone else = falling to the ground quickly.
4. Clumsy. Will most certainly land wrong and crack open skull and/or face.
5. Face. Will the wind give me weird Botox?
6. BREASTS. What will the wind do to them?!
7. What will happen if I am sick? Where will that go?
8. What if I am sick and someone catches it on camera and I become national laughing stock?
9. What if I meet an angry bird on the way down?
10. WHAT IF I MEET A PLANE ON THE WAY DOWN?
11. What if I wee myself (v. likely after Thorpe Park incident)

I fix my eyes on the back of Sally's hair, perfectly swishing from side to side as she leaps along the path like an elegant grasshopper. Whilst I try not to hyperventilate behind her like a congested worm.

This is really unfair. Of course running is easy for Sally. Her legs come up to my armpits.

We have been running for twelve hundred hours. Okay, we haven't. But it feels like we have. I'm sure we have definitely been running for more than twenty-three minutes (which is my absolute limit) and Sally has no intention of stopping. She hasn't asked if I'm okay once! It hasn't even crossed her mind that her only assistant could be dying a slow and painful death ten feet behind her. Well, the joke's on you, Sally, because if I die thanks to this ridiculous run then you will have to deal with Bianca all by yourself.

Except, obviously, the joke is much more on me because I'll be dead. Thanks to a run, of all things.

I push my burning legs into the ground in an attempt to catch up with her. How is she doing this so effortlessly? She doesn't seem out of breath at all. And I bet she's only wearing one sports bra. Sally's eyes flit towards me as I puff alongside her like a pitiful steam train, thankfully catching up as my legs tremble beneath me.

'How is your ankle?' she asks pleasantly.

I gape at her. How on earth is she speaking so normally whilst running?

'Okay,' I manage, using all of my internal oxygen and core strength to force the single word out. If she tries to start a general conversation with me then I will surely die, no doubt about it.

Sally's eyes dart towards me and then back at the road ahead.

'We're nearly back,' she says. 'You're doing well.'

I look at her in bewilderment. Am I? It doesn't feel like I'm doing well. It feels like I'm about to die.

I stagger behind her, desperate to keep up my speed as my feet drag along the ground. I tear my eyes away from Sally's immaculate skin and notice the entrance to the park, which was where we started the run one thousand years ago. My chest sags in relief. Oh thank God. She wasn't joking. We really are almost there.

I could hardly refuse running with Sally, even though it went against every ounce of my being to go on a run with someone who has four coffees before 11 a.m. and enjoys eating celery sticks (without hummus).

Sally lightly jogs up to a tree and I tumble behind her, grasping on to the tree for dear life, my chest convulsing under the pressure. Sally flicks up one of her feet and pulls it into a stretch.

'I enjoyed that,' she says, in a voice that suggests she didn't enjoy it at all. 'That was fun.'

'Me too,' I lie.

If this is Sally's idea of fun then I need to take her to Baskin Robbins.

Sally pulls her keys out of a pocket and gestures to her car, parked up next to the gate. 'Do you want a lift home?' she asks.

I pause. Sally has never offered me a lift home before.

'Sure,' I say, taken aback, 'thank you.'

Sally nods and clicks her car open. I slide into the front seat as my eyes scan over every detail of the perfectly manicured interior. Sally slots the key into the ignition and the car chugs forward politely. I lean back into the warm seat as my heart rate returns to normal.

'I enjoy running,' Sally says, as she pulls out into the road, 'it relaxes me . . .'

Right. It's official. Sally is mental.

'. . . I have always run,' she finishes.

I nod.

'This will be my first run,' I say, 'the 10k.'

'Oh yes,' Sally says. 'When is it?'

I shuffle in my seat, 'I'm not sure,' I say. 'I think we are going to make it a charity event to raise money for the MS Society. A sponsored run or something.'

Sally's face twitches.

'I would like to volunteer,' she says. 'I will help.'

I glance up at her, my chest inflating.

'Really?' I say. 'Wow, that's so kind, Sally. Thank you.'

Sally nods abruptly and steers the car around another corner. 'Anything I can do to help.'

★

I push my parents' front door open with my pointed elbow, my large bag tipping off my shoulder.

'Hello!' I shout, as I crash through the door. 'Is anyone here?'

'We're in here, love!'

I kick the front door shut and drop my bags on the floor, heat searing up my shoulders and scratching at my muscles.

I think I am the opposite of Mary Poppins. It doesn't matter how lightly I try and pack, my bag always feels like I've packed my entire bedroom and every available kitchen sink in Elephant and Castle.

I follow Mum's voice through the kitchen and spot her and Dad in the living room. I do a double-take as I see that Mum is holding Dad's hands in the air.

They both snap their heads round to see me, their faces animated.

'Err . . .' I manage, 'hi?'

What on earth are they doing?

'Hello!' they chime in unison.

'You're just in time!' says Mum in a jolly voice.

I sink on to their sofa and feel my eyebrows rise in alarm.

Oh God. Just in time for what?

'What are you doing?' I ask dubiously.

Mum and Dad look at each other, excitable grins spreading across their faces.

'Well,' Dad chortles, 'me and your Mum took a leaf out of your book.'

'Well,' Mum quips, 'your and Amy's book.'

I scowl at them. What are they talking about? Book? Me and Amy don't have a book.

'What do you mean?' I ask.

Mum lets go of Dad's hands and shoots me a look of exasperation.

'Isn't it obvious?' she cries. 'We've taken up dance classes!'

'Not Salsa,' Dad says quickly, reading the look of horror on my face.

'Oh no!' Mum giggles. 'We're doing ballroom. Like on *Strictly*! Look, we'll show you.'

Mum holds her hands up in the air like a well-stringed puppet, and Dad carefully slots his hands into hers.

Despite myself, I feel my appalled face break into a smile.

'Right,' Mum says, her eyes locked on to Dad's, 'sing us a melody, Georgie.'

What?

'What do you mean?' I manage, my face hot. 'I'm not singing anything. I can't.'

As if I'm going to sit here and casually serenade them. Who do they think I am, Paul Potts?

(A question I will never voice.)

'Oh, Georgia!' Mum snips, her eyes still glued firmly on Dad's face. 'Just sing us something. Don't be difficult.'

I stare back at them. They are both stood, frozen in time, as if they are the centrepiece of a music box.

Oh great. What on earth does she expect me to sing?

I sink back into the sofa awkwardly as every song except 'Hips Don't Lie' vanishes from my mind.

I am not having them dance to Shakira. No way.

'Okay,' Dad says into the silence, 'I'll sing something.'

My body jolts again.

He'll sing? Dad can't sing! Can he?

I look at my dad as he stares into Mum's eyes, and starts humming a tune. Together, they move their feet in time to Dad's song and slowly rotate around the room. At the third spin, Mum tilts back her head and laughs.

'What do you think?' she calls over her shoulder, as Dad twists her around the room.

Warmth spreads through me and I smile.

'You're actually pretty good!' I say honestly, sitting forward and resting my chin in my hands.

'See,' Dad flashes me a wink as he stops singing, 'Amy's list is benefiting us all.'

I look back at them as Dad dips Mum into a final position and they both grin at each other.

'I guess it is.'

★

I scowl at my laptop, propped on the kitchen counter.

The quick and easy way to make the perfect Victoria sponge!

I have a strong suspicion whoever wrote this didn't fully understand the words 'quick' or 'easy'. I glance down at the lumpy mixture in my bowl and feel a pang of dismay.

Why can't I do this? Amy said that this was the easiest cake to make. Children make cakes! Really old people make cakes! Why can't I do it? What is wrong with me?

I wipe my forehead with the back of my floured hand. Honestly, they don't make it look this hard on *The Great British Bake Off.* They just chuck it in, whisk it, chat to Paul Hollywood and poof! There you go, the perfect cake. I, on the other hand, have been whisking for what feels like four years and am being taunted by several stubborn lumps of butter. At least this recipe doesn't require any egg whites.

I toyed with the idea of baking in my flat. Then I realised you couldn't bake a cake with only a frying pan and a bread knife so gave up quite quickly.

I glare at the lumps as they poke out of the mixture arrogantly.

Melt! Why won't you melt? Why won't you bloody melt, you stupid thing?

My eyes scan the recipe.

Pour the smooth mixture into two tins and bake for twenty minutes.

Right. Well, my mixture is definitely not smooth but I can't

171

spend any longer on this. Decisively, I tip the mixture into the tins and shove them into the hot oven. The butter can melt in the oven. Assuming that is what the lumps are – not something else terrible that I have created by accident. Is that possible?

I look up as Amy walks into the kitchen. She flicks the kettle on and eyes me.

'Tea?' she says.

I smile and nod. This is the first time she has spoken to me since our fight. Well, her fight. I hardly fought with her. I just sat there.

'How's it going?' she asks, gesturing to the oven as I kick it shut with my slippered foot.

'Oh, you know,' I say sarcastically. 'About as well as everything else you put on that impossible list.' I stick out my foot, pointedly, and to my relief Amy smiles. She pours the boiling water into two mugs and we sit on the kitchen chairs. There is a silence as we both wrap our hands around the burning mugs and the familiar wave of anxiety creeps up on me, as it does every time I think of Amy.

Eventually, she speaks.

'I'm sorry about the other day,' Amy says quietly. 'I'm glad you're doing the list.' She raises her swollen eyes to look at me. 'Really glad.'

I reach forward and curl my fingers over hers. 'I'm worried about you,' I say.

A small laugh tumbles out of the side of Amy's mouth as she looks down at our hands. She drags her wet eyes back up to meet mine and my heart twinges.

'I'm worried about me too,' she manages, her voice thick. 'I don't feel well. I'm worried this is going to beat me. It's taking over my life.'

I grip my hands tightly around hers as tears fall down her face, a dull ache of sadness expanding in the back of my chest. Amy is always okay. She is never not okay. She's always fine.

'You can't let it,' I say, desperate to keep my voice steady. 'You have to look on the bright side. Mind over matter, like you always say to me.'

'What if I end up in a wheelchair?'

The thick words fire out of Amy's mouth and they strike me in the stomach like a physical blow. I take a deep breath and try to fight the hot emotion ripping up my throat and clawing at the back of my eyes.

'You won't,' I say firmly, squeezing her hands, 'you won't.'

At my words, Amy sags and her body seems to deflate like a punctured balloon. I stare back at her. I wish I had the power to make Amy better.

Amy pulls her hands away from mine and lifts her head. She wipes her eyes with the back of her hand and takes a deep breath, uncoiling her spine as if she is being pulled up by an invisible string until she is sat in front of me, the confident Amy I know. She faces me, her eyes suddenly bright and her wet face glistening.

'Thank you,' she says, 'I needed to hear that. I've been going mad, in my own head.'

I squeeze her hand. 'Whatever happens, Ames,' I say, 'we'll work it out. We'll always work it out.'

She nods, and I move my mug between my hands.

'I think,' I say, 'you need something to focus on. You gave me this list to challenge me, why don't you let me give you something to challenge you?'

Amy sips her tea. 'The run?' she asks.

I nod.

Amy places her mug back on the table and moves her eyes towards the window.

'I do think it's a good idea . . .' she says. 'Anything we can do to raise money to help people with this horrible thing is a good idea. And,' she looks up at me, 'I'm so proud of you. Everything you are doing, you are really pushing yourself out of your comfort zone.'

I meet her eyes.

'It's you, Amy,' I say, 'it's always you.'

★

I stick my head around Natalie's office door and spot her scowling at a stack of papers.

'Tea?' I ask, waving my empty mug in her direction.

Natalie holds her mug up towards me, her eyes still firmly glued to the paper. She must be counting. I take the mug off her, when I hear a loud ripple of female laughter from the kitchen and I stop in my tracks, my ear craning towards the sound.

The kitchen isn't very big. It can fit three people maximum, and that is if everyone stands completely still, which leads to very awkward, intense small talk.

Obviously I am always very cautious as to who I will go into that kitchen with. (Usually only Natalie or Jack. Unless Sally creeps up on me.)

I am also madly avoiding Sharon from HR, after Bianca's

whole coffee debacle. Sally's tried to put a call from her through to me five times in the last week and can't understand why it keeps 'mysteriously cutting off' every time I pick up the phone.

Although I can't keep that up for much longer, or she'll get Derek from IT involved.

Christ, that's all I need. Yet another person at work to avoid. I haven't even been at this job a year and I would have already created two enemies.

Well, three, if you count Shirley from reception and the whole Secret Santa scandal.

(I'm not getting into that now. You can guess what happened. Let's just say I was wildly inappropriate with her 'joke present' and Shirley does not approve of flashing Santa thongs.)

The woman squawks again and I pull out my phone, until I hear Jack's voice, quivering with laughter.

'Go on!' he cries. 'Do it again!'

My ears prick up and I feel myself leaning towards the kitchen like a malnourished sunflower.

Who is he talking to?

'Go on!' he repeats.

The woman's laughter rockets around the room, and I hear a gasp of breath, followed by a voice that I suddenly recognise as Bianca's.

'No!' she cries. 'I can't!'

That's her laugh? I've never heard Bianca laugh like that before! Usually her laugh is all tinkly and flowery, like she's made out of china.

'Please!' Jack manages. 'One more time! This is the best thing you have ever done!'

I hover awkwardly. I don't feel like I should be listening to this, but I can't bring myself to leave.

I hear another laugh rattle through Bianca. There is a silence as Bianca calms herself, then eventually she speaks, but not in her normal, composed voice.

'Diana is on the toilet, Billy!' Bianca growls, in a deep, throaty accent. 'You'll have to use ya coupon later!'

At this, Jack roars with laughter and I hear the familiar squawk erupt from Bianca.

'What . . . is . . . *that*!' Jack manages between laughs. 'What even is that? That isn't an accent! He sounded nothing like that!'

Bianca's laugh peals through the corridor. 'He did!' she squeals. 'He did!'

I feel a small laugh tickle its way through my body as a strange sense of warmth fills my chest. Me and Amy used to get the giggles all the time. All Amy has to do is look at me in the wrong way and it sets me off. It's how I got banned from her Pilates class. It's also how she got kicked out of her Year 11 leavers assembly. She's never forgiven me for that. She almost didn't let me come to her graduation.

I hear Jack burst into another splutter of laughter and I turn to walk back up the stairs. I'll make the tea later. When me and Amy get the giggles, it takes us hours to calm down.

CHAPTER SIXTEEN

Running schedule:

04/08	1k	✓	(August is not the time to start running. Sweat patches are uncontrollable.)
10/09	2k	✓	(Actually isn't that far at all. Who knew?)
05/10	3k	✓	(Am doing v. well. Kudos to me. I am superior to all. Bow to me, Usain.)

'That's so cool.'

I leap out of my seat and jerk my head around as Jack sticks his neck over my shoulder, peering at my illuminated screen.

I quickly minimise my open designs, my face burning. 'Thanks,' I mutter.

I thought I had the office to myself. I never would have worked on my designs if I thought there was a chance I would get caught.

He frowns at me. 'Why have you got rid of them?'

I glance around to check Bianca and Sally are out of sight. Jack pulls up a chair next to me. I shoot him a mock-annoyed look and pull the designs back up, a balloon of pride swelling inside me.

'Wow,' Jack says, 'these are really good.'

I cock my head as I let my eyes sink into the design, and my fingers coil around my pencil.

'It's the only thing I really know how to do.' I glance at Jack, 'I don't have to think about it, you know?'

Nobody ever looks at my designs any more. Except my family – and they don't count, because they think everything I do is brilliant. I glance sideways at Jack as he leans towards the screen.

I am particularly proud of this design. I have been working on it for weeks.

'What's it for?' Jack asks.

I shrug. 'Nothing,' I say. 'Well, it's following the supermarket brief.'

'You're working on that?' he asks. 'Does Bianca know?'

My stomach jumps and I quickly hide the design again.

'No,' I say, my face burning as if I have been caught red-handed doing something incredibly seedy.

Jack looks back at me, bemused. 'Why not?'

I click open my emails and angle my shoulder away from Jack, trying to feign great importance.

He really doesn't seem to understand this whole workplace scenario. I'm starting to think he used to work as some kind of celebrity socialite. Or, like, as a spy.

'You should show her,' Jack says, leaning back into his seat. 'I think she'd like them.'

'I can't.'

Jack frowns. 'Why?'

I shrug my limp shoulders, my face prickling with embarrassment. 'Well,' I flounder, 'she's busy. I will show her one day.'

Jack pulls out his phone and stands back up. 'Fair enough,' he says. 'What are you doing this weekend?'

I click on an email and tap a lame response.

'Nothing much,' I say, my eyes flitting between my screen and his face. 'Why?'

I hit send flamboyantly, when my eyes jolt back to the screen.

Argh! I just somehow added two kisses onto the end of that email! Like some sort of office creep!

'I think we should do the cycling in Hyde Park,' he says, 'it'll be fun.'

'Sure,' I reply, desperately trying to work out who I just accidentally flirted with.

Oh *no*. It was Colin from accounts! He's about fifty and happily married with three children. Great. Just what I need. The office Christmas party will be fun for me this year.

'Oh!' I pull my eyes away from the screen and face Jack as he goes to leave. 'I spoke to Amy. She's happy to go ahead with the run. You know, being a sponsored thing.'

Jack's face lights up.

'Well, let's get planning, then,' he says. 'We can start at lunch. You're free for lunch today, right?'

'Sure,' I say mildly as Jack walks out of the door.

'Great,' he says, 'see you at twelve.'

'See you then.'

★

I lean forward on the bike slightly as it wobbles. My jaw clenches and my fingers grip the handlebars as the bike rolls over a patch of crisp leaves scattered on the ground.

So, you know the saying 'you never forget how to ride a bike'? That saying that everyone says all the time? The saying that is pretty much a fact, it is said so often?

Well, what if I have forgotten? What if I can't remember what to do?

I try not to stare at my rigid feet, rooted to the floor, as Jack cycles up to me, grinning.

'Ready?' he says, pedalling slightly forward.

'Yes, wait!' I bark madly as he starts to wheel away from me. 'Do you know where you're going?'

Jack stops and grins at me. 'Yeah,' he says, 'we'll cycle round the park once and then we're stopping at the pub on the corner.'

'Right,' I say. 'Wait!' I yell again as he scoots forward again.

Jack turns his head and raises his eyebrows expectantly.

'Just,' I mumble, 'wait for me. I don't know how good I'll—'

Jack laughs. 'Nobody is bad at riding a bike, Georgie,' he shouts over his shoulder, and with that, he speeds off through the park.

Desperate to keep up, I ram my feet into the pedals and push off through the park as the bike rocks dangerously.

Oh my God. Am I doing it?

Jack glances over his shoulder and flashes me a smile. My stomach turns over as I feel a laugh creep up my spine.

I look up at a sea of vibrant trees stretching above and swaying gently in different shades of yellow and orange. Rays of sunlight seep through the gaps between the leaves and beat against my skin. I shake my head as the wind tickles my ears and plays with my hair, spiralling behind me. My chest rises and falls as I pedal, and for the first time in weeks, the tight knot around my heart isn't there. I feel happy.

I catch Jack's eye as I speed up towards him.

I feel happy being with him.

'Come on,' he grins, 'slowcoach. I thought you were supposed to be a runner.'

I cycle up next to him and smile.

'I was just enjoying the view,' I say.

Jack shoots me a look, his face still etched into a large smile. 'You know,' he says, 'I have never done this before. I lived in London for seven years and I never did this.'

I shake my head. 'Me neither.'

'It's fun!' he adds loudly, arching his back as we roll down a slight hill. 'I never did anything fun.'

My eyes flick over to him. He never speaks about his life before we met. He catches me looking at him and suddenly the smirk is back.

'Come on,' he says, 'the pub is just up there. Let's race.'

My stomach lurches.

'Race?' I repeat. 'No! I'm just getting the hang of pedalling!'

Jack laughs. 'Oh, come on!' he says. 'I'll make it interesting. If I win the race,' he says, 'you have to show Bianca your designs on Monday.'

My stomach flips over.

'If you win,' he continues, 'then I'll take you on a proper date.'

'Excuse me!' I say, grinning. 'Both of them are a treat for you.'

He laughs and a frisson of excitement pings through me.

'Ready?' he says.

I narrow my eyes in competition.

'Go!' he cries, and he shoots off.

I gape at him. 'You didn't say "set"!' I shout at the back of his head. 'That's cheating!'

I pedal in tight circles, propelling my bike forward across the dusty path. Excitement leaps through my chest when I spot the pub as we spin round another corner. I glance over at Jack as I speed up to draw level with him, side by side.

'Ha!' I shout triumphantly. I pump my legs hard as a zap of determination cues a fresh wave of energy, and I shoot past Jack. I spin the bike round as I reach the pub and throw my arms into the air.

'I did it!' I pant. 'I won!'

Jack skids to a halt next to me, his mouth curling in a smile. 'Date it is,' he says, 'lucky you.'

I shoot him a look. 'Lucky you, more like,' I say pointedly.

He meets my eye and my heart flips over again.

A date with Jack. Is that a good idea?

He looks up at the pub. 'Are they already here?'

I nod. After discussing the charity run with Amy and Tamal, we decided to meet so we can start planning it properly. It was Tamal's idea. As we walk towards the pub entrance I feel a flutter of nerves. Why am I nervous about them meeting Jack?

Covered in old thatching and peppered with strings of ivy, the fat pub sits on the corner of Hyde Park. As we push our way in, I'm greeted with a fresh wave of warmth and a light smell of coffee that swirls up around me. I spot Tamal and Amy instantly, perched in a corner and huddled around a board game. Amy's face is crumpled into a deep laugh and Tamal has his arms coiled around hers, like two snakes entwined. I beam at the sight of them. I haven't seen Amy laugh like that in weeks.

'There they are,' I grab Jack's arm and point towards them.

Jack smiles. 'She looks like you,' he observes as we make our way over.

I feel a warm glow stretch inside me at this. I love it when people say I look like Amy.

Tamal looks up as we reach their table and Amy wipes her streaming eyes with the back of her sleeve, still buckled over in giggles.

'Hey!' Tamal beams, enveloping me into a hug. He pulls away as his eyes land on Jack. 'You must be Jack?' he says, holding out a hand for him to shake.

I grin at Amy and notice her eyes are firmly locked on Jack, a slight smirk playing with the corners of her mouth. Jack shakes Tamal's hand and turns to Amy.

'This is Amy,' Tamal gestures, and Amy holds out her arms for Jack to bend down into a hug.

Amy smiles. 'Hi,' she says, as he lets her go, 'nice to meet you.'

We both sink into the squishy pub chairs opposite Tamal and Amy, who are pink-faced and still slightly giggly, as if they are two teenagers who have been caught kissing at school.

'I'll get some drinks,' Jack says. 'Do you guys want any?'

Amy and Tamal shake their heads.

Jack turns to me. 'Gin and tonic?'

I nod and Jack goes to the bar.

Amy shoots me a suggestive look.

'Ordering your drink for you?' she sings. 'That's very cou
pley.'

Tamal snorts into his pint and Amy laughs again, her eyes flitting to Tamal.

I roll my eyes at her. 'What's wrong with you two?' I say.

Tamal shakes his head, putting the pint back down. 'Nothing,' he says. 'We were just playing Scrabble and being childish—'

'*You* were being childish!' Amy interjects, jabbing Tamal in the ribs. 'Erection is a word. You can erect a building, or a . . .'

Amy's words are lost as another wave of laugher engulfs her. Tamal shakes his head, his eyes twinkling.

'How was the bike ride?' he asks. 'Where is the list? You need to tick it off.'

I pull my bag on to my lap and take out the list as Jack reappears, carrying two drinks.

'Thank you,' I say to him as he puts my drink down in front of me. 'I owe you one.'

Tamal looks down at the list, which is covered in large multi-coloured ticks.

'Wow,' he says, 'you've done quite a bit now.'

I feel my chest expand with pride. 'I know,' I say happily. 'I think I'll do it all before my birthday.'

I look at Amy and she nods at me. 'I know you will,' she says.

'Also,' Tamal adds, 'I think you deserve some credit, mate,' and he nods at Jack. 'Georgia said you've been helping her.'

Jack takes a sip of his drink and smiles. 'Yeah, it's been fun.'

I beam at Jack and catch sight of Amy, who is glowing with happiness. I feel my face flush, and pull my attention back to the list.

'We were thinking,' I say, flattening the list on the wooden table, 'about this charity run. Maybe we could hold it just before my birthday? As almost the final event of the list.'

Tamal nods. 'Sounds good to me. I said to Amy I'm going to

The List That Changed My Life

run it, and so are a few of my mates from work.' He glances over at Amy and she beams back at him.

'We should start fund-raising,' Tamal continues. 'Why don't I set up a page online and we can all share it?'

I nod happily. 'I think we can raise a lot of money.'

'That does mean,' Amy says, leaning forward to look at the list, 'that you need to hurry up with that skydive.'

My stomach lurches at the reminder that it's October.

'My birthday is a good two months away,' I mutter.

'There's a skydive on there?' Jack asks, peering over.

'Yeah,' I say, shooting Amy a look, 'Amy wants to kill me.'

'We were talking,' Tamal says, linking his hand back into Amy's, 'and we thought maybe the run could start at Amy's school.'

My eyes dart over to Amy. 'That's a great idea!'

Amy smiles, her cheeks blushing. 'Yeah,' she says, 'the school were very supportive.'

'We spoke to the head,' Tamal grins.

'This is so exciting!' I cry.

Amy looks back at me, a wide smile lighting up her face and turning her eyes into large, sparkling stars.

'I know,' she grins. 'I think it will be great.'

Chapter Seventeen

Georgie's list

1. Have a vindaloo on Brick Lane. ✓
2. Take a Salsa class. ✓
3. Do a skydive.
4. Go on a Tinder date. ✓
5. Cycle around Hyde Park. ✓
6. Run 10k.
7. Make the perfect Victoria sponge.
8. Go skinny-dipping in the sea.
9. Try skateboarding at Southbank. ✓
10. Show Bianca your designs!

My peripheral vision is blurred as Natalie sticks her head round the office door. She slinks in, holding a large mug of black coffee. Her hair is coiled into a knot and she has a thick, patterned scarf wound around her head.

'Sally in a meeting?' she asks, wheeling Sally's empty chair to my desk.

I shake my head. 'Lunch,' I say. 'How are you?'

Natalie tucks her legs under herself and smiles. 'Fine,' she says. 'How are you? How is Amy?'

I pick up my mug and nestle it on my lap.

'Good,' I say, a warm feeling of comfort stretching through my body. 'She's okay actually. She's feeling okay.'

Natalie smiles. 'I've come to say I'm going to sponsor you, for the run.'

I frown as I feel a flutter of confusion.

'It's in, like, two months, right?' she says, taking a sip of her coffee.

'Yeah,' I say, furrowing my brow. 'How did you know that?'

Natalie gestures over her shoulder. 'It's on the poster.'

I blink at her.

Poster?

I get to my feet and walk out of the office; Natalie follows. I peer around and suddenly spot several large, bright posters, plastered around the office.

Natalie cranes her head over my shoulder. 'Did you not put them up?'

I shake my head, my eyes widening as I recognise the posters in more detail.

Those are my designs. I designed them, but I didn't.

'Hey, Georgie.'

I look round as Jack walks down the corridor holding a stack of posters. I grab one off him.

'See,' Natalie points, 'it says it all on there.'

'How did you . . .?' I manage feebly. 'These are my designs.'

Jack looks down at the posters, grinning. 'I know!' he says. 'Don't they look great?'

'But how . . .' I look up at him, 'how did you get them? I didn't design these posters.'

Jack smiles. 'I took the designs you showed me from your computer and just made them into a donation sheet. Don't they look great?'

A quick zing of annoyance zaps my chest, until I spot Natalie ogling the sponsor sheet in amazement.

'Wow!' Natalie breathes, looking at the posters in more detail. 'Georgie, did you design these?'

I smile. I never show anyone my designs.

'And look!' Jack adds, gesturing to the poster pinned to the wall. 'Look at the donation list!'

I move my eyes over to the poster and gape at the scrawled signatures and amounts, stacked down the sheet.

'That's only about a third of this building,' Jack says, leaning against the wall. 'I'm about to go down to accounts. They always have a lot of money.'

'Not all of us,' Natalie laughs.

'And I've set up the Facebook event,' he adds, 'so we should get some more donations. I haven't checked the page, but if all these people stick to these donations then we've got about a grand here already.'

'This is amazing,' I say softly, running my hand over the poster.

Jack pulls out his phone and starts walking down the corridor.

'Glad you like it,' he says. 'I'll see you after work, for that meeting with the school?'

I nod after him. 'Right,' I say, as he disappears down the corridor.

I pull my eyes back to the signing sheet as my mind starts counting the different figures. I can't wait to tell Amy. She will be so excited. I've barely even spoken to some of these people.

'So,' Natalie says, breaking my concentration, 'meeting up after work, are we?'

There is a hint of amusement in her voice, and her small mouth twitches into a suggestive smile.

'Yes,' I say, as we walk back into the office.

'Will you admit that you fancy him yet?'

I drop back into my chair and shoot her a stern look, which breaks as soon as I catch her eye.

Natalie laughs loudly and slaps me on the leg.

'I knew it!' she laughs. 'I bloody knew it. You are such a terrible liar. Thank God you have admitted it. Finally. Does Bianca know?'

'No!' I cry in horror. 'Of course not.'

Natalie smirks. 'Hmmm,' she says, 'well, be careful. Shagging the boss's brother isn't very professional, Georgia Miller.'

'We are not shagging,' I mutter, my face flaming.

Natalie straightens up, her smirk still firmly in place. 'Well,' she shrugs, 'just be careful.'

'I'd never have sex with my boss's brother,' I say pointedly, as she slinks back out of the office.

I open an email and gnaw my lip.

I can't ever sleep with Jack, or have any form of real relationship with him, obviously. He is my boss's brother. But then, where am I hoping this is going? What am I doing?

★

I look up at my high street bank, standing ominously on the corner of our grey road and looming over the other buildings like an oppressive school teacher.

I take a deep breath and duck my head inside.

I hate coming in here. But I made a pact with myself that I would have to physically come into the bank to access any of my savings, to stop myself from dipping into them every time I fancied some sweet and sour chicken.

As I walk inside, I am greeted by a comforting blanket of heat that engulfs me and a delicious smell of air freshener and pine cones. I unwrap my scarf quickly as the heat spreads up my back and join the winding queue, readjusting my bag on my shoulder.

My goodness, it really is lovely in here. If I run out of savings and cannot pay my rent (very feasible) then maybe I'll just live here. I could fit under that desk easily. And look! It's right next to the coffee machine! It's like it's meant to be.

I really should ask Bianca for a pay rise. The amount she expects me to live off is ridiculous. Maybe I'll ask her when I show her my designs. If I ever actually do that.

'Next.'

I step forward as I reach the front of the queue and hop into a little booth, with a woman propped behind her computer. She has blonde hair that is twirled above her head in an immaculate bun and a neckerchief spun around her neck. She smiles as I sit down and I smile back gratefully.

She looks nice. She looks much nicer than the woman who served me last time and tried to convince me to take out a business loan when I joked about becoming a freelance busker because the man outside seemed to be making a fortune.

'Hello,' she says, 'I'm Shannon.'

'Hi.'

'How can I help you today?'

I shuffle in my seat, feeling my face redden with guilt.

For God's sake, why do I feel guilty? It's my money!

'I'd like to move some money about please,' I say, realising in alarm that I sound like a drug dealer.

'From my savings,' I add quickly.

The woman nods. 'Pop your card in,' she says, gesturing to the card machine sat proudly on the desk. I do as I'm told and tap my pin number in.

Argh. Any second now she is going to see my bank balance. I wonder what she will think? Probably something like: 'How on earth did this girl manage to reduce her bank balance to minus ten pence? Is she an actual moron?'

'How much would you like to move?' she asks.

'One hundred, please,' I say quickly, desperate to only say it once in case the ghost of my grandma is lurking, ready to curse me for spending my inheritance on tins of baked beans.

Shannon nods and taps at her computer.

'Okay,' she says, 'that will just take a moment.'

'Okay.'

'How is your weekend?' she asks politely.

I smile back at her.

'Fine, thank you,' I say, 'I'm training for a run.'

'Oh!' she coos in approval. 'For charity?'

I nod. 'Yeah,' I say, 'we're running a sponsored 10k to raise money for the MS Society. My sister got diagnosed with it earlier this year. So I'm training for that.'

Shannon looks back at me.

'I'm sorry to hear about your sister,' she says softly, 'my aunt has MS.'

I tilt my head. 'Really?'

She taps at her computer and then leans towards me. 'You know,' she says, 'the bank has a community engagement fund to make charitable donations. I'm sure we could donate something towards the run.'

I stare back at her.

'Really?' I say.

She nods and hands me a pen and paper. 'Jot down your email address, love,' she says kindly, 'and I'll speak to my manager and see what we can do.'

I take the pen and scribble down my details, my heart thumping.

'Thank you,' I gush, 'thank you so much.'

Chapter Eighteen

Running schedule:

04/08	1k	✓	(August is not the time to start running. Sweat patches are uncontrollable.)
10/09	2k	✓	(Actually isn't that far at all. Who knew?)
05/10	3k	✓	(Am doing v. well. Kudos to me. I am superior to all. Bow to me, Usain.)
19/10	4k	✓	(Finishes right by Burger King! Coincidence?!?!)

'Right,' Amy says, propped on the stool in the corner of the kitchen, 'so it says, cream together the—'

'Cream?' I interrupt, baffled. 'I don't have any cream. You didn't tell me that we needed cream. Cream wasn't on the recipe list, I'm sure of it.'

'Stop saying cream,' Amy says teasingly. 'It says, cream together the butter and sugar. Cream is the verb.'

I raise my eyebrows at her.

'Well that's stupid,' I observe. 'Why would they use a word that is a food to describe cooking two other foods? How ridiculous.'

'We're not cooking,' Amy says knowingly. 'Remember, we're baking.'

'You're not doing anything!' I retort, jabbing my wooden spoon in her direction. 'You're watching.'

Amy laughs and cups her head in her hands. I glance down at my bowl dubiously, and begin pushing the butter against the sides as the sugar dances around it.

Is this right? It doesn't look right. But I'm sure this is what Mary Berry does. I've seen her do it on BBC2.

'So,' I say, panting in between beats as I force the spoon into the thick lumps of butter, 'how has your week been?'

'Good!' Amy chirps, swinging her long hair over one shoulder and crafting it into a plait. 'I feel good this week. I've been in school every day. Some bits are harder than others, but generally speaking I feel good.'

I smile at her over my bowl, relief spreading through me.

'Good,' I say, 'that's so good to hear.'

'I mean,' Amy continues, 'the doctors have said that I will have good days and bad days, but it was nice to have a few good days in a row.'

'Of course,' I say gruffly.

Bloody hell, this is hard! Why is this so hard? My arms are killing me! And it looks nothing like cream.

'How are you getting on?' Amy asks, peering over from her chair. 'Does it look pale and fluffy? That's what it says in the recipe.'

I glower at the bowl. My mixture doesn't look pale and fluffy. It looks lumpy and ill.

'Screw it,' I say crossly, 'I'm going to whisk it. I'm sick of creaming. It doesn't bloody work.'

I drop the wooden spoon defiantly and begin searching in the kitchen for Mum's whisk.

'How has your week been?' Amy asks.

Mum has a really fun habit of rearranging the entire kitchen every time she throws a dinner party. She says it relaxes her, which makes me wonder how we can possibly be related.

Urgh. Where is this damn whisk? Where has she put it?

'Yeah,' I say, pulling my head out of the depths of a cupboard stacked with saucepans, 'good, thanks. Actually,' I say as the reminder dings in my brain, 'I forgot to tell you. We got another sponsor this week.'

'For the run?' Amy asks, her voice excited.

'Yeah!' I say. 'We spoke to a beauty parlour about donating something for the raffle, and it turns out that the owner loves running so is going to sign up! And we spoke to a florist who is going to donate something too.'

I stick my head in another cupboard.

'Wow!' Amy cries. 'I can't believe how well you're doing.'

Ah ha! There it is. Right at the back.

I angle my body forward and attempt to manoeuvre the whisk out without causing a culinary avalanche.

'Well,' I say, prying the whisk from the back, 'Jack has been helping me. He really is the brains, he just knows all of this stuff.'

'Hey,' Amy says brightly, 'maybe if I keep feeling this good then I could do the run too!'

'Yeah!' I say, as the electric whisk finally falls out of the cupboard. I jab it into the plug socket happily.

Right. Pale and fluffy. Let's have you.

'Georgie,' Amy says quickly, 'are you sure about that? It says, cream.'

'I need to get this bloody thing off my list. Cream is a food, not a verb,' I say. 'I'm sure it will be fine.'

Decisively, I shove the whisk into the bowl and switch it on. This is an action I regret immediately, as great chunks of butter cling to the whisk and propel themselves out of the bowl before splattering across my black top.

'Argh!' I yelp.

'See,' Amy laughs, 'I told you cream was a verb.'

★

I glance at my reflection in the mirror and feel a bubble of pride rise up my body.

I don't mean to be arrogant. But I look incredibly expensive today.

Not like a prostitute, obviously. Like a woman in her mid-twenties who is doing extremely well for herself, and not like a woman in her mid-twenties who has been eating butter-free toast because she can't afford a new tub until bloody pay day.

Today, I am wearing my cropped trousers, my favourite autumnal jumper and (the crème de la crème) my Prada shoes that I bought last year in a *charity shop*!

The only slight niggle is that they are extremely uncomfortable and I can barely stand in them. But, let's be honest, I can barely stand in any of my shoes with this fat ankle – and what's the alternative? That I wear trainers? No thank you.

I slink out of my flat and swing my bag over my shoulder as I make my way towards the bus stop and the autumn breeze nips my skin.

Me and Jack have been speaking to businesses about sponsoring the event, and so far they have all been thrilled to! Jack says that they always need to do their bit for charity, but he is especially good at getting their support. We're going to have a raffle, and some of the prizes are amazing! One of the travel agencies has offered a trip to Gran Canaria! I lightly suggested to Mum that I might fix the raffle so that I win that prize, but she got all shirty and called me 'immoral'. I was only joking. Sort of.

My phone buzzes in my hand and I flip it over, to see an incoming call from Jack. I smile as I answer the call.

'Hey,' I say, 'you okay? I'm on my way.'

Jack's voice cuts across me. 'I've had an idea.'

I pause as I turn a corner.

Okay. So, my feet are killing me. Oh my Lord. I didn't even pack any emergency flats. I toyed with the idea and then got all stupid and proud about being a 'real adult'.

Urgh. Why am I like this?

'Oh?'

'I think,' says Jack, 'we should take some of the money that one of these companies has given us and invest it.'

I frown.

Invest it? Like, buy a holiday home in Devon or put it in the pension pot?

I need to put something in my bloody pension pot. Actually, I need to start a pension pot.

Do I need an actual pot? Or is that just a figure of speech? I think I'd like a green one.

'What do you mean?' I ask.

'Well,' Jack powers on, not missing a beat, 'I think, with a bit of marketing, we could make this event pretty big.'

'Right.'

'So we could advertise it, online, using the money the investors have given us. We could advertise for more runners. If we say every runner has to raise, like, one hundred pounds each, then twenty more runners would be . . .'

'Two grand!' I cry.

Wow, that was quick maths! Where did that sudden stroke of genius come from? Maybe that bowl of bran flakes I stole from Tina is paying off!

Jack laughs. 'Exactly!'

I notice the bus stop and stride on, tottering on my impossible heels.

'We already have the artwork you designed,' Jack continues. 'It looks like such a great brand. What do you think?'

'Great idea!' I say. 'I really think—'

'Georgie?'

I almost drop my phone in shock as Bianca's voice pounds into my ears. I blink around hopelessly. Why is Bianca in Elephant and Castle? Finally, I spot her, hanging out of a black cab and staring at me in horror. I hang up my phone in haste.

'Hi . . .' I say in bewilderment, staggering forward, 'Bianca.'

Oh my God, why is she here? Has she followed me? What have I forgotten to do? It's a Sunday!

'What are you doing?' she cries in dismay. 'Why are you waiting at a bus stop?'

I pause, baffled.

'Err . . .' I manage, trying to avoid the eyes of the fellow bus travellers who are shooting Bianca looks of disgust, 'because I'm getting a bus?'

What kind of question is that?

Bianca looks at me as if I'm speaking in Finnish.

'I'm getting the bus,' I repeat in a slower voice.

Bianca flinches as if the very idea of getting a bus makes her gag. Suddenly, she throws open her cab door.

'Get in,' she orders.

I freeze.

'Really,' I protest, 'it's fine. I always get the bus. I—'

'Now!' she barks.

I glance around at the bus queue, and climb inside apologetically. Bianca is draped on the back seat, surrounded by a sea of large, square shopping bags and neat little boxes piled on top of one another.

'Where are you going?' she asks.

I falter as a bolt of panic shoots through me.

I'm on my way to meet Jack. Oh no.

'Clapham,' I say weakly, my brain freezing under the pressure and sacrificing every other place in London I could suggest.

Bianca nods towards the driver and we shoot forward, leaving my sad bus stop behind.

What's happening? Why am I sat in a cab with Bianca, on a Sunday in Elephant and Castle?

'Have you been shopping?' I ask conversationally.

Bianca's eyes flit down to the dozen bags propped by her feet.

'Yes,' she says. 'Jonathan is away this weekend.'

'Ah.'

'So,' Bianca continues, pulling out a nail file and buffing her long nails one by one, 'it is just me and Jack. He has decided to stay with me right up until the wedding, which is nice.'

My body jars.

Oh no. Why has she bought him up? Does she know? Is that why she has got me in this taxi, alone? Is she going to drive me to the middle of nowhere and then drop me in an abandoned quarry?

'Oh yes,' I say lightly. 'That's nice of him.'

I try to control the manic beats of anxiety reverberating up my throat.

I should never have got into this taxi.

'What are you doing today, then—' Bianca glances sharply towards me. 'In Clapham?'

I look up at her, my mouth dry.

Does she know? Is she playing with me?

'Just meeting a friend,' I manage weakly. Thankfully, this seems to satisfy Bianca and she nods.

'Well,' she says, 'that will be nice.'

'Yes.'

An awkward silence stretches between us and I glue my eyes to the view outside the window as we speed through London.

'What about you?' I say eventually.

My eyes flit back to Bianca and she screws up her nose. 'You know,' she says, 'I don't know. I might see what Jack is doing. Maybe we can go to the cinema.'

She pulls her phone to her ear and my stomach lurches.

Oh no. Is she calling him, now? What if he says that he is busy, meeting me? I have no escape. I can't throw myself out of the taxi, I'd splatter like an egg.

'Hi, Jack.' Bianca smiles into the phone as he answers. 'Listen, I'm just on my way back from shopping. Where are you?'

She pauses as he answers, then to my horror her eyes flit to me. I feel myself jerk in my seat, as if I'm preparing to throw myself out of the window.

'Oh really?' she says, her eyes fixated on mine.

Oh my God. He's told her!

My face burns as I pull out my phone, pretending not to listen to her conversation as I scroll through Twitter.

'That is so weird,' Bianca continues. 'I'm with Georgie and she is going to Clapham too. You know Georgie, right? From the office? One of my assistants?'

Heat flares up my face.

'Well, I'll see you later,' she says, and pulls the phone away from her ear. She looks up at me and laughs.

'Well!' she says. 'You'll never guess where Jack is?'

I blink back at her weakly.

'Where?' I manage.

'In Clapham!' she cries, laughing as if this is all just some big coincidence. 'You're going to Clapham, Jack is in Clapham. Maybe I should go to Clapham!'

Bianca slaps her slender leg lightly as she laughs at the idea. I look back at her, my face red hot and my cheeks burning. I force a polite laugh and cross my legs.

'Maybe you should.'

*

I look up from my computer screen as Jack darts into the office.

'Hi,' I say, as he drops into a chair and yanks it over towards me.

'I need your computer,' he says, grabbing the mouse.

I scowl, taken aback, as he stretches over me. Doesn't he have his own computer?

'Look at this,' Jack says, angling the keyboard towards him

201

and clicking on our sponsorship page. My eyes follow his gaze and widen as they fix on the screen.

'Oh my God,' I breathe.

'And . . .' Jack adds, now logging on to Facebook, 'look at this.'

He pulls Facebook up and suddenly my screen is filled with my design.

ARE YOU A RUNNER?
JOIN OUR 10K RUN ON 1 DECEMBER
AND
RAISE MONEY FOR THE MS SOCIETY
SIGN UP NOW!

'Wow,' I say quietly, my eyes lingering on the bright yellow advert.

I have never seen any of my designs in use before. Seeing one as an advert causes my heart to flutter with emotion. It's like looking at my child.

Six thousand likes. Two thousand shares.

I lurch forward and grab the mouse off Jack, then click on the 'like' section.

'Jack!' I cry. 'This is mad! How has it reached so many people?'

Jack grins. 'Well, we had to pay for it,' he says, 'it's the investment we spoke about.'

'So many people are engaging in it,' I whisper, my eyes scrolling up and down the list of people I have never heard of.

'That's because of your design,' Jack beams. 'It looks so great.'

A smile spreads across my face.

'And,' Jack adds, taking the mouse back, 'look at this.'

He clicks to pull up the sponsorship page.

'We've had thirty new runners sign up since we launched the campaign' he says, scrolling down the page. 'They've all agreed to raise one hundred pounds for the run.'

'Thirty?' I repeat.

'Georgie,' Jack turns to me, his eyes shining, 'I think we could make this event pretty huge.'

My eyes return to the sponsorship page and the staggering amount already raised.

'I think we could too.'

★

'You look like Miss Miller, Mrs Miller.'

I look at the small boy, his big eyes staring at me under a mop of matted red hair.

I smile. 'Thank you,' I say, 'but I am not a Mrs. I'm Miss Miller too.'

The boy cocks his head in confusion. 'You have the same name?'

I nod. 'At the moment, yes. Neither of us is married.'

'Are you not married to him?'

A lanky girl with cropped curly hair appears next to me and sticks her arm out towards Jack, who is doing some stretches in the corner with a bunch of teenagers.

'No,' I laugh lightly, 'we're not married.'

Jack flashes me a grin.

I shoot him back my best 'kids, eh?' look.

'But,' she says, 'he is your boyfriend?'

Oh God, I hope Jack didn't hear that.

'No,' I say, a more forced laugh pumping through me, 'no, no. No. We're just friends. No.'

Olivia Beirne

Stop saying no, Georgia. Why do I keep saying no? Nobody says no that much in one sentence.

'No.'

Argh!

'Why?' the ginger boy pipes up.

I swivel round to face him. My God, these kids are nosey.

'Because,' I say, trying to keep my voice light and superior, 'some adults are just friends.'

'Do you not like each other?' the boy persists.

If these kids don't stop asking me these questions in front of Jack, I am going to have to leave the country.

'No,' I say tightly, my face flaming. 'I mean, yes. Of course we do.'

This is ridiculous. I am being interrogated by a twelve-year-old.

'If you like each other,' he says, 'then why aren't you his girlfriend?'

'Is it because you are gay, miss?'

I spin back round to face the girl, whose eyebrows are raised in curiosity.

What?

'No!' I say crossly.

Did she just outwardly ask me about my sexuality? In a school gym? I only met her about eight minutes ago!

'Right,' Jack says loudly, causing all the children to snap their heads round to face him. 'Shall we start running?'

'Yes!' I say forcefully, internally commanding my cheeks to return to their natural shade of dull pink.

Led by Jack, all of the children stream out of the school hall and on to the tennis courts. The orange sun is low and masked by dark, heavy clouds that snake across the sky. I look around at the children, all hopping up and down on the spot to keep warm as the fearless wind whips past the backs of their bare legs.

'Right,' says Jack, 'who wants to lead the way?'

'Me!' squawks a small blonde girl, launching her arm into the air.

Jack nods. 'Cool,' he says, 'we'll follow you.'

All the children set off at a brisk pace and I follow, watching their small heads bob up and down in front of me. Amy set up the running club when she started at the school. She also set up a breakfast club for children who weren't getting a proper breakfast at home.

'Miss?'

I look up to see a small, skinny child bobbing next to me. Her large blue eyes are blinking up at me.

I smile. 'Yeah?'

'Where is Miss Miller?' she asks.

I glance down at her, unsure how to respond.

'She wasn't feeling well today,' I say honestly, 'so she asked me and Mr Lemon to run the club for her instead. We like running too.'

The small girl's face twitches.

'Is she sick, miss?'

I shake my head automatically. 'She's okay,' I say, 'she's got a nasty illness that makes her tired. But we're going to do a run here to raise lots of money for charity, to help people like Miss Miller get better.'

The girl screws up her face and narrows her eyes, focusing ahead of her.

'Can I run too?'

CHAPTER NINETEEN

<u>Note to self:</u>

P4 of *Grazia* magazine, gorgeous floral dress. Perfect for next year summer fun with Amy. Must save £40 so can buy (v. important). Enormous breasts and lack of bottom may be an issue, beware.

'Have you heard about the Shetland pony?'

I raise my eyes up from my computer screen, praying that Sally is about to spring an impromptu cracker joke on me.

'No,' I say dully, 'what Shetland pony?'

For God's sake, what now? What bloody Shetland pony? What else could Bianca possibly want? A pony who can tap dance? Or one that can manage the rap break in the middle of the bear number?

Oh, the bears. The bloody bears. I still haven't worked out how on earth I am going to wangle that one. I mean, I can't. I just can't. Contrary to Bianca's mad brain, singing bears do not exist. How will I ever explain in future interviews that the reason I got fired as an assistant designer was because I couldn't source a pack of singing bears?

Sally flicks open her Filofax and my body shrivels with irritation.

'Bianca has booked for the chief bridesmaid to arrive on a Shetland pony,' she says, her face deadpan. 'It's all booked.'

'Good.'

'But you need to meet with the trainer.'

'What?' I blink at her. 'The trainer? Why?'

'She wants to talk to someone before the wedding.' Sally flicks the book shut.

I roll my eyes at my computer screen as Sally totters back to her desk. 'Fine,' I say.

'The trainer is in Brighton,' Sally says matter-of-factly.

I jerk my head up. 'What?' I say. 'Brighton? How am I supposed to get to Brighton?'

Sally sticks her head over her computer screen blankly. 'You can catch the train,' she says.

I glower at my computer screen.

Can I now? Is that a fact? How am I supposed to work as a designer when I am constantly gallivanting across the country on the hunt for various bloody animals?

An email from Jack pops up and I drag my eyes to the side of my computer screen.

Have you heard about Brighton?

How does he know about that?

I tap a reply and his response crops up almost immediately.

I volunteered you. Thought it would be a good way to plan our date. I'm coming too. The trains are booked for tomorrow.

Jack is coming to Brighton with me? We're going together?

A final email pops up and my stomach flips.

Make sure you pack a bag.

'Also,' Sally says, making me almost fall off my seat in fright, 'I have signed up as a runner for the charity run. The fund-raising page is doing very well.'

With great effort, I pull my eyes away from Jack's email and look at Sally.

'Really?' I say.

Sally nods. 'I spoke to my running club,' she says, 'and a lot of them are going to sign up. You are going to raise a lot of money. I bet your sister is very proud of you.'

*

I don't know what to pack, I don't know what to pack!

What does one pack for an impromptu work trip to Brighton? Which is almost certainly not a work trip at all but, in fact, much more likely a sex trip.

My body convulses in panic as this thought bursts through my brain. I chuck my hair straighteners into my bag.

No. Not a sex trip. A professional business trip to see a woman about her pony (and that is, in no way, any form of innuendo or suggestive comment).

Or is it? Maybe the Shetland pony doesn't exist and it is all a euphemism . . .

I gape down at my open suitcase in dismay.

Argh! This is hopeless! What the hell do I pack? I am terrible at packing at the best of times, now I have to plan for two days (and a 'night') which I have no control over.

The List That Changed My Life

I can't cope with this. Maybe I should just call in sick and hide under my bed until this is all over and have a nice cup of tea.

I take a deep breath and evaluate my current outfits:

- *Travel outfit*: jeans, stylish roll neck (yes, they do exist) and heeled boots that I can walk in.
- *Date outfit*: slinky top, pencil skirt, nice heels, large hoop earrings.
- *Date outfit in case I accidentally eat too much cheese and my stomach swells out like a baked potato:* floaty dress, black tights, nice heels.
- *Date outfit in case I accidentally spill toothpaste down other options*: black cami top, nice jeans.
- *Date outfit in case the date is somehow underwater:* sexy swimming costume.
- *Date outfit in case date involves real swimming*: sensible, ugly swimming costume that at least covers my entire bottom.

I neatly fold each of the outfits and layer them in my suitcase. I shall not be packing any sex outfits. Mainly because I do not own any, and I can hardly shoehorn a trip to Ann Summers on my work expenses.

I check off my internal list as I place the final bits into my suitcase.

Toothbrush, make-up bag, phone charger. Check, check, check.

The only person I have told where I'm going is Natalie, which was a stupid idea as she almost burst with excitement the moment she found out and then continued to ask me when was the last time I 'had a wax'. She then tried to suggest we go together on our lunch break. I pretended to be called into a meeting and hung up on her instantly.

A joint wax? On our lunch break? Is she mental?

Also, I do not need a wax because that would imply that I will be having sex with Jack, which I will not. Definitely.

Although, I did have a wax this morning, just in case we do go swimming. Only because of that. I don't want him to mistake me for a walrus perched on a rock when I am giving him my best Ariel.

My phone bleeps and my eyes dart over to it.

Hey, booked something for 3 p.m. today. Meet me at the pier. Jack x

My stomach lurches.

Oh my God, he's booked something for today! Our date is happening today! I check the time. Right. I need to leave my flat in half an hour to get the 12.30 train. Any later than that and I'll have to do my date make-up on the train.

I flip my suitcase shut as Tina appears at my door. I do a double-take. Tina is nice enough, but we're hardly friends. She certainly never stops to chat. Unless she fancies a passive-aggressive exchange about how much Fairy Liquid is the correct amount to wash up a pan.

(The answer is the opposite of what I do. Apparently.)

'You all right?' I ask, digging my elbows into my suitcase in an attempt to zip it shut.

Come on. Shut, you stupid suitcase. You have to shut. I have just spent over an hour planning every last detail of these outfits. I cannot leave a single sock out. I refuse.

'Are you going away?' Tina asks in a lofty voice.

I look up and notice her hair, piled on top of her head and fastened with a large bow.

What is she wearing? She looks like a six-year-old.

'Yeah,' I grunt, 'just for a night. It's for work. I'll be back tomorrow.'

Tina nods, a look of satisfaction sweeping over her face.

'Why?' I add.

Tina pulls out her phone and leans against the door frame. 'No reason,' she says. 'I think I'm going to have a few friends over, then. If you're going out.'

My head snaps up.

Tina has had 'a few friends' over before, just after we moved in. I pretended to be totally relaxed about it and spent the night with Amy, and it was all going quite well. Until I came back and found one of her friends had used my bra as a slingshot for their tequila-filled balloons. When I raised it with Tina she said that they couldn't use her bra because her boobs weren't big enough and I should take it as a compliment.

'Err, Tina,' I say, pulling my body off the bulging suitcase.

Tina's heavily made-up eyes flick up to me. 'Yeah?'

'You're not having a party, are you?' I say, trying my best to sound aloof and unfazed.

Tina smirks into her phone. 'No,' she says, 'just a gathering. Only a few friends.'

I open my mouth to reply but Tina slinks away into the kitchen. I throw myself back on to my suitcase and wrench it open bitterly.

Great. So along with having to pack for the most stressful few days of my life, I now have to spend the next hour hiding every bra I own from Tina.

And pants. I definitely don't want any of her friends getting their hands on any of my pants.

CHAPTER TWENTY

11TH NOVEMBER

To do list (Shetland pony edition, from Sally):

- Find Jesus (*WHAT? What does this even mean!?*)
- Demonstrate walking motion/speed required of pony (*Absolutely not*)
- Ask if Jesus has dietary requirements (*Is this the name of the pony? Or human? Am I going on a pilgrimage? What's happening?*)
- Explain wedding schedule
- Ask if there are any larger Shetland ponies for taller bridesmaids (*. . . a horse. She wants a horse*)
- Monitor Jesus' natural walking speed to report back to Sally (*?!*)
- Ask if Shetland pony can smile on cue (*no*)

I take a deep breath as the wind whips my hair and a wave of goose pimples scatter across my skin. A great butterfly of excitement flutters in the pit of my stomach as I look out over Brighton Pier. The dark blue sea is simmering gently, swirling slightly in the wind, and not a single cloud is lingering in the bright sky.

It is really beautiful.

But I mean, it is also bloody freezing. It is November, after all.

I glance down at my right arm, all of my wispy arm hair standing to attention like blades of grass.

Why didn't I bring a coat? I know I wanted to look nice, but surely it is more important to be warm?

Oh great, now I sound like Mum.

I should be warm, considering I've spent the last hour trotting round a pen after Jesus the Shetland pony and his owner, Gabriel.

I flick my hair and command my body to keep warm.

It's okay. We'll be inside soon. Perhaps in a lovely restaurant, or in one of these nice bars. Although it does seem a bit early for drinking. But maybe Jack wants to get really drunk.

Maybe he's an alcoholic.

I shake my head as this thought wafts through my brain.

No, of course he isn't. I would have noticed by now if he was.

Thankfully, I stayed well away from cheese on my journey down, which means my stomach is the perfect size for my best date outfit: slinky top, pencil skirt, nice heels, large hoop earrings. My hair is behaving itself and even my liquid eyeliner flicked obediently in place. For once, everything has worked as it should. It really is meant to be.

I glance down at my breasts nervously.

Although, on reflection, I do think I should have worn a bra.

I need to get inside ASAP or my nipples will hail down a taxi all by themselves.

I glance down as my phone springs to life. I hold it up to my ear and hear Jack's voice.

'Hey, listen, I've been held up at this end.'

My stomach pangs.

'Right,' I say.

'I've ordered you an Uber,' he says, 'it should be just around the corner. It's going to bring you to me, so I'll meet you there. Is that okay?'

He's sent a car for me! How romantic!

'Sure!' I gush.

'Cool,' Jack says. 'I'll text you the car details so you can look out for it.'

'Great!' I cry. 'See you in a bit!'

The line goes dead and I peer down at it, until the text shoots through from Jack.

I can't believe that I am standing by Brighton Pier, waiting for a car to collect me and whisk me off to a secret location where a guy has planned a romantic date. This is like something you see in a film! This sort of thing never happens to me!

I glance up as I notice a car slide up next to me. My eyes scan the registration plate and I hop in the front, feeling like Audrey Hepburn.

'Hello!' I say giddily, clipping my seat belt on.

The driver's eyes flit towards me as he prepares to pull out into the road.

'You look nice,' he says, a smile pulling at the sides of his mouth.

The balloon of happiness forming inside me swells with excitement.

'Thank you!' I cry cheerily, looking at myself in the passenger mirror.

The driver nods and clicks his indicator on. I look at him, trying my best to stay silent like a sophisticated grown-up, until suddenly I cannot fight it any longer.

'I'm going on a date,' I blurt excitedly. 'He actually sent this car to pick me up. He has planned the whole thing.'

The driver's eyebrows twitch slightly. 'A date?'

'Yes!' I nod. 'It's all a total surprise. Isn't that romantic?'

The smile on the driver's face stretches wider. 'A surprise?' he repeats. 'Well, that is nice of him.'

'I know!'

'So,' he continues, twisting the car round another corner, 'you don't know where you are going?'

'Nope!' I cry. 'I have no idea!'

The driver nods, his eyes creasing in the corners. I angle my body to face him.

'Wait,' I say, 'do you know where I'm going?'

'Of course I do,' the driver says. 'I wouldn't be a very good driver if I didn't know where I was going.'

Excitement whizzes up me.

'Do you think I'll like it?' I gabble.

'Yes,' he says, 'it will certainly be a surprise.'

I grab my phone out of my bag and quickly jab a text to Natalie, telling her about the car. Maybe he's planned dinner on a beach, just the two of us. Although it is freezing. Maybe he's planned dinner on a beach, but he's organised some kind of heated marquee. Or! Perhaps he's got those big sticks with fire, like you see on all those Pinterest weddings!

'Okay,' the driver says, as the car slows down, 'we're here.'

I look around excitedly at my surroundings, desperate to find out where we are. My eyes land on a brown barn and a large, dank field. It looks like we're on a farm.

Oh, maybe we're going horse riding! I love horses! I didn't know Jack could ride? That is so romantic! That is so—

I stop in my tracks as I spot a large, ominous sign:

THE DIVE OF YOUR LIFE. TANDEM SKYDIVES!

*

I can't believe I am about to jump out of a plane in a pencil skirt.

Actually, no. Much worse than that.

I can't believe I am about to jump out of a plane when I'm *not wearing a bra*.

I have to wear two bras when I go running. Two! Now I'm expected to throw myself into the air with no support whatso-ever! What's going to hold them in place? I'm going to land back on earth and find them permanently dislodged under my armpits!

When I finally staggered out of the car, Jack took me inside and made me put on this hideous boiler suit over my perfectly planned date outfit - which, let me tell you, does absolutely nothing for my figure. I look like a sack of unwashed pota-toes.

Howie, the man running the skydives, then laughed at my choice of shoes (I retaliated by laughing at the name 'Howie' when he left the room, but nobody found it very funny). He returned saying that 'luckily' Jan had left her clumpy old trainers behind so I could wear them. Lucky me.

Oh, and also, I had to tie up my hair, without a hairbrush. Or a mirror.

The only part of my date image that is still intact is my liquid eyeliner. Which will, obviously, vanish immediately when I burst into tears after being thrown out of a plane to my death.

The rickety plane dips slightly and I grip on to my seat in panic.

Jack was thrilled at the idea. He was all 'what a great find' and 'another thing off the list'. Blah blah blah bloody blah.

I mean, hello? I shaved my legs for this!

'Right,' says Howie, 'we're almost there.'

My body seizes up and my eyes flit over to Dave, my tandem diver.

I almost had a fit when I realised I would be paired up with him. I don't have many qualms about being strapped to a strange man (obviously, I have a few, I'm only human), but Dave is absolutely enormous. He's about four times the size of me.

Howie said Dave is 'very experienced', but all I can think about is how much quicker I will be hurling to the ground with Dave strapped to my back like a baby rhino.

I look up as Jack squeezes my hand.

'Excited?' he asks.

I blink at him. 'You do know I'm terrified of heights?' I say bluntly.

Jack grins. 'I don't love them either,' he admits, 'but I've always wanted to do this. It will be an amazing experience.'

I nod feebly.

Bloody Amy.

Dave stands up and gestures. I copy. Feebly, I stagger over, my legs quivering like jelly.

Oh my God, I'm going to be sick. I am most certainly going to be sick. This isn't right. This isn't normal. You're not supposed to throw yourself out of a plane. Humans aren't supposed to fly, that's why we don't have wings.

Dave spins me round and I hold out my arms like a lifeless puppet. I glance over at Jack who is doing the same with Obé, his instructor.

'So why are you doing this, then?'

I jump as Dave speaks right into my unsuspecting ear. His gruff voice fires into my eardrum and I flinch.

'Charity?' he probes.

He wants to do small talk? Now? I'm so nervous I can barely speak!

'No,' I manage, 'it's for my sister. She wrote me a list of challenges to complete.'

Dave tightens a strap around us and I wince as the belt yanks all the remaining oxygen from my body.

'That's cool,' he says.

'Okay!' Howie stands up and rubs his hands together. 'Which one of you crazy kids wants to go first?'

'Jack,' I blurt before I can stop myself.

Jack shoots me a look of alarm and I scowl at him.

What does he expect? This was his bloody idea. I'm certainly not going first.

'Goggles,' Howie adds.

Reluctantly, I pull the goggles over my face. They squash against my cheeks and I try the fight the image of what I look like. Although I have a strong feeling I look like a beaver suffering from a very serious anaphylactic shock.

Jack and Obé move forward as the plane door slides open. A

ferocious gust of wind spins through the plane and I stagger backwards. Or I try to, but Dave stops me from going anywhere.

They drop to the floor and shuffle forward, until Jack's legs are swinging out of the plane door. Jack looks back at me and grins. I smile back weakly. Nothing about this feels natural.

'Right!' Howie shouts over the wind. 'Ready? Three, two, one.'

Jack screws up his face and Obé tips their combined body weight out of the plane. A soft scream falls out of my mouth as they disappear.

Oh my God. They've gone. They've actually done it. That means—

'Right,' Howie turns to me. 'Your turn, miss.'

Before I can open my mouth to argue, Dave moves our joint body forward and we drop to the floor, and before I know what's happening, my bandy legs are dangling over the edge of the plane like two pieces of limp spaghetti. My stomach plummets as I gape down at the swirls of white clouds, streaming across the sky like marshmallows.

Terrifying, deadly marshmallows.

'Ready?' Howie shouts.

'NO!' I scream back, but Howie ignores me.

'Three, two, one!'

Before I can register the count, Dave pushes his body weight against my back and I tumble out of the plane. My open mouth screams as we fall through the air, crashing through the clouds. The icy air rushes past my ears, and my eyes screw up tight and stream viciously.

'Are your eyes open?'

I flinch as Dave bellows in my ear.

No! Is he insane? What is the matter with this guy?

'Open them!' he shouts again.

No. Absolutely not. If I shut my eyes for long enough then I can pretend this isn't happening.

'Open them!' he screams.

Slowly, I peel one eye open and my stomach lurches in horror. The wisps of white cloud are swirling around us and snaking below like strings of cotton wool. Bursting between the clouds are flashes of green, and I see the tiny squares of land forming beneath us.

My stomach unclenches as my mouth edges into a smile and a wave of euphoria sweeps up my body. Dave pulls at my arms, which are clasped around my chest. They fling backwards into the air and I fall through the sky.

Oh my God. I'm doing it. I'm doing it!

Suddenly, Dave yanks a cord behind his back and we lurch backwards as the parachute springs out of the backpack. My eyes take in the sea of colour as we hang in the air like babies and float towards the ground, as light as air. I swing my legs back and forth as a burst of laughter fires from my stomach. Adrenaline shoots through me like a cannon filled with great fireworks that burst and crackle around my heart.

I have never felt anything like this before.

The sun spills through the clouds and I squint at the brightness as we float towards the ground, angling towards a large field. I notice a small figure already there, and realise that must be Jack. I wave enthusiastically.

I crash to the floor with a thud as me and Dave land in tandem. Dave unhooks us and I stumble to my feet, my weak legs trembling. I look up at Jack, whose entire face is masked by the giant smile plastered upon it. He reaches towards me and I throw my arms around him. He squeezes me back and throws me into the air, and I squeal in delight.

I have never felt anything like this before.

★

'Give me the list, then.'

I look up at Jack, my stomach clenching as I meet his sparkling eyes. His face is shadowed slightly by the flickering candle propped between us, and I take another sip of the red wine. My fifth glass.

(Fifth! It's a wonder I can still speak!)

After I recovered from this afternoon, Jack took me on a real date. We had dinner in a tiny restaurant, tucked behind the pier. I opted for the floaty dress.

I reach down into my bag and pull out the list. He pulls a pen out of his pocket triumphantly and ticks off the skydive. I laugh.

'We're nearly finished!' he says. 'We'll definitely finish it before your birthday.'

I cradle my wine and cock my head. 'Do you know when my birthday is?'

'December fifth,' Jack says, not missing a beat.

I grin. 'You listen to me, then.'

Jack's eyes flit up from the list. 'Always,' he says, his mouth softening into a smile.

I hold his gaze, warmth rolling up my body as I feel myself sink into his green eyes.

'So,' he says, moving his eyes slowly back to the list, laid out between us, 'what else have you got to do?'

'Well,' I say, peering down at the list myself, 'make the perfect Victoria sponge.'

Jack laughs. 'Oh yeah, how's that going?'

I roll my eyes. 'Not well.' I laugh as my eyes scan the list. 'And obviously, the 10k is still on there.'

Jack nods. 'Which we've got planned.'

I grin. 'Yeah, and then there's . . .'

I trail off as my eyes focus on the last remaining item.

'Go skinny-dipping,' Jack says eventually, his voice hoarse.

I look up and feel my heart jolt as Jack stares back at me.

We can't go skinny-dipping here. Can we? If we go skinny-dipping, that means we'll see each other naked. If we see each other naked, that means that we'll—

'We're right by the sea,' his voice interrupts my thoughts. 'It's the perfect time to.'

I hover, lost in his eyes.

'Okay,' I hear myself say, my mouth dry, 'let's do it.'

I tip the remainder of my wine down my throat and get to my feet as Jack pays. My stomach flips and exhilaration courses through me.

Am I really going to do this? This is not like me at all. But then, maybe that's a good thing.

'You ready?'

Jack links his hand into mine as we exit the restaurant. Within moments, we're right by the sea. Darkness stretches over the beach and only the crash of the waves reassures me that we are standing near the water. It is almost midnight. There is nobody to be seen. The alcohol in my body swirls up inside my chest and swims through my mind, fuelling me with a burst of confidence, and before I can convince myself otherwise, I pull my dress over my head. I hear Jack next to me, though I can no longer see him. I hear the chink of his belt and the light thump as his clothes fall to the floor. I gasp as the wind bites my bare skin. Jack reaches forward and takes my hand.

'It's so cold,' I manage, my teeth chattering.

He squeezes my hand. 'I'll keep you warm.' He pulls me forward. 'Come on!'

I suck in a great gulp of air and run after Jack, our arms swinging together as we run towards the sea. The icy wind whips at my skin and I feel as if I may turn to stone. Suddenly, my feet spark in shock as we reach the sea. The icy waters crash over us and I gasp.

'Oh my God!' I cry, as the sea surges right up to my waist. 'It's so cold!'

Jack doesn't respond, his hand still firmly around mine.

'We're doing it!' I laugh. 'We're skinny-dipping! We're—'

My final words are lost as Jack's hands grab my lower waist and pull me towards him. I am lifted slightly under his strong arms and, with my bare body pressed against his, he kisses me. Everything inside me explodes as I sink into him and my body lights up with excitement. With both of his hands still gripping my face, he pulls away and looks at me.

'God,' he breathes, 'you have no idea how long I've wanted to do that.'

CHAPTER TWENTY-ONE

My face twitches as I emerge into consciousness and the musky smell of Jack fills my nose. His arm is wrapped around my middle, the palm of his hand resting on my stomach. Slowly, I pull my eyes open as my head crashes into action, thick with red wine.

Oh God, I feel terrible. Why did I drink wine? And not just wine, red wine. I dread to think what my teeth look like. Instinctively I run my tongue over my teeth and clench my mouth shut.

My teeth! How could I have drunk an entire bottle of red wine and not brushed my teeth? What was I thinking?

Actually, I wasn't thinking. I didn't have time to think. I barely had time to breathe.

Jack stirs and I feel the familiar flame of excitement ignite in the pit of my stomach. My eyes scan the hotel room, and glance over to Jack, still fast asleep. We're both naked. We barely made it back to the hotel room, but when we did, we . . .

Well, I don't need to spell it out. You know the rest. Saying that, I thought I knew the rest. But Jack . . . he was . . . I mean, he was really . . .

Well, let's just say I'm bloody glad I had the wax. I really must buy Natalie a drink.

'Hey.'

I look round as Jack's voice whispers beside me. I smile at him and take in the sight of his familiar face. He really is gorgeous.

'Hey,' I whisper back, angling my body round to face him. He pulls me closer towards him and I giggle. His eyes peel open and he strokes my face with his hand. I smile at him, my heart inflating.

'Last night was fun,' I say.

He smiles back at me and kisses my face as I struggle to suppress another laugh.

'Tea?' he asks, pulling himself to sitting.

'Sure,' I say, stretching my arms above my head.

I haven't checked my phone since yesterday, I have no idea what the time is. I feel as if, since arriving in Brighton, I have left my London life behind. Jack flicks the kettle on, his boxers hanging low on his defined hips. I watch him and he flashes me another smile.

'What time is your train back?' he asks.

'I'm not sure,' I reply. 'Actually,' I reach over and grab my bag, 'I'd better check what the time is. I haven't got anything to rush back for. We could go try out those rides on the pier?'

The last sentence spills out of my mouth as excitement whips through me.

Oh my God, I would love to do that. I love rides.

'I can't.' Jack hands me a mug. 'I need to get back to London. It's the rehearsal dinner tonight.'

I take the mug with one hand as my phone springs to life. 'Oh yeah,' I say, 'I can't believe the wedding is this week.'

Jack takes a sip of his coffee and nods. 'I know. I still haven't written my bloody speech.'

I laugh as my phone vibrates in my hand. I glance down and my stomach lurches.

Fifteen missed calls from Tamal.

No.

I gape at the phone as fiery panic races through me and claws at my skin, burning my throat and tearing at my eyes, when suddenly the screen lights up with another call from Tamal. My fingers barely working, I manage to answer the call.

'Hello?' I stumble.

'Georgia? Where are you? Something has happened to Amy. You need to come to the hospital, now.'

*

I glare at Jack as he walks past me, plucking his belongings from the hotel room and slotting them into his open suitcase. My eyes snap back to my watch.

We need to leave. We should have left five minutes ago. Why is he doing everything so slowly?

I couldn't get much out of Tamal, only that Amy was in hospital. He said she fell down the stairs. My body burns with fear. I need to be with her. I am always with her. This is the first time something has happened and I haven't been there. I feel as if I've left an organ with Amy; I can't function knowing she's in hospital without me. I should be there. I have to be there. I need to get out of Brighton.

'You okay?' Jack asks.

'Fine,' I mutter, irritation pulling at my skin.

Jack cranes his head to look around the room. 'Have you seen my phone charger?'

'It's there.' I jab my arm at the socket next to the bed, refreshing my phone.

I tried to call Amy, but she didn't answer. Which seems obvious now. Tamal said she hit her head when she fell down the stairs. He said the whole family is with her.

The whole family, except me.

Jack pulls his charger from the wall and drops it in his bag. 'Are you sure you're okay?' he asks.

'Fine,' I snap. 'My sister is in fucking hospital and I'm trapped here with you but I'm fine.'

A wave of heat crashes over my face and I glare at my phone, as if Amy might call at any minute and tell me everything is fine. Or Mum, or Dad. There isn't any signal in the hospital.

'Trapped?' Jack repeats, looking up from his bag.

Why is he moving so slowly?

'Yes!' I lash out. 'I should be there! I need to get home and you're being so slow!'

Jack zips his bag shut and swings it over his shoulder. 'Let's go, then,' he says evenly.

I storm past him, out of the room and into the hotel lift.

We booked on the first train we could find, but it doesn't leave for another hour, and then it takes another whole hour to get to London. Let alone get to the hospital.

I should be there now. I should have been there from the beginning. I'm always there.

227

'You know the Uber has only just arrived,' Jack says as he follows me into the lift. 'I wasn't just being slow.'

I ignore him and refresh my phone again. The lift jolts as it jitters towards the ground floor and my heart clenches and unclenches like a stress ball.

'She'll be okay.' I hear Jack's soft voice and feel my body recoil in anger. 'I know you're worried, but she will be.'

'You don't know that,' I spit, my eyes locked on to my phone.

The lift doors creak open and I march out, tears clawing at the back of my eyes. I need to get home. I feel so far away from her. She's lying in hospital and I'm miles away, and for what?

I stagger out through the door and glare around hopelessly at the empty road stretching in front of the hotel. The icy November rain slices through the sky like knives and I scowl at the streets in fury.

Where's the taxi? Where is the taxi?

'Where is it?' I hurl at Jack as he appears behind me. 'It's not here. Where is it?'

Jack's face twitches. 'It's coming,' he says calmly.

'You said it was already here,' I snap, glaring at the empty roads.

I can't just stand here and wait. I've been waiting all morning. I can't wait any more. I need to get to Amy.

'I'm going to walk,' I say bitterly, and I begin to walk towards the high street.

I can roughly remember where it is. I'm sure it's in this direction.

'Georgie,' Jack calls after me. 'Georgie, don't be stupid. The cab will be here in a minute.'

'I can't just stand there and wait,' I shout over my shoulder.

I hear the thud behind me and notice Jack has followed.

'Georgie,' he says as he reaches me, 'come on. Waiting for the taxi will only take a few minutes.'

'I don't have a few minutes!' I cry, marching through the street and cursing my footwear. 'I should be with her now. I shouldn't be here with you.'

'Georgie!' Jack grabs my arm. 'Georgie, come on.'

I shake his arm off furiously and power through.

Finally, Jack stops chasing after me.

'It's not my fault,' he shouts after me.

His words root my feet to the ground and the anger bubbling inside me erupts.

'Yes,' I hurl my body round to face him, my eyes burning, 'yes, it is. If it wasn't for you, I would be at home right now. I would be with Amy, and if I had been with her then she wouldn't have fallen.'

A shadow passes over Jack's face and his mouth tightens.

'That's not right,' he says. 'You can't say that.'

I stare back at him, my chest rising and falling as the icy wind whips my hair.

'None of this should have happened,' I say coldly. 'I shouldn't be here with you.'

I turn back on my heels and storm back down the street, the burning tears streaming from my eyes and spilling down my cheeks.

I should be with Amy. I should always be with Amy.

CHAPTER TWENTY-TWO

I grasp my head with my hands, my fingernails sinking into my cheeks and breaking my skin as anxiety burns behind my eyes.

I should have been there.

I jump slightly as the clock chimes, standing proudly on the mantelpiece. My dry eyes snap up to look at the time, my head splitting with the sudden movement.

I should have been there and I wasn't. I was miles away. In bed with someone I barely know. I never do that, that isn't me.

I shouldn't have done it. I should have been here. It took me hours to get back, and by the time I did Dad told me to wait at home. Alone.

I let my head fall back into my hands, anxiety snaking around my body and squeezing my organs like a python.

I feel like I can barely breathe.

Amy fell. Tamal said she fell from the top of the stairs. He had to take her to hospital; she wouldn't wake up. She hit her head.

This thought causes my body to jolt violently and I try to fight the balloon of fear that is swelling inside me, when I hear the crackle of the car rolling on to the drive. I leap to my feet and rush towards the door. I pull it open and my eyes mist as I spot the family car on the drive. Mum is clipped into the front seat. Her face is as white as paper and she looks as if she hasn't slept. Dad climbs out of the car, his face bright and cheery as always. My heart aches as my eyes search his face. Dad flicks open the boot and places something by the rear passenger door. Panic storms through me as I realise what it is. My hands grip on to the door frame in fear.

It's a wheelchair.

Tamal climbs out of the car next. His face is grave, a sober smile stretched across it, pulling his mouth into a shape I've never seen before. He walks round the car and opens the door for Amy. She folds herself out of the car and drops straight into the wheelchair like a rag doll. Her arm is hooked in a sling and I notice an ugly purple bruise smeared across her face.

I hover at the door, my heart cracking every time my eyes fall on another dent on Amy's battered body. Then suddenly, my stomach plummets as Amy's eyes look up and lock on to mine. Her face doesn't move, but I know instantly what she is thinking.

I should have been there.

★

Amy looks up at me as I place a mug down beside her. She smiles weakly.

'How are you feeling?' I ask, as I curl on to the sofa next to her, guilt chewing every part of me.

Her eyes flit to the mug, and I flinch as I realise she can't pick it up. She's only got one arm.

'Here,' I say quickly, handing her the mug.

She shakes her head. 'Not yet,' she says, 'it's too hot.'

'Right.'

Amy stares forward, her eyes glazed over and locked on to the TV. My eyes ache as I look back at her hopelessly. Tamal left about an hour ago to go to work, and I texted Sally to say I wouldn't be in. It's the big pitch tomorrow, but she understood.

'How are you feeling?' I ask again.

'Where were you?'

Amy's soft voice cuts through me, her eyes still fixed ahead of her. The guilt pierces my insides with blunt blades of anxiety, and I try to fight the hot panic tearing at my skin.

'I was with Jack,' I manage. 'We were in Brighton.'

Finally, Amy looks at me. Her eyes are red and inflamed, and her left eye is blurred with a deep stain of sickly yellow. I reach forward and grab her hand, my fingers coiling around her cold fingers. Amy lets her fingers hang limply in mine and I grip them, desperate to instil some warmth into her.

'Are you okay?' I ask.

She doesn't speak, but slowly I see her grey eyes blur with a layer of tears that spill over and fall down her face. I lunge forward and cradle her head into my body, unable to fight the tears pricking at the back of my eyes.

'I'm sorry,' I say, holding her tightly against my chest. 'I'm sorry I wasn't there.'

Amy shakes her head and pulls away. I sink back down into the settee, and try to wipe my wet face dry.

'Don't be,' Amy says quietly, 'I'm glad you were out doing something fun.'

'No,' I argue, 'I shouldn't have been. I should have been here, with you and . . .'

I trail off as Amy shakes her head at me.

'Do you know what I was doing?' she says. 'When I fell?'

I look back at her helplessly.

'I was about to run a bath,' Amy continues, 'and I thought, wouldn't it be nice to have some bubbles? I knew that Mum had that nice scented bubble bath we bought her for Christmas that she never uses. So I went upstairs to find it, and then halfway back down, my legs stopped working.'

Amy has stopped crying now, and the words fall out of her mouth like stones dropping into water. I watch her, unable to speak.

'And now,' Amy laughs, gesturing down at herself, 'now I'm like this! I'm in a wheelchair. It's really happened. I'm actually in a fucking wheelchair—'

She breaks off.

'You'll get out of it,' I breathe. 'Tamal said it's only temporary.'

Amy turns her head sharply away from me.

'No one knows that,' she says coldly. 'I'm supposed to be at work today. The kids have their first netball game next week. How am I supposed to teach in this?' She slaps her free arm on the wheelchair and I wince as it rattles under the force.

I angle my body towards her. 'They'll understand,' I say, 'they know you're not well at the moment. They all want to run for you. They want to help with the event and—'

Amy rests her head against the back of her chair and scrunches up her face.

233

'The event's off,' she says scathingly. 'I don't want it.'

'But Amy, we've raised . . .' I falter.

'I can't watch everyone I love run a 10k while I'm sat in this chair.' Her words slice across me as her eyes flash. 'I just can't.'

I stare back at her, my final glimmer of hope slowly vanishing.

'Okay,' I manage, wrapping my fingers tighter around her hand. 'It's off.'

CHAPTER TWENTY-THREE

Running schedule:

04/08	1k	✓	(August is not the time to start running.
			Sweat patches are uncontrollable.)
10/09	2k	✓	(Actually isn't that far at all. Who knew?)
05/10	3k	✓	(Am doing v. well. Kudos to me.
			I am superior to all. Bow to me, Usain.)
19/10	4k	✓	(Finishes right by Burger King!
			Coincidence?!?!)
13/11	5k	✓	(Christ)

Natalie places a cardboard cup of tea in front of me and smiles sympathetically. I slept at my parents' house last night. I didn't mean to. I didn't want to leave Amy. When I woke up this morning nobody was there.

I run my hand over my face as Natalie passes me her compact.

'Here,' she says, 'I always carry one in my bag. In case I have too much fun on a night out.'

'Thank you,' I say, snapping it open and trying not to wince at my grey reflection. 'I slept at my parents' last night. I wanted to stay with Amy.'

'How is she?'

'Terrible,' I say honestly. 'I think she'll be okay, though. She doesn't even want to come to the run.'

Natalie's eyebrows shoot up her face. 'But the run is in a few weeks, isn't it? You've raised a fortune. I looked this morning and you're on about eight thousand. She has to be there, it's all for her.'

I shrug and wrap my hands around the milky, sugar-infused tea.

'That's what I told her,' I say quietly. 'I managed to talk her out of cancelling it completely but she says she won't come.'

Natalie nods as I stare into my tea, willing myself not to cry.

I have never seen Amy so defeatist. She has never given up on anything.

'So,' Natalie says airily, swirling her latte in her hand, 'is there any other reason why you look so sleep deprived?'

I click my eyes up at her teasing face and, to my annoyance, feel the sides of my mouth pull into a smile. I can never stay miserable in front of Natalie for long.

Natalie slaps the table with her hand and an enormous hoot of laughter escapes from her mouth.

'I knew it!' she cries. 'I bloody knew it! I think I have a sixth sense. A sex sense.'

I scrunch up my nose at her. 'Ew,' I say, 'don't say that.'

'How was it?' Natalie says, leaning forward. 'How did it happen? Tell me everything. Have you seen him since?'

I falter.

Of course I haven't seen him since. We barely spoke on the train journey home. He tried to call me but I didn't answer. What would I say?

'No,' I say quietly, 'we had a fight, actually.'

Natalie's face changes and I, begrudgingly, tell her everything. Each detail drags up a familiar feeling of guilt as I relive every horrible word I threw at Jack. He was only trying to help.

'And you haven't spoken since?' Natalie asks when I finish.

I shake my head, taking a generous sip of tea. 'He tried to call me.'

'But you didn't answer?'

'No.'

Natalie leans back into her seat, holding her coffee with one hand and pushing her long braids off her shoulder with the other. 'He'll understand,' she says. 'He knows what's been going on with Amy, doesn't he?'

I nod. 'He's been helping me.'

'This is just a blip,' Natalie says. 'Everyone fights. He'll understand, I wouldn't worry about it.'

I smile slightly as the knot in the pit of my stomach loosens.

'So,' Natalie starts again, 'apart from that, how was it?'

I meet Natalie's excited eyes as a warm glow spreads through me.

'It was amazing,' I say honestly. 'It was one of the most romantic days of my life.' I look into her shining eyes. 'I really like him.'

Natalie leans her head against her hand and grins.

'I always knew you fancied him.'

★

I look up as Sally strides into the office, stopping next to my desk. Her crisp bob is perfectly tucked under her chin and she is dressed head to toe in an immaculate suit. The big pitch is today. Even though me and Sally have very little to do with it, Bianca instructed us to wear our 'most expensive-looking outfits'. Which, for me, is my Topshop blazer and my only pair of trousers without frayed hems – certainly not the pair that has little bristles of elastic that sprout all up my bottom.

I should really throw that pair away.

'Hello, Georgia,' Sally says.

'Hi, Sally,' I say, raising my glazed eyes to meet her. 'How are you?'

'Fine,' Sally says. 'How is Amy?'

I hesitate.

'She's okay,' I say eventually. 'She fell down the stairs, so she's quite bruised. She's actually in a wheelchair.'

Sally's face twitches. 'That's bad,' she says.

I almost want to laugh at her attempt to be sympathetic.

'Yeah,' I say, pulling my eyes back to my computer screen.

Sally walks back to her desk and sinks into her chair.

'I have received a lot of sponsorship,' she says abruptly. 'Almost one thousand pounds.'

My eyes snap up from my screen and I angle my body round to see Sally over the monitors.

What? Sponsorship?

The List That Changed My Life

'One thousand pounds?' I repeat.

'Yes,' Sally responds, 'people have been very generous when I've explained what it is for. And five people from my running club have signed up too. They all want to meet Amy.'

I blink at her, trying to make sense of it. She's been telling people? She's been fund-raising? I just thought she liked running.

'Wow,' I breathe, 'that's amazing, Sally. But I'm not sure Amy is going to be there.'

'What?' Sally barks, alarmed. 'Why not?'

I falter. A weighted ball of sadness lodges in my chest as I remember Amy's face.

'She doesn't feel up to it,' I manage.

Sally opens her mouth to respond, when Bianca charges through the office door. Her red hair is sculpted into an impressive ponytail and her cat-like eyes are framed with sweeping black eyeliner. Today, she is dressed in a magnificent blue dress that wraps around her slim frame and tumbles down her long legs. I try not to flinch as I notice her spiked heels, poking out of the bottom of her dress like glamorous hedgehogs.

'Georgie,' she says as her eyes land on me, 'good, you're here. I need you.'

She turns and walks out of the office, and I spring to my feet and follow her obediently. I've given up worrying about Jack telling her about us. She can't fire me before the wedding, I'm the only one who knows how to control the doves.

We march down the corridor and into her office, which is covered in various wedding sketches. Why she planned her wedding for the weekend after our biggest pitch I will never know.

'How are you?' she asks, dropping into her large chair and

gesturing for me to do the same. I sink into a much smaller chair quietly.

'Fine, thanks,' I say. 'How are you? How are you feeling about this weekend?'

Bianca flips open a file and she smiles. 'I am very well,' she says. 'Thanks to you and Sally, I think it will be a wonderful day.'

I nod, feeling my cheeks pinch in embarrassment.

Maybe she's forgotten about the bears.

'So,' she hands me a large piece of paper, 'I just wanted to run over the seating plan one last time before the pitch. My great-uncle has just pulled out. Apparently he's sick. Anyway, now I need to find a new place for my Great-Aunt Julie, who won't want to sit on her own.'

I pull out a pen and look at the table plans.

'So,' she continues, 'I just want to go through it and see if there is anyone we can move. We've got about ten minutes before we need to get ready for the pitch; that should be enough time.'

I nod again. 'Okay.'

She stretches out her own seating plan and sighs.

'So,' she peers down at the paper, 'obviously on the top table are myself and Jonathan; my parents; Jonathan's parents; Jack and Lulu. They all have to stay together, although Jack would be the perfect person to stick with Aunt Julie because he will just chat to anyone.'

'I'm sure he wouldn't mind not sitting on the top table,' I comment, 'if you move him to the table next to it.'

'Oh no,' Bianca says, 'we can't separate Jack from Lulu. They need to sit together.'

I feel a pang of envy.

I've never heard of Lulu before.

'Oh,' I say, trying to keep my voice light, 'why? Who is she?'

Bianca swishes her pen across the paper. 'She's Jack's wife.'

My stomach drops.

What? She's . . . what?

'Bianca . . .'

I jump as Sally appears at the door.

'. . . the clients are downstairs. They're early.'

Bianca springs to her feet and shoots Sally a knowing look.

'Great!' she says. 'Go bring them up, will you, Sally? Georgie,' she turns back to me, 'follow me. I'll need you to get coffee.'

Slowly I get to my feet, my legs threatening to buckle beneath me, as if all my bones have dissolved. I can feel my heart cracking and splintering in my chest and releasing a thick ooze of panic through my body, turning every spark of happiness within me to ice. My throat twists as I struggle to breathe.

His wife?

My entire body numb, I follow Bianca out of the room. My mind feels like it has been turned into thick, grey paste as it tries to compute that sentence.

His wife?

That's why he didn't tell Bianca about me. That's why I know nothing about his life. It's because he's married. He's married.

He can't be. He can't be married.

He's married?

'Right!' Bianca says briskly as we push through the doors. 'Let's . . .' she trails off as we enter the meeting room. My eyes follow her in brief confusion, until I reach the centre of the room and my heart stops entirely.

241

Spread across the room are my designs. Pinned up and scaled up into giant posters. The designs I have been working on for the big pitch, in private. My designs.

What are they doing here? How did they get here?

My stinging eyes pulse in panic and I stumble back towards the door, desperately reaching for support. Bianca storms up to one of the posters, a look of fury on her face.

'What the fuck is this?' she cries, outraged. 'These aren't my designs! Where are mine? Who put these . . .' her words are lost as she turns abruptly to examine the corner of one poster. My stomach lurches into my throat as she reads my name, etched in dark ink. Bianca hurls herself round to face me, her eyes like balls of fire.

'Did you do this?' she hisses between clenched teeth.

'No!' I splutter, trying to control the anxiety erupting in my body. 'Those are my designs, but I didn't—'

Bianca claws one arm into the air and rips my poster down. I wince as it crumples to the floor.

'How dare you!' she bellows, her words striking me like daggers. 'Who do you think you are, to swap my designs for yours? You're an assistant!'

'I'm sorry,' I manage, my voice heavy, 'I'm sorry. I didn't—'

By this point, her flaming red hair is flailing behind her and her expression is murderous. Her teeth are bared, like fangs, and her voice is firing out of her mouth like bullets. My body convulses in fear and I feel the scorching heat of tears making my eyes burn.

'You think these people want to see your shitty designs instead of mine?' she thunders. 'You think these people have come here to see you? You could have lost us our biggest client—' She breaks off, her chest rising and falling dramatically and her eyes watering in fury. Her burning face is twisted with a look of disgust as she takes a step towards me. I step back against the wall instinctively. I open my mouth to speak but all the words die in my throat and I'm trapped there, helpless.

'Get out of here,' she snarls at me. 'You're fired, Georgia. Get the hell out.'

CHAPTER TWENTY-FOUR

<u>Georgie's list</u>

1. Have a vindaloo on Brick Lane. ✓
2. Take a Salsa class. ✓
3. Do a skydive. ✓
4. Go on a Tinder date. ✓
5. Cycle around Hyde Park. ✓
6. Run 10k.
7. Make the perfect Victoria sponge.
8. Go skinny-dipping in the sea. ✓
9. Try skateboarding at Southbank. ✓
10. Show Bianca your designs! ✓

I bury my head in the cushion, my cheek squashed up against a corner, and my body draped across the sofa as if it's made of lead.

I ran. After that, I ran. I didn't let Bianca speak, I didn't go back to get my things. I just ran. I had to. I didn't know what else to do.

244

I scowl as another episode of *Don't Tell the Bride* begins on the TV. I have been lying here for hours, drifting in and out of sleep, only peeling myself off the sofa to go to the toilet, and even that is a struggle. Then, every half an hour or so, when I think I'm finally able to face the crippling reality of today's events, a wave of anxiety crashes over me and squeezes my throat with such force that I can barely breathe.

Today I was fired. Today I found out I slept with a married man.

I slept with a *married man*.

I pull my eyes away from the TV as I hear the front door click open, and I feel my body shrivel in dread.

Urgh, Tina.

I came back to the flat today for the first time since Brighton, and the entire living room was littered with a sea of cans and half-empty beer bottles with a rogue bra of mine hanging from the flickering kitchen light bulb.

Obviously I can't reach it alone, and I am not risking balancing on another one of our kitchen chairs. My deposit can't take another hit after the shower curtain fiasco.

I swing a flailing arm over the side of the sofa and hook the remote under two of my fingers and jab up the volume uninvitingly.

Hopefully, she'll get the message and leave me alone.

I scowl at the TV as I hear the door creak open. My eyes flick towards the sound in irritation when, to my alarm, they land on Amy, pushing her way through in her wheelchair.

'Amy!' I cry, pulling myself up to sitting so fast that my entire blood flow rushes to my head.

Amy rolls through the door, and scowls down at the floor.

'Please don't tell me you drank all of this?' she says in disgust.

I push the bottles out of the way, slumping back against the sofa cushions.

'Of course I didn't,' I say. 'What are you doing here? How did you get here?'

Amy wheels over to me and parks her chair next to the sofa so that my face is propped next to her armrest.

'Tamal drove me over on his way to work,' she says. 'I used the spare key. What are you watching?'

'*Don't Tell the Bride*,' I say, glueing my eyes back to the screen.

'Surely you've seen every episode of this by now,' Amy says.

I scowl in her direction. 'Why are you here?'

Amy reaches into the side of her chair and pulls out a Diet Coke. She slots it in front of my face and I take it.

'Sally called me,' Amy says, and I hear the fizz as her can opens. 'Wow, look at her dress.'

I pull myself up on to my elbows.

What?

'Sally?' I repeat in bewilderment.

Amy glances at me, sipping her Coke. 'Yeah,' she says, 'she said something happened at work and you left crying.'

'How . . .' I manage, 'how does she have your number?'

Amy shrugs. 'We've been messaging about the run. She's been helpful.'

I blink at Amy, winded by this news.

Amy has been messaging Sally?

'So,' Amy looks at me, 'do you want to talk about it?'

'No,' I say childishly, flopping back down on to the sofa, my face squishing into the armrest.

'Okay,' she says, 'well, I brought some supplies.'

My body twitches as I hear four light thumps. I look at the floor and notice Amy has dropped a cheesecake, a bottle of wine, two face packs and some ginormous slippers. My eyes scan the items as I feel an overpowering ball of emotion block my throat.

'There are some benefits to this chair,' Amy says lightly. 'It has great storage.'

It's our care package. It's what me and Amy buy for each other whenever something has happened. We haven't done it since Amy got sick.

'Thank you,' I manage, my voice thick.

I lie back down on the sofa as Amy moves her hand, and links it into mine. She squeezes my hand in hers and I feel the knot clenched around my stomach loosen.

'Bianca saw my designs,' I murmur into the sofa, my face burning at the memory.

Amy doesn't move, her eyes still fixed on the TV. Her thumb strokes my hand.

'And?' she questions. 'What did she think?'

My eyes burn as I force the words out of my mouth.

'She fired me,' I manage. 'She hated them. Someone put them up in the pitching room and she thought I was trying to sabotage her.'

My head pounds as my eyes stream. I don't know how I can still cry, there can't be anything left inside me.

'Oh, Georgie,' Amy sighs. 'That's so unfair. Your designs are really good.'

I shake my head, defeated. 'They're not,' I say. 'She said so.'

Amy's grip on my hand tightens. 'She's an idiot,' she says fiercely. 'Everyone always says how talented you are.'

'Oh yeah?' I grunt. 'Like who?'

'Me,' Amy says, 'and Mum and Dad, and Tamal, and Jack.'

'He doesn't count,' I say bitterly, betrayal gripping my chest.

Amy looks down at me, her eyebrows raised. 'What do you mean?'

I glance up at her. I slowly peel my wet face away from the sofa and hang my head in my hands. My heart flips over as I try and find the courage to say the words out loud.

'He's married,' I say weakly. 'He's got a wife.'

Amy's mouth falls open.

'I don't know what to do.' The words tumble out of me. 'I can't believe I was so wrong about everything. I don't even have a job any more. What am I supposed to do now? I've just wasted the last six months of my life.'

My face is wet again as my eyes leak tears down my cheeks. Suddenly, Amy twists her hand round my arm and yanks me upright. I stumble up ungracefully.

I always forget how strong she is.

'You have not wasted anything,' she says firmly, her fierce eyes staring into mine. 'You have achieved things in the last few months that you never thought you could.'

Amy cups my face with her hand and wipes away my tears.

'You have planned an incredible event,' she continues, 'and you're going to raise a lot of money for a really important cause. Do you know how many people that will benefit? Because of what you are doing?'

The tight vice of worry clasped around my chest vanishes as a new feeling snakes through my body.

'And most importantly,' she says, her voice softening, 'you've helped me. You've kept me afloat during the hardest time of my life. Those two arseholes may not be able to see it, but you have done some pretty incredible things, Georgie.'

I rest my head in her hand and Amy smiles. 'You haven't finished yet, either,' she grins. 'This run is going to be incredible.'

Amy looks into my eyes, and her kind face cues a fresh wave of tears that rise up inside me.

She tilts her head to one side. 'What is it?'

I rub the tears off my face, my body crumpling like tissue paper at the relief of having Amy here.

'I just . . .' I manage, 'I just don't know what to do now. I feel like everything I thought I knew has been taken away from me.'

I pull my watery gaze up to Amy. She moves her hands and coils them around mine. My clammy hands relax under her strong grip, and her eyes shine back at me.

'Sometimes,' she says slowly, 'life turns you upside down and you just have to keep moving. It can feel like you don't know what to do, but that's what I'm here for—' she moves her hand back to my face as tears stream down my cheeks 'And that's what you do for me. It doesn't mean life is over. We just find new things to do, together.'

Amy pinches my cheeks and I feel my face relax into a smile as I rest my head against her hand. The tight anxiety gripping my body starts to vanish.

Amy is all I need. She's always been all I need.

Her eyes scan the room and her face scrunches up into a grimace.

'Did Tina do this, then?' she asks.

I flop my head back against the sofa and peer around the dank living room. Along with the dirty carpet, strewn with cans and bottles, there are several dark stains splashed up the walls and a bucket skulking ominously in the corner.

'Yeah,' I reply.

'Why don't you come back and live with us for a bit?' Amy says. 'I know you wanted to move out, but just until you get back on your feet?'

I shake my head and pull myself upright.

'No,' I say, 'I can't. I need to stay here. I can't go backwards.'

Amy frowns. 'But why is it moving backwards?' she asks. 'Are you honestly telling me that you would rather live here—' she gestures towards the grey living room. 'Than back at Mum and Dad's, just for the sake of pride?'

My eyes flick up to her. 'Yes,' I lie.

Amy raises her eyebrows at me and I avoid her gaze.

Obviously, I want to go home. Of course I'd rather live back with my parents than in this dirty, rickety flat. I hate living here. But if I go back to live with my parents with no job, no relationship and no income then what will I have to show for the last year of my life? It will be like nothing ever happened.

'So,' Amy says tentatively, 'if you're staying here then you will need to pay rent.'

'Yup.'

'How will you do that?'

I try to squash the rush of anxiety that squirms up my body. 'I will get a job,' I say steadily, my eyes fixed on the TV, 'in a bar or something.'

At this, Amy puffs loudly.

'Right,' she says, grabbing the remote and switching off the TV, 'that's enough. You're coming home with me. I'm going to give you a job.'

Without the TV to distract me, I'm forced to look at Amy. I almost jump at the sight of her. Her cheeks are flushed and her eyes are narrowed with determination. Her lips have disappeared into a flat line and she is scowling at me.

This is the face she used to pull whenever she would try and force me to go to Zumba. I haven't seen this face in ages.

I haven't seen this face since Amy got ill.

'You'll give me a job?' I repeat.

'Yup!' Amy nods fiercely. 'Georgia Miller, you are now employed by Miller Enterprises. This is a fixed-term contract, from now until January.'

A small laugh tickles my chest and Amy's face glows with satisfaction.

'I'm not doing all your washing,' I say, 'or helping you peel lemons or whatever weird thing you like to do.'

Amy's face quivers with laughter.

'No,' she says, pulling a mock stern face, 'your sole job will be to assist me in planning this 10k event and making it a bloody huge success. This will include some weekend work – and you will be working alongside Amy Miller, your business partner, as a part of The Miller Project.'

At this, her mouth widens into a grin.

'Do you accept?'

I look back at her, an identical grin spreading across my face. I can never say no to her.

'I accept.'

CHAPTER TWENTY-FIVE

Running schedule:

04/08	1k	✓	(August is not the time to start running. Sweat patches are uncontrollable.)
10/09	2k	✓	(Actually isn't that far at all. Who knew?)
05/10	3k	✓	(Am doing v. well. Kudos to me. I am superior to all. Bow to me, Usain.)
19/10	4k	✓	(Finishes right by Burger King! Coincidence?!?!)
13/11	5k	✓	(Christ)
16/11	6k	✓	(Life flashed before eyes. Can't go on much longer. Go on without me, Mo.)

'Hello, Georgia!'

I beam up at Hamish, our local baker and owner of The Loaf, the town's independent bakery. Hamish has a mop of sand-coloured hair and a great moustache that tufts over his face and jiggles every time he laughs. He has been running the bakery ever since me and Amy were tiny.

'How are you?' he asks. 'How's the big smoke?'

'Good,' I respond, unwinding my scarf from my neck as the heat of the fresh pastries swirls around my face. 'I'm back for a bit. I was wondering whether we could put some flyers in your window?' I hold up my poster.

Hamish scowls at it and takes the poster from my hand. 'What's this?'

'We're holding a sponsored run,' I say, 'to raise money for MS.'

Hamish looks up. 'Is that what Amy's got?'

I nod. 'Yeah. We're trying to get sponsors, or donations or whatever.'

Hamish runs his eyes over the poster and then looks back at me. 'Well, if you're looking for donations, why don't I hold a bake sale?'

I grin. 'Really?' I say. 'That would be amazing. Thank you.'

Hamish puffs out his chest and nods. 'My pleasure,' he says, 'it's for a good cause. Leave a load of posters and leaflets, and I'll put them in the window.'

I tease out a handful and place them on the counter. 'Thank you so much,' I gush.

I buy a packet of iced buns and push my way out of the door and on to the quiet high street, a welcome change from the high street of Elephant and Castle.

Amy took me home with her that night. I currently have seven missed calls from Jack, three from Natalie and a text from Sally. I can't face any of them. Not yet.

I stop in my tracks as I reach the corner shop and smile as

I see Mrs Felix, perched behind the counter and doing the crossword. My heart swells at the sight of her. Everyone knows everyone here. It was Amy's idea to go into town to try and put up the posters.

'Hello, Georgia,' Mrs Felix says kindly. 'Nice to see you.'

I smile at her as I shut the door behind me. 'Hello, Mrs Felix,' I say. 'How are you?'

Mrs Felix nods and puts her crossword down and standing up. 'Oh, I'm fine,' she says. 'How are you? How is Amy?'

'Actually,' I say, pulling the poster from my bag, 'that's why I'm here. We're holding a sponsored run at The Elmrud School next month, to raise money for the MS Society. I wanted to see if you could put some posters up to spread the word?'

Mrs Felix takes the poster from me as her face stretches into a smile.

'Oh yes!' she says. 'I think my grandson is running. He goes to the school. Give them to me—' she gestures at my hands, clasping the posters, and I hand her more. 'Of course I'll put them up and spread the word. What a great cause. Are you running?'

I nod, smiling. 'Yeah. I think a few of us are.'

Mrs Felix smiles. 'Good for you,' she says.

I thank her and leave the shop, feeling a glow of satisfaction. Last time I checked, we had raised almost £15,000. I slip the last few posters into my bag and make my way to my parents' house. When I get back, Tamal is in the living room with Amy, who is cuddled up on the sofa next to him.

'Hi,' I say, as I walk into the living room.

Amy's face lights up as she sees me.

'Hey,' she says. 'How did it go?'

I drop on to the floor, cross-legged, and grin. 'Really well,' I say. 'Hamish is going to do a bake sale, Mrs Felix took posters, and the barbers and the wine shop said they'd contribute to the raffle.'

Tamal squeezes Amy's shoulder. 'Amazing!' he says.

'And,' I press on, 'I think we're on about fifteen thousand now.'

'Seventeen!' Tamal quips.

'We just checked,' Amy grins. 'We've just hit seventeen thousand pounds.'

I beam at them.

£17,000!

'How are you feeling about the run itself?' Tamal teases. 'Reckon you're ready?'

Amy slaps him playfully on the arm. 'Of course she is!' she says. 'She'll smash it.'

I smile gratefully, when my phone buzzes in my pocket. I pull it out and scowl at an unknown number.

Who is that?

I quickly scurry out of the room and up to my old bedroom.

'Hello?' I answer.

'Hello? Sorry. Left! LEFT! Hello? Hello?'

I jump as a racket of noise cannonballs into my ear. Who on earth is this?

'Hello?' I repeat, baffled.

Maybe I should just hang up. Although they sound quite distressed.

'Hello?' the woman barks again.

She sounds mental. Surely this is a wrong number.

'Georgia Miller?'

I jump and look at the phone. How does she know my name?

'Yes?' I say suspiciously.

Who is this crazy woman?

'Georgia Miller!' the woman squawks. 'This is Penny Pamdarny.'

I blink into the receiver.

Who?

'I have the birds and I— STOP! I said LEFT!'

I almost drop the phone in fright as her piercing voice assaults my eardrum. I should just hang up. But then this woman knows my name and telephone number, what else does she know? Does she know where I live?

Oh God, she's not outside, is she?

I peer out of the window and scan the road for any signs of crazed women.

'I have the birds!' she shouts down the receiver.

'Sorry,' I say, trying to sound calm, 'the birds? What birds?'

'Yes!' she cries, almost hysterical. 'I have the birds! You ordered birds!'

I open my mouth to respond when realisation dawns on me. The birds. Bianca's bloody birds. It's 17 November. It's her wedding day.

'Oh,' I say tightly, 'no, I didn't. Sorry.'

'You're Georgia Miller?' the woman bellows, and I jump again. Bloody hell. Doesn't she know what an inside voice is?

'No,' I say, my face prickling. 'No I'm not. Sorry.'

'Oh,' the woman says, 'well, I shall redial the number. The number I have here is . . .'

She starts reading out the number and I roll my eyes.

'That is my number,' I say irritably.

I hear a rustling down the phone.

'So you are Georgia Miller?' she pipes accusingly.

'Yes,' I sigh, 'yes, I am.'

Yes I bloody am. Yay me.

'Right,' the woman puffs, 'I need you to come out here and help me.'

I frown in bewilderment.

'Come where?' I say stupidly.

'Out here!' she barks. 'Outside! I need some help!'

I squint at the phone screen. 'Outside where?'

I peek through my curtains uncertainly.

'Outside Richmond Manor House!' the woman cries in fury. 'Outside the wedding venue! I need you to come out here and help me!'

I falter as a rush of heat storms up my neck.

'I can't,' I say mindlessly.

'What?' the woman snaps. 'I need some help. I don't know where the birds are going!'

I slump on to the bed.

'They need to go round to the left side of the manor house,' I say wearily, 'away from the dogs.'

'Dogs!' the woman yells. 'Dogs? I didn't know there would be dogs! You never told me there would be dogs! These doves are one of a kind, I am not leaving them around dogs!'

I hold the receiver away from my ear as her voice trumpets down the phone.

'If you go to the left side of the manor house,' I say patiently, 'there is an area for the doves where they will be safe.'

'I am not taking the doves anywhere without being escorted!' the woman puffs indignantly. 'You have misled me, Georgia Miller. You did not inform me of this. Did you not fill in our safety questionnaire? Did you not read our terms and conditions? If you do not come and personally escort me, right now, then I will hold you responsible and I shall ensure that you personally—'

'Fine!' I shout down the phone, desperate to stop her from yacking on for another second. 'Fine! I'm coming. Stay bloody there.'

I end the call and pull it away from my hot ear. The wedding venue is a five-minute drive from my parents' house, and if everyone is sticking to schedule then the guests will be having their wedding breakfast. I can nip over, sort out this lunatic, and then drive back home without anyone ever knowing I was there.

I mean, I should just leave her to it, but she sounded like she might have a heart attack if I don't help, and I don't want a crazy lady's blood on my hands. I mean, what would her relatives be like?

I shove my Ugg boots back on over my leggings and wrap my Puffa coat around my body. I charge back down the stairs and stick my head round the living-room door.

'Tell Mum I'm borrowing her car,' I say. 'I'll be back in twenty.'

I speed down the country lane leading up to the manor house and try to smother the anxiety snowballing up and down my body. Jack and Bianca are in that house.

Anger bites at my skin as the car skids to a halt and I turn the ignition off.

Two people who took advantage of me, used me, and dumped me. I don't know which one of them I hate more.

'Georgia!'

I look up to see a mad-looking woman, yelling across the lawn to me. She has great tufts of white hair sprouting from her scalp and she is dressed head to toe in bright green gardening gear.

'Hello,' I say politely. 'Penny?'

Penny nods at me aggressively and I gesture her to follow me. As we get closer to the tent, I notice four crates with neat doves perched inside.

Wow. They are very white.

'Okay,' I say, 'they're just going round here.'

'Away from the dogs?'

'Away from the dogs,' I echo, fighting the urge to roll my eyes.

My feet crunch over the stiff grass as I escort Penny through the gardens. Bianca made me and Sally visit the venue every other week, to undertake various 'vital checks', which included measuring the speed of the grass growing and testing the brides-maid shoes on the gravel.

'Right,' I say briskly, as we reach the section mapped out for the doves, perfectly laid out and meticulously organised.

Sally must have done all of this.

'So,' I say, 'this is where the doves go, okay?'

Penny stares back at me. 'Here?'

'Yes.'

'And when do you want them to fly?'

Irritation scratches at my skin as I glare back at her.

'I don't know,' I say curtly.

'But you booked it.'

'Yes, but it isn't my wedding!' I shout, suddenly unable to control myself. 'Look at me!' I throw my arms out in exasperation, gesturing at my body. 'Do I look like a bride to you? I'm barely wearing underwear!'

Penny looks at me as if I have sprouted an extra head.

'Georgia?'

I turn on the spot and see Sally. She is dressed in a crisp suit and is clasping a clipboard, her fingers white.

'Ah!' I say, flailing my arm towards Sally. 'There you go, Penny. Sally will be able to advise you about the bloody pigeons. Doves. Whatever the hell they are.'

I stalk past them both and stomp back up the field, my feet sliding in the thick mud.

'Georgie? Is that you?'

My body stiffens in fury as I recognise the voice of Bianca. I turn around and notice her, walking down from the manor house, alone. She is wearing an extravagant gown that hugs her body and spills into a deep train. She looks beautiful.

'What are you doing here?' she says accusingly. 'You were no longer invited.'

I stare back at her, dumbstruck. When, suddenly, an overpowering burst of anger fires up inside of me and overtakes the fear.

'What am I doing here?' I repeat, my voice thick with fury. 'I'm here because your wedding needed help. Even after everything you put me through, I still came here to help you, because I am a good person. And not only that, I am a damn good member of staff. And do you know what else? I am a great designer. All right? I know you don't believe that I didn't put my designs up, but you can't deny that I am bloody good. So don't worry—' I shoot her a look of disgust as I charge past her. 'I'm not staying.'

I storm down the field as my ears pound and anger throbs

through my veins. I pick up my pace as I hear the voice I least wanted to hear, chasing me down the field.

'Georgie!'

As quickly as I can, I race towards my car. But I am no match for him in my slippery Ugg boots, and he gets there first. I almost flinch when I meet his eyes. He looks thunderous.

'Why are you yelling at my sister on her wedding day?' he cries, blocking me from getting into my car. 'What's the matter with you?'

I push past him towards my car. 'Move,' I snap. 'Get out of my way.'

'No!' Jack yells, grabbing on to my hands. 'What's wrong with you?'

My eyes snap up to his face and I wrench my arms away from him. Anger ripples up my body and thunders around my chest. As I look into his eyes, my heart begins to throb in pain.

'You're married!' I scream, staggering backwards. To my alarm the tears pricking at my eyes spill over, and I wipe them away furiously. 'I know you're married!'

Jack stares back at me, his face helpless.

'Bianca told me,' I spit. 'I know about Lulu. You're fucking married, Jack. All you've done from the start is lie to me. Now get out of my way.'

I try and reach past him to open my car door but Jack grabs my arm and spins me back round. I whip my arm away furiously.

'I'm not married,' he says quietly.

'Don't lie to me!' I bellow, throwing my arms in the air. 'Bianca told me! To Lulu! You're married to Lulu!'

'No,' Jack's sharp voice cuts across me. 'You're wrong. Me and Lulu were married. We separated, about six months ago.' His eyes latch on to mine. 'We didn't want to tell Bianca. Lulu is Bianca's best friend, so we didn't want to ruin her wedding. I'm not married, Georgie,' he says earnestly. 'I'm not.'

I stare back at him. The wind speeds through my hair and, for a moment, we just stare at each other.

'You're not married?' I manage.

Jack's eyes bore into mine. 'No.'

The anger in my body is replaced with a ball of emotion than ricochets up my body and strains at the back of my eyes. I attempt to blink the tears away.

'I believed you were,' I say, the words falling out of my mouth.

Jack takes my arm. 'I'm not.'

'That's not the point.' I push him away. 'I believed you were married,' I manage. 'I believed you were. I believed you could be that guy. I don't—' I take a deep breath in an attempt at controlling my quivering voice. 'I don't know anything about you.' I look into his eyes, my vision blurred by a mist of thick tears. 'I can't see you any more.'

Jack takes a step closer towards me. 'Georgie,' he says, 'come on.'

'Right from the start,' I cry, quickly losing the power of control over my thoughts, 'I haven't known anything about you, and you know so much about me. You read my diary!' I yell, throwing my arms into the air.

'I didn't,' Jack says firmly.

'You opened it!' I lash back. 'You read my list!'

'You're upset,' he says. 'I understand, but—'

'No!' I yell, unable to control the anger firing up inside me. 'You don't understand! You're married, Jack! And Bianca fired me for something I didn't do! Amy is sick, and there is nothing

I can do to help her. You don't understand anything. You never have.'

Jack stares back at me, winded.

'Bianca . . .' he manages. 'Bianca fired you? Why?'

I run my furious eyes up his body.

'She saw my designs,' I say tightly. 'Someone put them in the pitch room. She thought I was trying to screw her over.'

Jack's face crumples and he runs his fingers through his hair.

'I'm so sorry,' he says weakly. 'I wanted Bianca to see what you had done. I meant to tell her, but I got called out and I . . .'

He trails off and I stare back at him, my heart pounding.

He did it? He put my designs there? He set me up?

Jack opens his mouth to speak, but no words come out. I stare back at him, my chest aching under the pressure.

'Georgie,' he manages, 'I am so sorry. I'll make it right. I'll—'

'It doesn't matter,' I cut across him coldly. 'I have to go,' I say, turning towards my car. 'Enjoy the wedding.'

Chapter Twenty-Six

'And take a deep breath in. In through the nose, out through the mouth.'

I inhale deeply, the moist scent of clammy women filling my nostrils and swirling down the back of my throat.

Urgh. Why aren't there any windows?

'In through the nose, out through the mouth.'

After four days of constant planning and late nights with Amy, this morning I thought I'd allow myself the treat of a lie-in, and had planned to sleep until 10.30. The dream.

Sadly, I didn't account for Mum having a day off today, and she burst into my room at 8.30 a.m., horrified at the idea of me lying in bed all day and 'wasting my life'.

Shortly after, she tipped me out of bed and dragged me along to her yoga class, insisting that all I need to do is clear my mind and then I will feel better. So now, I am propped in the back row of a sweaty sports hall, using all of my core strength to breathe when the instructor says so, which is bloody hard. I feel like I'm going to pass out. Surely she is doing it wrong. No one can be expected to breathe like this.

The run is now less than two weeks away. I don't have time to squat in a hall and puff out air like a deflating balloon. I should be running. I did try and explain this to Mum, but she shooed me into the car before I had the chance to hide under the bed, and here I am.

'And now,' the instructor coos, 'I want you to bend your body forward, into the smiling lion.'

One of my eyes pings open.

The smiling lion?

My open eye darts around the room as all of the women angle their bodies accordingly, as if she just said something completely normal. Begrudgingly, I copy.

Is this my life now? Spending my days at odd yoga classes with my mum and learning how to breathe properly?

I guess it will be. Now that I have to move back home I'll never be able to escape Mum and her endless invitations for me to do things I never want to do, ever. Like flower arranging or joining the village committee as the 'social secretary'. When I asked what being the social secretary would involve, Mum started talking about their 'annual knit off' and, before I could register what was going on, she had begun a knitting lesson.

I hate the idea of moving back home. It's not like I didn't enjoy living at home. But I had finally moved out. I'd got a job on my own, found my own place, and moved on with my life. I finally felt like I was moving forward.

Amy has tried asking me what I am going to do now, but I can't answer. Designing is all I want to do, it's the only thing I've ever known how to do. I was so excited when I was offered the job at Lemons.

This thought cues a small pang in the pit of my stomach.

I shake my head quickly. Don't think about that. Think about something else.

I take a deep breath.

I can't believe I have been fired. How am I ever going to get employed with that on my CV? Well, I won't, I suppose. Maybe I'll just have to become a blogger and pray someone finds me interesting enough to pay me thousands of pounds to rank the best Chinese takeaways in south London.

I flinch slightly as I feel a gust of air waft past me.

What's that?

I peel open my eyes surreptitiously, and to my alarm, spot Mum, shuffling over whilst in full smiling lion pose.

I gawp at her. What the hell is she doing?

I glance up at the instructor, who hasn't noticed, and scrunch my eyes back shut, when I suddenly feel Mum inching up next to me.

Oh no. What is she doing?

'Darling,' she whispers, her voice close to my ear, 'are you okay?'

I keep my eyes tightly shut. 'Yes.'

'Okay,' the instructor says gently, 'now we can move into the singing duck.'

What? The singing duck?

She's making this up! That is not a yoga position!

I feel Mum next to me, moving her body into the pose, and reluctantly open my eyes to copy. I jump when I see that Mum is staring straight at me. I snap my eyes shut and move my body to copy the other women.

'Well,' Mum whispers again, 'I want you to know that I am here for you.'

'I know,' I say.

'Breathe in through the nose,' the instructor repeats, 'and out through the mouth.'

I suck in a deep lungful of air and feel it inflate my stomach and uncoil my taut muscles.

In through the nose, out through the mouth.

In through the nose, out through the mouth.

In through the nose, out through the—

'Because it will all work out in the end.'

I jump as Mum sidles up closer to my ear.

Why does she keep trying to talk to me? You can't talk during yoga!

'I know,' I say, my mouth not moving, willing her to go away.

'And you'll find another job,' Mum continues, 'I know you will.'

'Mhmm.'

'And another boyfriend,' she says pointedly, 'much better than that nasty married chap.'

My eyes fly open and I snap my head round to glare at Mum. To my horror, the three women in front have done the same.

Oh my God, they heard! They're going to think I'm some form of harlot! Mum has just confessed to a room filled with strangers that I was dating a married man. This will be on the town's Facebook group within minutes.

'Have you spoken to him?' she says in a loud whisper.

'No,' I snap. 'Please stop asking me about it.'

I hear Mum puff indignantly and I clamp my eyes shut, irritation dancing up and down my body.

This is why she was so desperate to get me here. She wanted to interrogate me. How does she even know about Jack? I've made a point of never telling her about any boyfriends after she found out I was dating Jimmy Davids in Year 11 and tried to arrange a coffee morning with his mum to talk about 'the importance of safe sex'. I only found out because I discovered the leaflet she was intending to give Jimmy's mum, poking out of the corner of her handbag. I burned it immediately.

'Well, good,' Mum says in a tight whisper. 'You'll meet Mr Right.'

I shoot her a look, but Mum's eyes are now shut.

Oh God. She's about to start her pep talk. She usually saves this for Christmas Day.

'He's out there somewhere,' she whispers knowingly, 'so don't you worry.'

'I'm not worried,' I assure her, desperate for this conversation to end.

'No talking, please!' the instructor coos from the front. 'Now into the perching koala.'

Really?

This woman is a bloody fraud. She's making it up as she goes along. I should know, I do it all the time.

'Well,' Mum starts again, 'I'm not worried.'

'Good.'

'If you're not worried, then I'm not worried.'

She's just saying words now. She's not even making any sense.

'Good.'

'But if you do ever need to talk about anything, you know I am here.'

'Yes.'

'Anything at all.'

'Yes.'

'Anything.'

'Yes!' I snap back, shooting daggers at the side of Mum's face.

The three women in front angle their heads around and shoot us a disapproving glare. I shrivel back down into my perching koala and make an apologetic face. Mum hasn't even noticed.

Right, that's it. I'm revisiting the idea of living on the tube. Anything is better than this, even the Bakerloo Line.

★

I lean back into the sofa as Tinder spins on my screen and my finger launches into action.

Nope. Nope. No way. Nope. No. Nope. Never.

Amy looks up, sat next to the sofa in her wheelchair. Her arm is finally free of the sling. She hasn't been back to work since her fall.

'What are you doing?' she asks.

'Tinder,' I reply groggily, my face slumped into my hands.

Amy peers over my shoulder. 'Have you heard any more from Jack?'

I shake my head, my eyes still glued to the phone. 'I blocked his number,' I say, my throat swelling at the mention of his name. 'I didn't want him trying to contact me.'

Amy leans away from me and picks up her mug of steaming coffee.

'Would you definitely not forgive him?' she asks gently.

'He's married, Amy.'

'Yes,' she says, 'but not really. You said they'd been separated for half a year.'

I look up from my phone.

'Yes,' I say irritably, 'but that's not the point. He lied to me. He's still married. He never should have asked me out if he was married. That's just something you should never do.'

Amy cocks her head and holds her mug up to her lips. 'I guess.'

I blocked Jack's number as soon as I got back from the wedding. I blocked Jack's, and then I blocked Bianca's. I never want either of them to find a way to reach me. After what they did to me, I never want to hear from them again.

'I just want to forget this entire year,' I say glumly, fixing my eyes back on the men flying off my screen. 'It's been horrible.'

'Yeah,' Amy laughs, 'well, it hasn't been great for me either, George.'

I look up at her.

'I didn't—' I say feebly. 'Sorry. I didn't mean—'

'Georgia?'

I look up as Dad walks into the living room. 'There is someone here for you.'

I sit up quickly and run my fingers through my hair.

What?

Someone here for me? I'm not expecting anyone! I'm barely dressed! I haven't even brushed my teeth!

Dad steps back and I look up anxiously, when I see Natalie. She is carrying a battered cardboard box and has a small smile etched upon her round face.

'Natalie!' I cry, springing to my feet. 'Hey!'

I stumble over and wrap my arms around her neck. She squeezes me back as best as she can, her arms full.

'Hi!' Natalie smiles at me. 'Hey, Amy.'

Amy raises her free hand. 'Hey, Natalie. How are you?'

I quickly push aside the magazines stacked on the sofa and make room for Natalie to sit. She sinks down into the space next to me and places the box down in front of her.

'Would you like a tea, girls?' Dad pops his head round the corner.

'Yes, please,' I say.

Natalie nods and Amy shakes her head.

'I've still got a coffee,' says Amy, 'so just the two.'

Dad leaves and I look back at Natalie, suddenly feeling a wave of hot emotion creeping up the back of my throat. I haven't seen Natalie since my last day at work.

'I had some leave to take,' Natalie says, 'so I thought I'd come and check up on you. Sally mentioned that she thought you'd gone back to stay with your family for a bit.'

I look back at her.

'Yeah,' I say, 'Amy came and rescued me. After, you know. Everything.'

Natalie folds one leg underneath her on the sofa.

'What?' she says. 'What do you mean? Nobody really knows what happened. One minute you were there, and then suddenly you'd gone. Sally said you left crying, and some people thought you'd been fired.'

I blink at her, my heart thudding.

'Here you are . . .' Dad bustles in, carrying two mugs.

I take mine gratefully and cradle it between my hands.

'Bianca fired me,' I say, looking down at my steaming mug of tea. 'Jack put my designs in the pitch meeting and she lost it . . . and she also told me that Jack's married.' I look up, my face burning in humiliation at having to relive it.

Olivia Beirne

Natalie's face barely moves.

'Does Bianca know about you and Jack?' she asks.

I shrug. 'I don't know,' I say, 'and I don't care. That company was horrible anyway – you are the only person there who cared about me. I'm glad to have gone.'

Natalie's eyebrows creep up her face.

'I wouldn't be so sure,' she says quietly. 'I've brought your things from the office.' She gestures down to the box. 'Look at this.'

Natalie digs around and pulls out the sign-up sheet that had been pinned on the office wall. My eyes widen as I see that it is covered in black and blue biro. All donation signatures. I gape at it, and I feel Amy's hand rest upon my shoulder.

'They're all coming to the event,' Natalie says, leaning over so she can read the list of names and amounts herself, 'and they've all pledged this much online too. Sally made sure of it.'

My eyes flick up. 'Sally?'

Natalie nods, pushing her glasses back up her nose. 'Oh yeah,' she says, 'she's been rallying the troops like we're going into battle. She keeps trying to make me run but I said I'd stick to making a donation.'

'I can't believe people have been so generous,' I breathe.

'Well,' Natalie shrugs playfully, 'I think you had more of an impact on people than you realise.'

★

I stretch a large piece of paper out on the kitchen table and look up at Amy and Tamal, sat on the opposite side. I pull out a Sharpie pen and snap off the lid with my teeth.

Amy winces. 'I hate it when you do that.'

272

'I know.'

'You'll crack your teeth one day.'

I look down at the paper and begin to scribble.

'So,' I say, 'the run is starting at the school. The runners will need to arrive and register—'

'Where Mum and her gardening club will give them their numbers and badges,' Amy interjects.

'Right,' I say, glancing up at Amy, 'then we will all get together and do a group warm-up.'

'Led by Laura,' says Amy, 'my old Zumba instructor.'

'Then for the run,' I say, looking back down at my paper. 'We're running through the school field, on to the common, round the parade of shops, and then back again.'

Tamal frowns. 'Is that 10k?' he asks.

Me and Amy nod in unison.

'We checked,' says Amy.

'While people are running,' I continue, 'Hamish will be in charge of the bake sale, and Marianna will be selling hot drinks. She runs our local coffee shop,' I add for Tamal's benefit, seeing him shoot Amy a confused look.

'So,' Tamal says, 'how many people do you think we'll have at this event?'

I move my hand towards my laptop and refresh the fund-raising page.

We've raised almost £20,000.

'I think about forty,' I say. 'We've had thirty runners sign up.'

Tamal gapes at me. 'Didn't they all have to raise one hundred pounds each?'

I nod sheepishly. Thanks to all the work donations, I've raced past my own target. I've raised almost £1,000.

'Wow,' Tamal says.

'Well,' I say, grinning, 'you've got eight people from your work running, Tamal.'

He cocks his head and smiles. 'That's true.'

'Georgia!'

I jump at the sound of Mum's pinched voice. All three of us whip our heads around as Mum scurries in, her scarf flapping behind her and her face pink and excited.

'Hi, Mum,' I say cautiously. 'Are you okay?'

Mum pulls up the spare seat and drops into it. 'I have got great news!' she cries.

I blink back at her. Mum's idea of great news can vary from Alexandra Burke being in the *Strictly* final to Laura Ashley having a surprise sale.

She leans forward and wraps her hands around mine.

'Now,' she says, 'do you remember Pamela?'

I look back at her blankly. I really hope she isn't about to try and set me up with someone. That would not be welcome.

'You know!' she cries, slapping my knee. 'Pamela. She's married to Duncan, who teaches cricket at the boys' school, at St Margaret's.'

I blink back at her.

'I know who you mean,' Amy chips in. 'What's happened to Pamela?'

Mum looks at Amy gratefully and turns back to me.

'Well,' Mum continues, 'Pamela's husband Duncan plays golf with Nigel Dunst, who works at Mix FM. You know,' she looks at Tamal, 'the radio station?'

I nod, completely baffled as to where she is going with this.

'Anyway,' Mum presses on, 'I was telling Pamela about all the great work you've been doing,' she squeezes my hands, 'for Amy, and all the charity work, and she just thought it was a wonderful idea.'

I nod, my cheeks reddening.

'And she spoke to Duncan, who spoke to Nigel, and you're in!'

Mum throws her arms up into the air excitedly and I blink back at her.

What?

'I'm in?' I repeat in bewilderment.

I'm in what? Their golf game?

Mum turns back to me. 'They want you to come in,' she says, 'and talk about the run on the radio! They thought it was marvellous and they love talking about the local community.'

My stomach plummets.

They want me to . . . what?

'They want me to talk on the radio?' I manage.

Amy squeals.

I can't do that! I can barely talk to strangers.

'Yes!' Mum cries. 'Isn't is great? They've slotted you in for Wednesday morning. The breakfast show – Pamela says it's the best time.'

Amy claps her hands together. 'Georgie, this is so exciting!' she says. 'You're going to be famous!'

I puff at her, and Tamal grins.

'But,' I gape back at them both, 'what will I talk about? I can't do this. I don't have anything to say.'

Amy grins at me, her eyes glittering.

'You just need to talk about all the amazing things you've been doing.'

Chapter Twenty-Seven

1 WEEK UNTIL RUN

Running schedule:

04/08	1k	✓	(August is not the time to start running. Sweat patches are uncontrollable)
10/09	2k	✓	(Actually isn't that far at all. Who knew?)
05/10	3k	✓	(Am doing v. well. Kudos to me. I am superior to all. Bow to me, Usain)
19/10	4k	✓	(Finishes right by Burger King! Coincidence?!?!)
13/11	5k	✓	(Christ)
16/11	6k	✓	(Life flashed before eyes. Can't go on much longer. Go on without me, Mo.)
23/11	7k	✓	(How does anyone do this for pleasure?)

'Are you sure about this?'

'Yes.'

'Because I'm not, okay? I'm really not sure. If anything, I am unsure. I am very unsure.'

I blink, looking around desperately. Oh God, what am I doing here?

Natalie throws me a look out of the corner of her eye. 'Stop gabbling,' she says, 'just play it cool. It will be fun.'

I shoot her a look, doubt itching at the back of my brain.

Fun? How is this anyone's idea of fun? I can't believe this is Natalie's idea of fun, but she hijacked me last week and forced me to attend, claiming that she knew 'I wouldn't have anything else planned'. Which I found slightly insulting.

'Hi.'

Why is there a deck chair in the corner? What is that doing there? It's almost Christmas, for goodness' sake.

I nod weakly at the girl sitting at the reception desk in front of us, a loose smile fixed in place. Her arms are decorated with a smattering of ink that snakes up her pointed elbows and under the arms of her bright, tight T-shirt. Her purple hair is wound into three buns that sit on her head like door-knobs, and her beady eyes are rimmed with a thick layer of kohl.

Natalie steps forward, flicking her long hair over her shoulder.

'Hi,' she says coolly, 'I'm Natalie and this is Georgie. We're here for the speed dating.'

Hearing the words spoken aloud make me want to protest loudly in denial and hide under the table.

Urgh. Here for the speed dating. What have I become?

I blink at the girl and try to force my taut, disapproving face to slacken. She flicks open a notepad, pops off the lid of a gold Sharpie and writes our names on two large stickers.

I glare at the stickers in horror as she peels them off and hands them to us.

A name badge? We have to wear name badges?

I take mine limply and let it hang off my index finger.

Great. Where am I going to put it? I can't put it anywhere near my boobs (obviously), but then, where else? My stomach? People might think I'm crazy and that Georgie is the name of my unborn child. Or I could stick it on my forehead as a joke, which nobody will find funny, and I'll have to constantly justify it all night until nobody wants to talk to me.

Although, that might be a good thing.

'Right,' the girl instructs us, 'so we're going to start in five. The boys sit and the girls move round, so just choose where you want to start. There will be a bell once your six minutes are up, and then you will have to move on. You will need to fill out these—' she hands us two cards, and Natalie takes them. 'To say who you liked. Okay?'

Natalie nods as she links her arm in mine and steers me into the hall. I clomp alongside her like a reluctant horse.

After much thought and (vastly unhelpful) input from Amy, I decided to wear jeans, heeled boots and my low-cut Christmas top that makes my boobs look about two sizes bigger than they actually are.

Har har. Merry Christmas.

I smear my name badge on to my chest, just below my right collarbone. Even with my super bra on, my breasts are obviously nowhere near my collarbone. So I should be fine.

My eyes scan the room manically, and I try to take everyone in.

Bearded man, bearded man, humungous man, twelve-year-old.

My grip on Natalie's arm tightens.

'I still don't feel right about this,' I mutter into her ear.

Natalie said that I needed to 'get out there'; she's convinced I'm heartbroken over Jack. Which, you know, I'm not. I mean, yes, I'm still furious at him and never want to see his face again. And yes, I'm mortified that he was married the whole time we were together. But heartbroken? As if. No, sir. No way. Absolutely—

My chest lurches as my eyes land on a man with dark stubble, curly hair, green eyes and . . .

A nose ring. Jack would never have a nose ring. He once told me that he's never understood facial piercings, which led to an hour-long discussion on what people with nose rings do when they sneeze.

Stop that. No more thinking about Jack. He's gone. He was married, and now he's gone.

My eyes continue to sweep over the room and I feel my body relax as Natalie scoops up two glasses of wine from the bar.

Maybe tonight will be really fun. Maybe I'll actually meet the love of my life and we'll end up having a six-minute wedding as a big joke and everybody will call us charming and original. But no deck chairs. I still don't understand who puts deck chairs in a bar.

'Okay!' the girl from reception calls, as she saunters into the bar, hips first. 'So we're going to start. Ladies, choose your starting man.'

Olivia Beirne

My body shrivels in embarrassment.

Choose your man? I need to be much more drunk to handle this.

I take a generous gulp of wine and look around as the men drop into chairs dotted around the room. Natalie walks forward and I scurry after her, until we are face-to-face with two men. I look at the guy sat in the chair and my stomach twinges.

He has minimal hair on his head and an enormous beard sprouting from his chin. He looks like an upside-down parsnip.

'I was sat there!'

I jump as a girl with large earrings claps over and barges me out of the way.

'Sorry,' I mumble, staggering backwards.

I glance down at Natalie, who has already sunk into her chair, and then turn to face the room. Pretty much all the chairs are now filled with excited girls, all sat upright and ready to go.

Oh, great. Have I not got a chair? What am I supposed to do? Stand in the middle and boycott people's dates? Or cheer everyone on from afar whilst shouting weird innuendos like Paddy McGuinness?

'There's a spare seat over there.' The woman holds out a non-committal arm, gesturing towards the corner of the room, and I shuffle forward as quickly as I can and slide into a grey chair. I look up at the man sat opposite me. He is slumped backwards into his seat and is chewing gum like a camel toying with spit. His dirty-blond hair is long and droops over his face in lank curtains and he is wearing a checked shirt that pulls open at the chest to reveal a stretch of manicured skin.

I watch as his eyes flick over my body randomly, lingering on my chest.

'Ready?' the girl calls. 'Your six minutes start . . . now!'

She dings a bell and I jump slightly, feeling as if I have been pushed into some sort of sumo wrestling ring.

'Hi,' I say quickly, desperate to speak before we're both drowned by an unbearable silence, 'I'm Georgia.'

'Hi,' he says back, 'I'm Rocko.'

I pause, stumped.

Rocko? Did he just say Rocko? His name is Rocko?

That's . . . that's a dog's name.

I feel my lips quiver and I will my expression to remain neutral. 'Hi.'

'Hi.'

Rocko remains draped over his chair like a castaway outfit from the night before. I remain uncomfortably upright, as if I am scared to sink into the back of the chair in case I need to escape.

'How are you?' I offer.

'Good,' Rocko says idly. 'So tired, man.'

I nod politely.

Did he just call me man?

'Oh, really?' I say, trying to keep my voice light.

'Yeah,' he looks over his shoulder and exhales deeply, 'I've literally come here straight from the gym.'

I feel my shoulders sag.

Oh, great. Here we go.

I take a sip of my wine. 'Oh, right,' I say.

'Yeah,' he continues, apparently unfazed by my bored expression, 'I try and go twice a day.'

'Mhmm.'

'I'm really into it. I've just finished my cardio, now I'm moving

281

back to the weights.' He flexes his arms under his shirt and a smug smirk crawls on to his face.

'Oh, cool,' I reply.

He hasn't even asked me how I am. He hasn't even finished the small talk.

'Do you do any fitness?' he asks, shooting me a look that suggests he thinks it doubtful.

I puff out my chest indignantly.

'Yes,' I say firmly, 'I'm actually training for a 10k next week.'

Rocko's eyebrows twitch. 'Really?'

'Yes!' I say. 'And I—'

'I ran a 10k yesterday,' Rocko interrupts. 'I run them almost every other day, when I'm not doing weights. It was a staple part of my cardio. Yeah,' he stretches his arms above his head, 'now that I've moved on to weights I don't have to run as much, but I reckon I will. Just to keep the fitness up.'

I stare back at him.

What on God's green earth is he talking about?

'Really?' I manage.

This is the longest six minutes of my life.

'Do you go to the gym?' he snaps his gum loudly.

Urgh, really? Is that the best question he can ask me?

'No,' I say shortly, craning my neck around to see how everyone else's dates are going.

That girl is laughing! That is so unfair. How did she manage to sit with a funny guy and I'm stuck with someone who has the personality of a wooden spoon?

I force my eyes back to Rocko and, to my amazement, realise he is still speaking.

'. . . the weights are the hardest part, for what I want, but the cardio and the HIT workouts I've done will give me a good leg-up. So I won't find it as hard. I'm thinking about personal training too, maybe running my own business. Or some modelling.'

I gawp back at him, failing to control my eyebrows, which are creeping into their sarcastic expression.

Oh God. Come on, six minutes. I can't listen to much more of this. What is he even talking about? All this has stemmed from me asking how he bloody was.

'Right!' the girl shouts as the bell rings. 'Okay, lovebirds. Next date.'

Without looking at Rocko, I jump to my feet and race over to the guy next to him. I quickly pull out my piece of paper and write in large letters:

Rocko: NO.

'Hi there.'

I look up and focus on the guy sat opposite me. He has olive skin, salt-and-pepper hair and a neat beard. His bright eyes are framed with square glasses, and he is wearing a colourful Christmas jumper.

Okay, well, I don't think this guy goes to the gym.

'Ready,' the girl calls, 'and, GO!'

'Hi,' I say back, 'I'm Georgia.'

'Hi there, Georgia,' he says pleasantly. 'I'm Lewis.'

I feel my body relax slightly. Okay, I managed the first six minutes, I can survive this one. This guy seems quite sane – if nothing else, we will just have a pleasant conversation.

'Nice to meet you,' I smile. 'What do you do?'

'I'm actually a student,' Lewis replies, in a posh drawl that oozes out of his mouth as if it has been soaked in cream. 'I'm studying for a PhD.'

'Oh, wow,' I say, genuinely impressed, 'that's amazing.'

Lewis cocks his head to the side and lets out two long, horsey laughs.

'Har, har. Yes, I suppose it is.'

I blink back at him.

Oh no. Is he weird? He's weird, isn't he?

'So,' I say eventually, 'where are you studying?'

'Cambridge,' he slurs.

'Wow,' I pick up my wine, 'impressive.'

I'm dangerously close to needing another drink. Why don't they offer table service? Maybe I'll write that on the score card as some constructive criticism.

Lewis smiles again. 'Yah,' he says, 'I'm actually studying on a scholarship.'

'Oh?' I say.

Come on, six minutes. Come on, six minutes. Hurry the bloody hell up, six minutes.

'Yah,' he drawls again.

I feel my body slump against the back of my chair. I take another glug of my wine.

'What did you get a scholarship for?' I force myself to ask.

He runs his hands through his hair, a wry smile creeping on to his face.

'Oh, for being gifted,' he says, as if it is the most obvious thing in the world. 'You know, in the arts, sciences, maths, humanities, music, literature . . .'

I gawp at him, aghast, as he slowly lists every subject ever created.

'Theology, philosophy, languages . . .'

What?

He must be lying. Surely he isn't a real person. A real person could not sit opposite a stranger and deem themselves remarkably gifted in every subject ever invented.

'Technology, sports, politics—'

'Right!' the girl shouts again. 'Time's up!'

I sag in relief. Oh, thank God for that.

I nod Lewis a quick goodbye and scuttle on to the third person. Come on, one of these dates has to be passable.

I drop into my third chair and almost fall out of my seat in fright at the man opposite, who is looking at me as if he hasn't eaten in four weeks and I am a delicious carve of roast beef. His mouth is hanging open slightly and a line of saliva is visible between his cracked lips. His veined, bulbous nose is purple in the centre of his otherwise waxy face, and his yellow eyes are wide and staring. I glance down at his hands in alarm and the first thing I notice are his hairy knuckles and fat fingers, followed by nails that are chipped and rotting.

Oh my God.

This is it. This is how I'm going to die. This is the guy who is going to kill me and hide me under his floorboards. For years I have mentally panicked about this moment and now I have to endure a six-minute date with him. I'm going to kill Natalie. If he doesn't kill me first, that is. Which he will. Obviously.

I feel myself deflate in my seat as my eyes dart around the room, avoiding eye contact with him at all costs.

Oh God, this is going to be terrible. This will be the worst six minutes of my life.

My gaze accidentally crosses with his and I feel a pang of guilt.

Am I being mean? Maybe it won't be terrible. Maybe it will

be okay, he might actually be really nice. After all, he can't help how creepy he looks, can he?

'Okay,' the girl shouts, 'ready? Go!'

Maybe this will be the best six minutes of the night. That will teach me for being so judgemental and disapproving. Maybe this is the life lesson I have been waiting for.

The man leans his crusty elbows on the table and cranes his neck forward.

Maybe this will be really fun and I'll leave with a new outlook on life.

I look at him, trying to listen intently as I wait for him to speak.

'So,' he drawls longingly, 'what's your favourite colour?'

Nope. I was right. He is going to kill me.

CHAPTER TWENTY-EIGHT

Running schedule:

04/08	1k	✓	(August is not the time to start running. Sweat patches are uncontrollable.)
10/09	2k	✓	(Actually isn't that far at all. Who knew?)
05/10	3k	✓	(Am doing v. well. Kudos to me. I am superior to all. Bow to me, Usain.)
19/10	4k	✓	(Finishes right by Burger King! Coincidence?!?!)
13/11	5k	✓	(Christ)
16/11	6k	✓	(Life flashed before eyes. Can't go on much longer. Go on without me, Mo.)
23/11	7k	✓	(How does anyone do this for pleasure?)
25/11	8k	✓	(Urghhhhhhhhh. Whyyyyy do I have to run, whyyyyyyy???)

I drill my fingers on the desk and cross my legs, and then immediately cross them back over the other way.

I don't know how to sit. How is one supposed to sit when waiting for a radio interview, when you have no idea what they are going to ask you?

I mean, I know what they're going to talk about: the run. Unless they're lying. Or they've got me confused with someone else and think I'm here for an interview on quantum physics.

I shake my head.

That won't happen. That can't possibly happen.

But what has Mum told them? I don't trust her judgement at the best of times. What if she's told them I am an experienced runner and they want to ask me for fitness advice?

This thought makes my eyes stray to the mini sausages poking out of the top of my handbag. I shove them back inside quickly and glance around.

Much like Amy's hospital appointments, the entire family have decided to troop along today. Thankfully, we were all directed to a green room upon arrival, and I stashed them inside and made a run for it. I don't want them anywhere near me when I have to speak live on the radio.

I run my fingers through my hair.

A 10k run. A 10k run for charity, raising money for research into Multiple Sclerosis, on Saturday. Right. I can remember that. That's what I have to say. Worst comes to worst, I'll just manically repeat that sentence until they're forced to play a song.

Mum has told everyone that I'm going to be on the radio. She even tried to send out a last-minute family newsletter. When we pointed out that she has never sent anything like that in the past, she retaliated by saying that she's never had anything worth writing in it. Which was a bit harsh.

I mean, hello? What about the time I won the gin drinking contest at university? That was a pretty big deal.

'Georgia Miller?'

I twitch in alarm as my eyes snap up and land on Lenny Hilroy, my Year 12 boyfriend.

'Lenny!' I yelp, leaping to my feet. 'Hi!'

His once bristly hair has grown out into a sweeping, blond quiff and his teeth have shuffled back to their original crooked position. The weight around his face has dropped down to his stomach, which strains against a woollen Christmas jumper, and his chin is masked by a matted beard that springs from his chin. I haven't seen him in about eight years.

'Hi,' he says back. 'How are you feeling?'

'Yeah, fine,' I say, slightly confused. 'Do you work here?' I add.

'Yeah!' Lenny nods. 'I program the shows. I work with Nigel. We're almost ready for you,' he adds, pulling his sleeve up to check his watch. 'Do you want to follow me?'

I jerk forward. 'Sure,' I mumble, my stomach churning with nerves. I follow Lenny down a dark corridor, dragging my feet as if they are made of lead.

I can't believe I am about to be interviewed on the radio when I can't even answer calls from unknown numbers.

'How is Amy?' Lenny asks, as we push through a set of double doors. 'I think it's amazing,' he adds, 'what you are all doing for charity.'

I feel my cheeks burn.

'She's okay,' I say. 'We're all focusing on the run.'

Lenny nods. 'It's this weekend, right?'

'Yeah,' I reply, 'on Saturday.'

Lenny stops walking and I glance around as we reach a glass studio, filled with computers and large equipment, with strings of gold and silver tinsel draped across the ceiling. Greg, the radio presenter, is leaning into his microphone and chatting merrily, and another woman is sat next to him, tapping away at her computer and smiling.

'Well, let's hope that we drum up some more support today,' he says, picking up a clipboard and scanning it quickly. 'It's a great cause.'

'Thank you,' I say, my heart swelling. 'I think so too.'

★

'One last time, Georgia,' Greg says into the microphone. 'Remind us of the details for Saturday.'

I smile and pull my body towards the microphone.

'The Miller Run,' I say slowly, 'this Saturday, the first of December. The run starts at 1 p.m. and we're going to have a raffle, and hot drinks and a cake sale, and lots of fun things to raise money for the MS Society.'

'Great cause,' Greg replies. 'You heard it here, folks. Hope to see lots of you down there on Saturday. Now, up next we're checking in with the news, but before then here is some James Blunt for you.'

Greg clicks a button, and my body sags in relief.

I did it. It's over. I take a deep breath and feel my nerves slowly evaporate.

I can't believe I just took part in a live radio interview.

'That was great,' Greg says, standing up. 'You're a natural.' He

290

holds his hand out for me to shake. 'Best of luck with the run on Saturday.'

'Thank you,' I say, getting to my feet, 'thank you so much.'

'Georgia!' I turn and see Lenny sticking his head around the studio door. 'Can we borrow you? We've got an idea.'

I shake Greg's hand and follow Lenny out of the studio and back into the blue corridor, my heart rate slowly returning to its normal speed. Lenny shuts the door behind me and leans against the wall.

'So,' he says, 'how did you find that?'

I smile and take a sip of my water, desperately trying to add some moisture to my dry mouth. 'Fine,' I say honestly, 'I actually really enjoyed it. Which I was not expecting.'

Lenny nods. 'You were great,' he says. 'We had a lot of social media activity while you were being interviewed. People wanting to get involved.'

'That's great!' I cry.

Lenny smiles. 'We were thinking,' he says, 'how about we come down and cover the run? We could push people to donate whilst the run is happening, create a buzz. What do you think?'

I stare at him, my eyes expanding to the size of dinner plates.

They want to cover the run?

'Really?' I breathe in amazement. 'Lenny, that would be amazing. Thank you so much.'

Lenny claps me on the shoulder and grins.

'You've got the community behind you on this,' he says. 'We'd love to get involved.'

★

I slide my foot into my trainer and pull the laces tight.

'You were so brilliant!' Mum chirps, dancing around me excitedly. 'We were all listening, weren't we?'

'Oh yes!' Dad says merrily. 'And so was everyone from the golf club.'

'And everyone from yoga!'

'And I think Uncle Jim recorded it.'

'We can play it at Christmas!'

I laugh, unable to fight the jolly atmosphere circulating around the room. The interview went well, really well. Everyone there was so enthusiastic and desperate to talk about the run. I've had loads of messages too – from people I used to go to school with, who must have been listening – all promising to come down on Saturday. Everyone wants to help Amy in some way. Everyone remembers her.

I look up at Amy, who is smiling at me from her wheelchair. Her face is lit up, and the creases that were once drawn around her eyes have vanished. Her cheeks are bright pink, and her whole face is glowing as if she has been dusted with sugar. I beam back at her. She looks like the old Amy. The positive Amy. The happy Amy. I lace up my other trainer and stand up.

'Oh,' Tamal says, quickly getting to his feet, 'before you run off, Georgie. We've got a surprise for you.'

Amy grins at Tamal as he sidles out of the living room. I wait, curiosity spinning through me.

A surprise?

'Oh!' Mum coos excitedly. 'Of course!'

I look back at Mum, when Tamal reappears in the doorway carrying an enormous brown box, which he dumps on the floor with a thud. I look down at it as Tamal and Amy grin at each other. Tamal bends down and sticks his arm into the box.

A surprise for me? What is it?

Is there a puppy in that box?

Tamal straightens up and holds out a white T-shirt that unfolds to reveal the words:

THE MILLER RUN
01.12.18.
RAISING MONEY
FOR THE MS SOCIETY

My stomach flips as I read the words over and over.

'Isn't it fun?' Mum cries. 'Amy and Tamal have had T-shirts made up!'

I walk forward and take the T-shirt. The words are entwined with my design, which runs behind the words and across the body of the shirt. My eyes sink into it as my heart swells with pride.

That's my design! My design is on a T-shirt!

'Do you like it?' Amy asks.

'I love it!' I cry, pulling my eyes reluctantly away from the T-shirt. 'It's amazing!'

Tamal sits back down and laughs.

'We've had about thirty made,' Amy says, holding her hand out to reach Tamal's. 'Do you think that will be enough?'

I put the T-shirt back in the box and smile.

'Yeah,' I say happily, 'I'm sure it will be.'

★

'Georgia, be careful.'

'I am being careful.'

'Mind the clutch!'

The car jolts forward and I snap my head round to glare at Amy.

'Amy,' I say tightly, 'I have been driving for eight years. You don't need to instruct me. I am a very good driver.'

Amy slumps back into her seat and rolls her eyes.

'Apart from the time you ran an old lady over.'

I scowl at her and turn the key in the ignition again.

I did not run an old lady over. I just didn't see her on the zebra crossing – and she had to, ever so slightly, jump out of the way and into a bush.

She was fine. My car was fine. Everyone was bloody fine.

The car springs back to life and we judder forward towards the school gates. For the first time in years, we woke up this morning to a layer of crisp snow coating the streets like royal icing. Everyone was excited and hopping around the garden like merry elves. I joined in for about four minutes until I slipped on a frozen snail and landed in the recycling bin.

Me, Amy and Tamal stayed up last night and plotted the route for the run, while Dad put together the signage. And now, in the tiny Fiat, me and Amy are wheeling around the school to map it all out.

'Right,' I say, as I wrench up the hand brake, 'this is the 1k mark.'

Amy nods and holds up a torch. She shines it out of the car window and I kick the door open with a thud. We had to wait for all the children to leave before we could begin, so it's now almost pitch black. The icy air rattles through me as I grab the first sign off Amy and ram it into the ground.

'Can you pass the hammer please?' I ask, steadying the sign with my bodyweight and holding one arm out towards the car. Amy pushes it towards me, her eyes glued to her phone screen. I grab the hammer roughly.

'Thank you,' I say stiffly, whacking the hammer on the sign. The sign breaks through the icy earth and I give it one final kick, before jumping back into the car.

'Right,' I say, slamming the door shut, 'now where?'

Amy doesn't answer and I glower at her.

'Amy?' I say sharply.

'What?'

'You're meant to be telling me where to go!' I say. 'Where next?'

Amy doesn't look up from her phone but flings her arm out in a vague gesture. 'Over there,' she says unhelpfully.

I ram the car forward, irritation niggling at me. Why is she being so difficult?

The car slowly grinds across the school field, sliding under the mushy snow. My hands grip the steering wheel and I narrow my eyes in an attempt to see into the darkness.

'Here?' I ask.

Amy ignores me, and I bite my tongue.

'Right!' I say crossly. 'Here it is, then. Can I have the sign, please?'

I twist my body round to face Amy, her eyes mindlessly running up and down her Facebook feed. She doesn't answer.

'Amy?' I snap.

'It's there!' she cries. 'It's under my foot. You can reach it.'

I glare at her, anger fizzing under my skin.

'Fine,' I say tightly, whipping the sign out from underneath her feet and kicking my way out of the car.

Two signs down, only seven more to bloody go.

I stab the second sign into the frozen earth and whack it into place with the hammer, the beam from Amy's torch light hanging limply in the air. Once the sign is firmly in, I jump back into the car.

'You know,' I mutter, jabbing the key back in the ignition, 'if you didn't want to come, you could have stayed at home.'

'Oh yeah,' Amy says scathingly. 'Like I always do.'

The car jolts forward again and we roll through the snow. My eyes flick over to Amy.

'What?'

Amy angles her body away from me and I turn my attention back to the field, now engulfed in a blanket of darkness. My car lights are swallowed by the night sky as the car crackles over the field, leaving an icy snail trail.

I glance down at the map and slow the car down.

'Okay,' I say, trying to sound more upbeat, 'here?'

I pull the hand brake up and look at Amy. Once again, she doesn't answer me.

'Here?' I press on, a wave of anger rising inside me.

'I don't know,' Amy says, 'I don't care.'

I glower at her, my ears ringing with frustration.

'What's the matter with you?' I cry. 'Why are you being so difficult?'

Amy lets out a dry laugh as she refreshes her phone.

'Oh yeah,' she says coldly, 'I'm always difficult. Sorry for being so difficult. You won't have to deal with me much longer.'

I stare back at her, dumbfounded.

'What?'

'It's almost over!' Amy cries, finally raising her eyes to meet mine. 'What am I going to do with myself? I can't work. I can't do anything!'

The last words fall out of her mouth, and she stares back down at her phone defensively.

I feel a thick ball of emotion swelling in the back of my throat.

'Come on,' I say weakly. 'We haven't got many left to do.'

CHAPTER TWENTY-NINE

Running schedule:

04/08	1k	✓	(August is not the time to start running. Sweat patches are uncontrollable.)
10/09	2k	✓	(Actually isn't that far at all. Who knew?)
05/10	3k	✓	(Am doing v. well. Kudos to me. I am superior to all. Bow to me, Usain.)
19/10	4k	✓	(Finishes right by Burger King! Coincidence?!?!)
13/11	5k	✓	(Christ)
16/11	6k	✓	(Life flashed before eyes. Can't go on much longer. Go on without me, Mo.)
23/11	7k	✓	(How does anyone do this for pleasure?)
25/11	8k	✓	(Urghhhhhhhhh. Whyyyyy do I have to run, whyyyyyyy???)
28/11	9k	✓	(Cause of death)

I take a deep breath in an attempt to dispel the anxiety snaking up my body as I look at my reflection in the mirror. I glance down at my new sports watch, strapped to my arm: 11.01.

It's today. The run has finally come. I shuffle my legs to try and kick-start my blood flow, which seems to have stopped somewhere around my heart. I'm wearing black sports leggings, two sports bras and – my favourite part of the outfit – the charity T-shirt.

I've been awake since five, which – obviously – is unheard of, for me. I couldn't sleep. I couldn't believe something I created was really going to happen.

Well, something me and Jack created.

'Hey.'

I look round as I see Amy enter the PE Office, which I have turned into my dressing room. She is also wearing her matching T-shirt, and her chestnut hair is spun down to her waist.

'Hey,' I say back. 'You okay?'

'Yeah,' Amy says quietly, as she moves closer to me.

I turn from the mirror and drop into a swivel chair, fighting the urge to spin round in it like a child. I'm glad I never had one of these at Lemons, I'd never have got anything done.

'So this is your office,' I say. 'Was this your desk?'

'Of course,' Amy says. 'Look.'

She points behind me and I swing the chair around and follow her gaze.

'Oh!' I cry, as I notice photos of Amy and Tamal together, and then a photo of me. 'You have a photo of me on your desk!' I say, touched. 'I had no idea.'

Amy smiles. 'Well, you know.'

'Is it because I'm so inspiring?' I say, flashing her a grin.

A small laugh falls out of Amy, which dies almost instantly. I look back at her. The usual spark in her eyes isn't there.

'Are you okay?' I ask, swivelling round to face her.

Amy tilts her head to the side. 'Yeah,' she says in a small voice. Her eyes drop, and she looks down at her lap.

I frown at her and reach out to take her hand. 'No you're not,' I say. 'What is it?' I squeeze her palm. 'Tell me.'

'Nothing.'

'Amy!' I say sternly. 'Tell me, what's wrong?'

Amy's body shakes as she exhales deeply and I feel a splash of wet on my hand as a tear falls from her eyes. She shakes her head quickly and dabs at her eyes with her other hand.

'I'm really proud of you,' she says. 'I'm so proud of you, Georgie.'

I look back at her, feeling my heart contract at her expression.

'Well,' I say lightly, 'you're not crying because you're proud, are you?'

A rush of tears drown Amy's smile and she shakes her head, then looks back down at our entwined hands.

'What is it?' I say again. 'Come on, Amy, tell me.'

'It's just,' she says, 'I just wish I could run too.' The tears are gathering around her swollen eyes. 'It's just hard for me, not to be a part of it.'

I look back at her, my eyes blurring..

'Amy,' I say gently, 'this whole thing is because of you. Everyone in the community wanted to help you. You inspired this event. You inspired me. This list changed me. You may not be able to run the 10k, but you can't say that you aren't a part of it. You are it.'

'Georgia?'

I look up from Amy to see Tamal standing in the door frame. He clocks Amy and rushes over.

'Hey,' he says, hooking his arm around her shoulder, 'what's going on?'

Amy wipes her eyes with the back of her hand quickly and shakes her head.

'Nothing,' she says quickly. 'I'm just being silly. Emotional.'

Tamal looks at her questioningly, and then back at me.

'Err . . .' he starts, 'Georgie?'

'Yeah?'

'Have you looked outside recently?'

My eyes snap up to meet his.

Oh God, what's happened? Tornado? Hurricane? Alien invasion?

No. Don't be silly, Georgia. We never get hurricanes in England.

I get to my feet quickly, push my way out of the office door and head towards the nearest window. My mouth falls open as my eyes scan the school playground, which is overflowing with people. Runners of all different ages, shapes and sizes are limbering up, jogging on the spot and stretching across the playground. There are pockets of families scattered about, chatting excitedly and taking photos. My eyes alight on some younger children, who I recognise as Amy's school running club, all bouncing up and down excitedly. I smile as I spot Larry and Nigel, setting up their radio booth, and Mum, perched in the mini marquee we bought, barely visible in her giant scarf, which is coiled up to her nose like a festive woollen snake.

There are so many people. How are there so many people?

I push through the doors and scurry over to Mum, my body

pounding with adrenaline as the cold air takes my breath away. Tamal and Amy follow.

'Mum!' I say as I reach her. 'Mum?'

Mum twists round to face me. Her cheeks are pinched and her nose is glowing in the cold.

'Darling!' she cries, leaping to her feet. 'Darling, look! Have you seen? We've run out of T-shirts! Tamal,' she leans over, 'do we have any more?'

Tamal shakes his head, laughing.

'What are all these people doing here?' I manage, as Dad appears and drapes his heavy arm around my shoulders.

'I've just been talking to that group over there!' he chortles. 'They're a running club from Sutton. And we've got some chaps over there who heard about it on the radio.'

'Have you seen my yoga class, Ian?' Mum asks quickly. 'Have you said hello?'

'They're all here for the run!' Tamal says, clapping me on the shoulder. 'Georgia, have you checked the money?'

'The money?' I echo mindlessly.

'How much money we've raised?' Tamal says. 'Georgie, we've raised a fortune!'

Mum squeals as a smorgasbord of runners stream up to the desk, all dressed in Lycra and grinning.

'Hello!' one of them says. 'Can we sign up, please? We've all donated to the page. We couldn't quite get one hundred each, but we've done it between us.'

I spin round to face the woman speaking. She looks about forty and has a wide smile, which is mirrored in the faces of the women running with her.

'That's amazing!' I gush. 'One hundred pounds is amazing!'

The woman blinks back at me, bemused, and turns to Mum, who hands out stickers with numbers on them.

'So, you're number eighty-one,' she says, adopting a professional voice, 'through to eighty . . . err,' she counts with her pen, 'nine. Okay?'

'Eighty-nine?' I spin round to face Dad. 'There are eighty-nine people here? There can't be eighty-nine people here!'

Dad surveys the sea of people and laughs. 'Oh no,' he says, 'there are eighty-nine runners here. There are far more people here, love.'

I step back from Dad, feeling as if all the air in my body has escaped through my ears.

'Now,' Dad says quickly, steering me back round, 'I've put a stage up over there, can you see? We used some bits from the school hall. It should be okay for Laura to do her warm-up.'

'Is she here?' Mum says, sticking her head up like a meerkat.

'She's just setting up, love,' says Dad.

I stare around and spot a small stage in the corner of the school playground, where Laura is setting up a music machine. She is dressed head to toe in fluorescent pink sports gear, and she has a large fur hat wrapped round her head.

'Hello, can I help?'

I jump at the sound of Amy's voice and realise she's slipped in next to Mum, behind the desk. I feel a pang of worry, when Tamal grabs my arm.

'Georgie,' he says quietly, 'listen, before the run starts. I need to talk to you.'

★

'Okay! Are we ready?'

I feel a balloon of excitement inflate inside me as I look around at the runners, all spread out across the playground, as Laura's high-pitched voice booms over the speakers.

'Let's get you all warm!' she calls. 'We're raising a lot of money today for the amazing MS Society, so please do keep donating! For those of you who aren't running, we have hot chocolate for sale, a raffle, and lots and lots of charity buckets.'

My face reddens as I hear Mum 'whoop' loudly from the corner, and a clatter of laughter spreads like dominoes through the audience.

'Come on!' Laura calls. 'Let's go!' She leans over and hits a button on the machine, and the music pumps out and fills the playground. I jump up and down on the spot to keep myself warm.

I don't know why I decided that December was the best month for a 10k. It's bloody freezing.

'Georgia?'

I see Sally stride towards me on her long, stick-like legs. My eyes widen at the sight of her. I know she always said that she was going to come, but I never thought she actually would.

'Sally!' I cry, and before I can stop myself I fling my arms around her. I feel Sally's rigid arms hang behind my back as I squeeze her.

Might as well make the most of it. This is probably the first and last time I will ever hug Sally.

'And let's do some star jumps!' Laura calls, as Sally moves next to me and we leap in unison.

'You came!' I cry. 'I can't believe you actually came.'

Sally frowns at me. 'I told you I was coming,' she says, her face still red under the shock of my hug, 'my whole running club is here.'

She gestures over her shoulder and I spot a large crowd of people all jumping on the spot. I smile, warmth spreading across my chest.

She actually did it. She brought all of these people.

'How are you?' I gush, as we move on to a different exercise.

'Fine,' Sally says immediately.

I smile with fondness at the familiarity of her fast response.

'Good,' I grin.

'It's not the same without you,' she says quickly, as if saying the words out loud causes her great discomfort. 'Everyone says so.'

I falter.

'Really?' I manage.

'They are all here,' she adds, pointing. 'Natalie invited everyone from work to come and support you.'

I look over and gasp as I spot Natalie, waving manically. I do a double-take as I spot the horsey face of the guy stood next to her, his arm draped over her shoulder.

Is that *Lewis*? Lewis from the speed dating?

Oh well. Each to their own, I guess.

I wave my arms back at her as I take in the sea of people behind her. Everyone from my office is here.

Well, almost everyone.

'Bianca and her family have left now,' Sally says tightly, 'for the honeymoon.'

I pull my eyes away from her. Bianca and Jonathan were going to the Maldives, with their entire family. Jack told me.

He's really gone, then.

'Okay!' Laura commands. 'Stretch it out!'

I lean on one leg, my ears pounding. I can't believe there are so many people here.

'Hey,' I say to Sally as my eyes focus on her body, 'you're wearing one of the T-shirts!'

Sally looks down at herself and then at me.

'Yes,' she says stiffly. 'You designed it.'

I blink back at her, failing to stifle my laughter.

'Yeah!' I say, swapping legs. 'Do you like it?' I can't help but add.

Sally swaps legs, her stretch considerably deeper than mine.

'Of course,' she says matter-of-factly, 'your designs are very good.'

I pull myself back up to standing and stare at her. Sally has never said I was good at anything.

'Okay!' says Laura. 'I think you're all ready now. Let's get running!'

She clicks a button and a loud claxon trumpets through the playground, and everyone jogs in unison towards the starting line. I see Mum waving excitedly and Larry chatting quickly into the microphone as the sea of joggers troop forward. Finally, my eyes stray towards Amy and she gives me a thumbs-up. I feel a swell of determination fire through my chest, diminishing any anxiety left inside me. I push myself forward to the front of the line and feel the icy air rattle in my lungs.

To my annoyance, I feel my spirits dip slightly as the idea of Jack coming today falls out my mind. I shake my head crossly and power forward.

This isn't for Jack.

It's for Amy.

★

I push my legs into the ground and they tremble beneath me.

I feel as if I have been running for one hundred hours.

Every part of me is ice-cold, apart from my chest, which burns every time I suck in another intake of breath. The only thing that has kept me going is Amy. I have to get to the finish line. I can't let her down.

The run began with all of the runners bobbing forward in unison, but the crowds quickly parted when the real running started. I gave up trying to run with Sally. There was no way I was going to willingly try and keep up with her again.

Upon reflection, it is simply unreasonable to expect me (a smaller than average sized person) to keep up with Sally (a taller than average sized person who I once caught eating a raw egg and couldn't see what the big deal was when I almost threw up in the sink).

Tamal and all of his friends from the hospital overtook me a while ago, and I don't recognise any of the runners near me.

I glance over my shoulder and lay my eyes on two women, chatting happily behind me.

How on earth are they speaking whilst running? It is taking all of my internal strength just to breathe.

'Miss?'

I jolt in alarm as a lanky, blonde girl springs up next to me, her arms pumping alongside her and her blonde hair flailing in the wind. I smile as I recognise her from the running club. My eyes flit down to her knobbly knees in alarm; she must be freezing.

'Miss Miller?' the girl says again.

Oh God. Does she want to talk to me? I don't think I can! I can't talk and run this race! But then I can't ignore a child, can I? That just feels morally wrong.

'Hi,' I manage. My brain fumbles madly.

Oh God. What is her name? What is this child's name? What the bloody hell is this child's—

'Molly?' I guess, as the name drops into my mind.

Thankfully, the girl smiles. Thank God. How on earth did I remember that?

'Nice to see you,' I add, looking fixedly ahead to indicate that I cannot possibly manage a single word more and that we must now run in silence for the sake of my health.

'I think we're nearly finished!' Molly chirps.

I nod solemnly.

We'd better be nearly finished. Please let us be nearly finished.

'Where is your boyfriend, miss?' Molly asks. 'Why aren't you running together?'

My heart jars.

'I don't have a boyfriend,' I say stoutly.

I see Molly's brow crease out of the corner of my eye.

'Oh,' she says, 'I thought he was your boyfriend. Mr Orange.'

'Lemon,' I correct her, before I can stop myself.

Molly continues to bound alongside me and I try to focus all my energy on the run as Jack's face seeps back into my mind.

Don't think about Jack. He's not here. He's left. He's not coming back, and that's a good thing. That's what you wanted.

'I liked him,' Molly quips.

How is this child not out of breath? How is she managing to speak so conversationally? Why is it that everyone seems to be able to manage talking and running, whereas for me I feel as if I can only do it if I'm prepared to sacrifice my own life?

'Did you not like him, miss?' she probes.

Why did Amy ever want to work with kids? She must be lying when she says that she misses them. I mean, this is unbearable.

'No,' I say tightly, 'I didn't.'

And neither should you, I want to add. But I don't. Don't open that can of worms.

'Oh,' Molly shrugs, 'that's a shame.'

I keep my attention focused ahead and I feel a surge of determination as I spot Dad and Amy, at the 9k sign.

'Right,' I say to Molly, feeling a new burst of energy spiralling up inside me, 'see you in a bit, Molly.'

I pat Molly on the arm and pound my feet into the ground, steering my way off the track towards Amy and Dad. Amy looks up at me in alarm.

'What are you doing?' she asks as I reach her. 'You're nearly finished, Georgie, you can't give up now.'

'I'm not,' I pant as I reach her.

Amy opens her mouth to speak, but before she gets the chance I run behind her wheelchair and push her forward. Amy almost falls out of the chair in shock and grabs on to the armrest.

'Georgia!' she screams, as I charge back on to the track, pushing Amy in front of me. 'Georgia! What the hell are you doing?'

'We're doing this together!' I scream back, as we rejoin the track.

The wheelchair rocks uncontrollably on the uneven path and I grip the handles determinedly with my icy fingers, a new fire of strength powering up inside me and filling every part of my body with a burst of scorching heat. My legs power into the ground as we storm forward together and Amy screams.

'Georgie!' she cries. 'Georgie! Stop! You can't do this!'

'You always say,' I shout back, 'there's no such thing as can't!'

I steer Amy round the bend and my eyes widen as I notice the finish line. We're almost there, we've almost done it. My body burns under the strain of our combined weight and my chest convulses under the pressure.

'We're a team,' I manage, using every ounce of energy left in me to force the words out, 'we do everything together, Amy. Everything I have done has been because of you.'

I keep my eyes focused on the finish line, thronged with people waving and cheering. We're almost there.

'We will work this next part out together,' I yell through the screams.

My legs hit the ground as we get closer to the crowd of people. My heart is racing and my chest is burning. I look down and notice that Amy has held up her hand; she twists it round and grips mine. I wrap my icy fingers around her gloved hand and power through as we are engulfed by the cheers of people and we burst through the finish line. My hearing is blocked by the wave of cheers that crash around us, and I grip Amy's chair as my legs crumple beneath me. Amy's hand tightens around mine and she turns her head to face me.

'Thank you,' she says quietly, her face wet, 'thank you.'

I squeeze her hand back and notice Tamal appear. His face is flushed, and I feel a wave of emotion at the sight of him. Amy follows my gaze and the grip on my hand loosens as she spots Tamal. He steps towards her, his eyes shining. Slowly, he sinks on to one knee.

I step backwards as Mum squeals uncontrollably and I hold

on to my parents. Amy's hands fly up to her face in shock. Tamal's mouth moves, but his words are inaudible over the cries from the runners. Amy's eyes are locked on to his as if they are the only people in the world. Eventually, she nods and Tamal dives forward and wraps his arms around her. Before I know it, Mum and Dad split apart from me and run towards Amy, wrapping their arms around them both.

'Georgie?'

I turn my head, suddenly realising my face is wet from tears that have seeped out of the corners of my stinging eyes. I wipe my eyes with the back of my hand, when my stomach drops.

'Hi, Georgie.'

It's Bianca.

She's dressed head to toe in black, with a large expensive hat propped on top of her head. Her hair tumbles down her back and her lips are painted a shade of dark red. Her sharp eyes are dusted with glitter and, for once, they are round with worry.

I blink back at her.

What is she doing here?

'Bianca,' I manage, 'hi.'

There is a silence as we both stare at each other, and slowly the heat of the adrenaline that has propelled me to the finish line vanishes and I feel the icy wind nipping at the back of my neck.

'I thought you'd left for your honeymoon,' I hear myself say.

Bianca's face doesn't move. 'We're leaving in an hour.'

'Oh.'

Bianca's eyes are flitting between my face and the school field, and she is opening and closing her mouth as if she's lost the ability to speak. Bianca is always so composed, I have never seen her like this.

'Congratulations,' she says eventually. 'The run seems to be a huge success.'

I hold up my chin as I feel a rush of pride flood over me.

'Thank you,' I say.

'I donated,' she adds quickly, 'via the page. Sally showed me the link.'

I nod, my body tensing with dislike.

Good old Sally.

'And,' Bianca continues, 'the branding looks very good. The design is superb.'

I stare back at her. To my annoyance I feel a wave of pleasure at her comments.

What does she want?

'Thank you,' I say again. I hear Amy laugh loudly and I turn my head. 'If you don't mind, I need to go. So I'll—'

'Georgie!' Bianca cries, stepping forward as I turn to leave. 'Georgie, wait.'

I turn to face her and feel the icy chill creeping down my back and gripping on to my clammy skin.

'I want to apologise to you,' she says, 'for the way I treated you. Jack explained to me what happened. Your designs are really good. I think the client would have liked them.'

I blink back at her.

She's apologising?

'I'm sorry I reacted the way I did,' she finishes.

I look back at her blankly. Her face is twitching and her eyes are wide circles, deeply shadowed with worry. To my surprise, I feel a pang of sympathy.

'Thank you,' I say, lost for words. I look back over my shoulder and catch Amy's eye; she beckons me over. I look back to Bianca. 'I really need to—'

'And,' Bianca interrupts quickly, 'and I want you to come back and work for me. If you'd like to.'

I stare back at her, stumped. My stomach flips.

She's offering me my job back? My old life?

I look into Bianca's face, and then pull my eyes back to Amy.

'Thank you,' I say. 'I really appreciate you coming here and apologising, but I can't come back.'

'Is it the pay?' Bianca blurts desperately. 'We can up your pay.'

I try to control my mouth dropping open in shock. She's offering me a pay rise?

'Sorry, Bianca,' I say, looking back over towards Amy, 'but there are some things that are more important than money. Thank you for coming— ' I reach forward and touch her arm. 'I really appreciate it. Make sure you enter the raffle!' I add, as I run back towards Amy and leave Bianca, standing alone, flummoxed.

I reach Amy and she flings her left hand in front of my face. I grab her hand and stare at the sparkling ring.

'Look!' she cries, her eyes streaming. 'Look!'

I throw my head back and laugh, my fingers curling around Amy's hand. My heart feels as if it could burst.

'I know,' I manage, 'I'm so happy.'

Amy squeezes my hand and cranes her head around me. 'Who was that you were speaking to?'

I look back over and see Bianca tapping at her phone.

'Bianca,' I say. 'She offered me my old job back.'

Amy gasps. 'Wow!' she cries. 'Georgie!'

'I said no,' I say quickly. 'I turned it down.'

Amy blinks at me, her face astounded.

'Well,' she says eventually, 'what are you going to do now?'

I shrug, feeling a wave of hysteria crash over me.

'I don't know!' I laugh. 'Whatever you want to do.'

'Georgia?'

I tear my eyes away from Amy as Mum bustles over with three women.

'Georgia,' Mum says again, 'this is Joanna from the MS Society. She'd like to speak with you.'

CHAPTER THIRTY

Georgie's List

1. Have a vindaloo on Brick Lane. ✓
2. Take a Salsa class. ✓
3. Do a skydive. ✓
4. Go on a Tinder date. ✓
5. Cycle around Hyde Park. ✓
6. Run 10k. ✓
7. Make the perfect Victoria sponge.
8. Go skinny-dipping in the sea. ✓
9. Try skateboarding at Southbank. ✓
10. Show Bianca your designs! ✓

I drop three sticks of butter into my mixing bowl with a thud.

Right. Butter measured correctly. Tick.

My eyes scan down the recipe, staring back up at me from Amy's iPad. I can do this. I will do this. My birthday is tomorrow, and I will not be defeated by a bloody cake of all things.

I mean, it's a cake! It has to be easy. Surely, that's where the expression 'piece of cake' comes from?

Hmmm. Why don't I ever use that expression? Maybe that's where I'm going wrong. They say, dress for the job you want. Maybe it's also, speak for the job you want? Maybe if I used the expression all the time then I would actually be a terrific baker.

Well, from now on I shall endeavour to slip that expression into any conversation I can. Perhaps I will do so tomorrow! Maybe this cake will be the making of me, and I am secretly an incredible baker. I shall buy a polka-dot apron and a Cath Kidston purse and a big chef's hat.

Although, Mary Berry doesn't wear a chef's hat, does she? I don't want to look silly.

Okay, forget the chef's hat.

Then tomorrow, I will lay my perfect cake on the table and everybody will gasp in amazement. They will turn to me in shock and cry, 'How did you do it?' and I will say, 'Oh this? It was a piece of cake!'

And then everybody will laugh and I will become such a baking sensation that it will be my catchphrase.

My eyes scan the recipe. Right, add the sugar.

I pick up the bag of sugar and tip the contents out experimentally.

The run was three days ago now, and we're just about getting back to normal. I can almost sit down without groaning like a pre-menstrual pig, so that's something. The event was bigger than I could ever have imagined. We raised over £30,000.

Just thinking about this causes my insides to squirm in delight. £30,000!

Everyone loved it too! A story was run in the local paper,

and people were donating online whilst listening to the radio. People started asking me if we were going to organise another run. I didn't know what to say.

Then, if that wasn't mad enough, me and Amy were approached by the head of the MS Society. She asked the same question. Then she asked how we'd feel about running their events. I tried to argue that I didn't know anything about organising events, but the people around me proved me wrong pretty quickly.

Cream together the butter and sugar until pale and fluffy.

I scowl at the recipe. Pale and fluffy sounds like an anaemic duckling, not a cake mixture. I push my spoon against the bowl obediently and feel a zing of satisfaction as the ingredients blend together.

I still don't know why Amy put this on the list. For starters, she can easily make a cake. I've seen her do it! Nothing about her MS restricts her from baking.

Right, I think that's enough 'creaming'. My eyes flit down to the recipe.

Beat in the eggs.

I pick up the eggs and crack them into the bowl; they gloop in and sink into the mixture as I pick up the whisk.

Amy and Tamal are out collecting the wedding rings. Finally, for the first time since Amy's diagnosis, she seems to be happy. In fact, I don't think I've ever seen her happier.

The whisk spins impressively and I watch as the ingredients ricochet against each other.

Fold in the flour.

I put the whisk down and look over at the large bag of flour, slumped over in the corner. I pick it up with both hands.

Natalie was devastated when I told her I wasn't going to come back to Lemons. I even think Sally was upset too. I really think that—

WOOMPH!

I jump as the bag of flour flops over into the bowl and a great white cloud puffs in front of my eyes. I blink madly as the flour clings on to my eyelashes and attempts to suck the moisture from my exposed eyeballs.

Argh! How the hell did that happen?

I drop the bag of flour crossly and wipe my face with the back of my hand, smearing flour into my hair. I tip the flour into the mixing bowl aggressively and flick the whisk back on.

Urgh. Stupid flour. It was all going so well! Why can't I cook a bloody cake? What the hell is wrong with me?

I chuck the mixture into the baking tray and shove it into the oven.

Stupid cake. Stupid Amy. Why can't I do it? Why can't I do anything?

I slump down on to the kitchen floor and hang my head in my hands, feeling a familiar emotion creep up inside me.

I am happy. I keep telling myself that: I am happy. The event was a huge success. We raised an enormous amount of money for an important cause. I was offered a job out of it, doing something that really matters. I am happy. I am.

My head lolls in my hands as the back of my throat burns.

I'm happy that Amy is happy. That is the most important thing. I am happy for her. I am happy that she is engaged, and that she has found love. But it also reminds me that I haven't, and I'm not even close.

I tried signing back up to Tinder and going through the

swipes, but it's just not the same. I connected with Jack, really connected with him. Or I thought I did.

I look up as I hear the thump of post hitting the doormat. I screw up my eyes and take a deep breath that rattles through my slumped body.

Come on now. You have plenty to be thankful for. The future is really exciting. You are going into the new year with Amy by your side, doing something really important. You should be happy. You are happy.

I pull myself to my feet and walk towards the post.

I am happy.

I turn back towards the kitchen. Obviously, I never get any post as I don't actually live here.

I stop as my eyes register a brown, square package on the top of the pile of post, addressed to me.

Why is it addressed to me?

I frown in curiosity as I lean my body against the hall radiator and pick up the package. Who is sending something to me?

As carefully as I can, I pull the paper off. A small diary lands in my lap. There is a note taped to the outside that reads OPEN ME, and my breathing quickens as I recognise the handwriting.

It's from Jack.

Before I have a chance to order my thoughts, my hands flip the diary open and I start reading his untidy words, scrawled across the page in black ink.

Jack Lemon's Diary

1. I'm scared of slugs. Terrified, in fact. I know it makes
    no sense.

2. I grew up in Brighton and moved to London when I was eighteen, with Bianca.

3. Our parents separated when we were kids, which made me and B very close.

4. My Tinder bio says: 'I'm 60% water, and who doesn't love a drink?' I thought it was hilarious. Most disagreed.

5. I set up my own marketing company. It went bust.

6. I love dogs and my dream is to have a husky called Hugo.

7. Me and Lulu separated because she cheated on me.

8. Bianca once wrote a letter to me from Dumbledore. Twelve-year-old me believed it was real.

9. I'm named after my great-uncle who was an artist.

10. Doing the list made me appreciate life again, and everything I had been missing.

11. Meeting you made me appreciate everything else.

12. I watch *Made in Chelsea* religiously.

13. I have been told by multiple people that I am tone deaf.

14. I used to skateboard a lot as a kid. I also had a side parting and a fringe that covered one eye.

15. I have accidentally killed seven goldfish in my lifetime and I feel terrible about it.

16. I cried the first time I watched *Love Actually*.

17. I think Easter is the most underrated holiday.

18. I have been thinking of nothing but you since the wedding.

19. I swallowed a safety pin when I was in Year 9 and have never seen it since.

20. I had a huge crush on my Year 10 maths teacher, Mrs Gunner. She was in her forties.
21. When you came up to me in The Hook, I had just had a three-hour argument with Lulu. She found out I'd left to go to London.
22. You are like no one I have ever met.
23. My whole life changed the moment I met you.

My eyes fill with hot tears as I flick through the pages. There must be over a hundred notes in here, all randomly scrawled in different colours. Some bigger than others, and some barely legible. I hold the diary in my hands as my mind swims with confusion and a dawning feeling of elation. He cares. He's written me a—

I jump as the door behind me rattles with great force when a hand raps on it.

Who is that?

I quickly blink my tears away and pull open the door. I almost drop the diary in shock as I see Jack standing in the doorway.

'Look,' he blurts angrily, 'I'm sorry but I can't just walk away. I need to talk to you. I need to—'

His words are lost as I drop the diary on the floor and throw my arms around him. Jack grabs my waist as my hands cling on to his face and I kiss him firmly. His light stubble brushes against my lips and he presses his body against mine and kisses me back. My insides explode with excitement as we grip on to each other as if we will never touch each other again. Finally, I let him go. The original anger on his face has gone, his eyes flit down to the diary and then back up at me.

Olivia Beirne

'Why are you here?' I manage. 'I thought you were away, with Bianca or . . .'

Jack smiles and shrugs. 'I had more important things to do.'

I stare back at him, my heart racing, when suddenly a sharp smell fills my nose.

What? What is . . .?

Oh my God.

'The cake!' I scream, letting go of Jack and launching myself in the direction of the kitchen. I tear along the hallway, as a pungent smell of burning wafts out of the kitchen.

Oh my God. Oh, bloody hell.

I wrench the oven door open and blink as I am blinded by a fog of thick smoke. I pull the cake out, which is blackened and shrivelled. I gawp at it in dismay.

'Oh,' I whine, 'look! I can't bloody make a cake! I don't know why, I just—'

My words disappear as Jack spins me round to face him and kisses me again.

Suddenly, the cake doesn't seem so important any more.

CHAPTER THIRTY-ONE

5TH DECEMBER: MY BIRTHDAY

'Wow, I can't believe you made that.'

'Well done, darling! It looks fantastic.'

My cheeks redden as everyone gathers round me and ogles the sponge, glistening impressively on a large cake stand.

'Thank you,' I say in a small voice.

Well, I can hardly say 'piece of cake' now, can I?

Okay, full disclosure: I bought the cake. I mean, what was I supposed to do? I fully believe that the cake I made yesterday would have been perfect and fully edible, if Jack hadn't got in the way.

My stomach flips as he flashes me a wink.

I mean, it was totally worth it. Obviously.

Although he'd better not give me away. He did promise he wouldn't.

I make the stupid decision to catch Amy's eye. She is raising her eyebrows at me knowingly. I look away quickly.

She totally knows. I mean, who am I kidding? This cake has seven different kinds of fruit on it. I didn't even realise seven different kinds of fruit existed.

'Well!' Mum says, springing to her feet. 'I am very impressed, darling. We will sing you Happy Birthday soon. Would anyone like a nice cup of tea?'

Everyone responds politely and Mum bustles back out of the living room, carrying the cake carefully.

'Okay,' Amy grins, 'where is the list, Georgie?'

I feel a swell of excitement as I pull it out of my bag and spread it out on the coffee table, for everyone to see. A wave of pride sweeps over me as my eyes scan the list.

'I still cannot believe you completed everything,' Dad says quietly, leaning over my shoulder to look down the list.

I beam at him, pride fluttering beneath my skin.

If you'd told me at the beginning of this year that I was going to complete all of these things, I would never have believed you. I hated doing anything outside my comfort zone, I even struggled with things that were inside my comfort zone. I never challenged myself or did anything out of the ordinary. I just existed.

Amy passes me a pen and I take it off her happily.

'There you are, champ,' Dad says, clapping me on the shoulder as he gets to his feet, 'you can tick the last thing off your list!'

He leaves the room and Amy shoots me a look.

'I know you didn't make that cake,' she says out of the corner of her mouth.

I lift my chin in the air.

'I don't know what you are talking about,' I say airily, avoiding eye contact at all costs.

Jack sinks into the sofa next to me and takes my hand, and I notice a look pass between Amy and Tamal.

'So, Jack,' Tamal says, readjusting himself in the armchair next to Amy, 'has Georgie told you how successful The Miller Run was?'

I feel my face flush, like it does every time someone brings this up.

'No,' Jack says, and I turn my head to look at him, 'but Bianca did.'

'Bianca?' I blurt, baffled.

Why was she talking about it?

'Yeah,' Jack says, 'she thought it was great. She said the whole branding was brilliant. Didn't she tell you that?'

'Well,' I mumble, 'yeah, but I didn't think she meant it.'

She said that to Jack?

Jack laughs. 'Of course she did!' he says. 'You know Bianca never says anything she doesn't mean.'

Well, I guess that's true.

'She also donated a shedload of money,' Jack adds, 'when you turned her job offer down. She said she wanted to do something for her karma, because of how badly she treated you.'

'Really?' I say quietly.

'Yeah,' Jack nods, 'she's like that. She never means to hurt anyone. Her heart is in the right place.'

I open my mouth to respond when all the lights click off and we are plunged into darkness while Mum juggles a box of matches and attempts to light the candles on the cake with Dad's help.

The tiny flames dance as my body shrivels in dread at the prospect of the dreaded song.

Urgh. If there is one thing I cannot bear (who am I kidding? There are many, many things I cannot bear) it is people singing Happy Birthday to me. I mean, for one, the song lasts about four years. Nobody can sing the high notes, and the whole thing is so dreadfully awkward.

I hear Mum take in a deep breath and I force an unnatural smile on to my face.

'Haaaaaaaaaaaaappy birthday to you,' she begins, and slowly everyone joins in.

I cringe inwardly, smiling awkwardly like I'm waiting for my prom photo to be taken.

'Happy birthday to Georgie!' Mum sings in her best soprano.

Oh. Someone has been watching *Songs of Praise*.

'Happy birthday to you!' The entire living room sings in unison, and I smile at them gratefully.

Amy grins at me. 'Make a wish, then!' she says, her face bright.

I look around the room and shut my eyes tight, the wish forming in my mind.

The only wish I have ever had.

The wish that has strayed over the past year and, at times, almost vanished entirely:

I wish that me and Amy can be happy for ever.

I blow out the candles and open my eyes.

Amy's eyes are shining brightly at me and my heart swells as I know that my wish, swirling around in the smoke from my birthday candles, is coming true.

The List That Changed My Life

Georgie's List

1. Have a vindaloo on Brick Lane. ✓
2. Take a Salsa class. ✓
3. Do a skydive. ✓
4. Go on a Tinder date. ✓
5. Cycle around Hyde Park. ✓
6. Run 10k. ✓
7. Make the perfect Victoria sponge. ✓
8. Go skinny-dipping in the sea. ✓
9. Try skateboarding at Southbank. ✓
10. Show Bianca your designs! ✓

ACKNOWLEDGEMENTS

I need to start by thanking my super agent, Sarah Manning, who believed in me right from the start, championed me endlessly and made all of this possible. An enormous thank you also goes to my editor/literary wizard Jess Whitlum-Cooper, who saw things in the book that I would never have seen and loved Georgia as much as I do.

Thank you to my publicist Phoebe Swinburn and everyone at Headline for all the amazing things you do.

Thank you to my cheerleaders: Andrew and Adam, Gemma and Ziggie, Mel, Jamie, Kristie, Georgina and Jodie.

Thank you to Jess and Varsha from the MS Society for all of your help.

Thank you to Ari, for repeatedly saying to me 'You should write a book' since we were eleven, and for always, always believing in me.

Thank you to Laura, James and Anna for constantly allowing me to take over the living room and teaching me how to think.

Thank you to Catherine and Maynie, for always laughing at my jokes and inspiring me endlessly.

Thank you to my favourite bookworms: Kiera, Shannon, Lucy, Natalie, Evangeline, Silke and Vivien.

Thank you to my girls for their infinite support; Claire, Lib, Kate, Hayley, Becca, Georgia, Rosie, Jess, Lauren and Alice.

Thank you to everyone who has read snippets over the years and spurred me on: Ciara, Emily, Cheri, Emma, Beanie, Catherine, Holly, Ami, John-Webb, Annie, Luke, Lydia and Alex.

Thank you to my grandparents, for always sparking my imagination.

And finally, thank you to my family for everything you've always done for me. To my parents for teaching me how to laugh at myself, to my brothers Tom and Dominic for their undying belief in me and to Elle, for teaching me how to be a sister.